The Incident at the Merry Hippo

By the same author

On the Edge of the Rift

A New Earth

The Flame Trees of Thika

The Red Rock Wilderness

The Incident at the Merry Hippo

ELSPETH HUXLEY

WILLIAM MORROW & COMPANY
NEW YORK, 1964

 Printed in the United States of America by H. Wolff Book Manufacturing Co. Library of Congress Catalog Card Number 64–10735.

NOTE

THE Protectorate of Hapana is not to be found on any map, and its citizens, together with the members and staff of the Connor Commission, are equally imaginary. I am, however, indebted to the Anglo-American Corporation of South Africa, Limited, for their help over the technicalities of copper extraction, which I have assumed to be very much the same in the fictional plant at Shooting Star as in their real ones in central Africa.

The Incident
at the Merry Hippo

The Connor Commission

The Royal Commission on Constitutional Changes in the Protectorate of Hapana—generally known as the Connor Commission—was appointed early in 1961 "to consider and report on such future constitutional arrangements as may seem appropriate in respect of the Protectorate of Hapana, in view of that territory's impending attainment of full independence within the Commonwealth."

The members of the Commission were as follows:

Sir Christopher Connor, K.C.M.G., Q.C. (*Chairman*)
The Earl of Bagpuse, T.D. (*Vice-Chairman*)
Sir Jeremy Maxwell-Palmer, K.B.E., M.C.
Mrs. Amelia Tripp, M.P.
Chief Erasmus Faustus, M.B.E.
Dr. Alexander Burton, D.LITT.
Mr. Mansfield Matunda
The Rev. Goliath Zaza
Dr. Horatio Rumble, PH.D.
Secretary: Mr. Merthyr Evans, O.B.E.
Personal Assistant: Miss Thomasina Labouchère
Public Relations Officer: Mr. Stephen Partridge

Following instructions received by Letters Patent, the Commission, after preliminary meetings in London, proceeded to the Protectorate of Hapana for the hearing of evidence and receipt of memoranda. After touring the Protectorate, the Commission returned to London for further meetings and for the preparation of their Report, which they presented to the Prime Minister at the end of the year.

Chapter 1

"Mrs. Tripp and gentlemen, good morning." The Chairman looked round suavely, like a self-confident swan. It was his black eyebrows and beak-like nose, not an extra long neck, that suggested swans; they gave him a predatory look, mitigated by a smile full of charm. Mrs. Tripp smiled her acknowledgement right back at the Chairman. Except for the Secretary's Personal Assistant, sitting in a corner with a pad, she was the only woman in the room.

"I shan't waste your time making speeches," the Chairman said. "Only just to welcome you, and say we've got a stiff task but I think we're equal to it, and we'll push ahead just as fast as we can. The Cabinet wants a quick answer. That suits me, and I'm sure it suits all of you."

"Hear, hear," said Sir Jeremy Maxwell-Palmer.

The Chairman spread shapely fingers over the documents lying on his blotting-paper. "Our aircraft is laid on for Friday week. Arrive Saturday, a week-end to sort ourselves out, then straight into the hearing of evidence. Our highly efficient Secretary has everything in train, I think. May I ask whether everyone's agreeable?"

The brisk, business, man-to-man approach Alex Burton recognized. Sir Christopher Connor had in his time played many parts, nearly all with great success; and now he was confronted with a situation full of land-mines—or game-pits perhaps, as they would soon be in the back-blocks of Hapana, a Protectorate just emerging from colonialism into the full sunlight of political freedom.

Like snakes-and-ladders, Alex thought: a single false step could send his number sliding down a long, twisty snake, but if he handled things well, and had a bit of luck, he might shoot right up a gilded ladder. The gamble had certainly appealed to this ex-barrister, ex-Advocate-General and ex-Governor with an Irish name, and political ambitions.

"Mr. Chairman, what arrangements have been made about our other colleagues? With respect, surely it wouldn't be proper to start without them?"

Commissions, Mrs. Tripp believed, were like marriage: you went on as you began. The right technique was to plunge in at once and make your number; if you didn't, others said what you wanted to say and you were left silent, or had to repeat points already raised. A commission soon sorted itself out into the talkers and the silent. As the only woman, she felt she owed it to her sex not to be pushed into a corner. She looked the Chairman in the face across a green baize table, one hand fingering her cultured pearls, the other tapping ash off a cigarette.

"Quite right, Mrs. Tripp. Two of our members have not yet joined us: Chief Faustus from Hapana, and the United Nations nominee. The Chief can't meet us till we arrive on the scene. He's got some private business, hasn't he, Hugo?"

The Secretary, sitting on Sir Christopher's left, looked up with just the correct blend of respect without obsequiousness and authority without arrogance. His voice was melodious and his accent exactly right—crisp, not drawling, and without diphthongs. He had learnt it at the Berlitz School of Languages after arriving from Carmarthenshire on a bicycle, with a change of shirts and only the rudiments of the English tongue, to take up a scholarship at University College. His name was Merthyr Evans but his friends called him Hugo.

"As Mrs. Tripp says, we oughtn't really to start without Chief Faustus," he agreed, "but I had a telegram this morning asking us to."

"What exactly does it say?"

"It's from the office of the Chief Minister in Umpah. 'Faustus joining Commission here later proceed without him provided salary paid.' That happens automatically, of course."

"I should like to raise a point, Mr. Chairman."

The speaker's voice was plump and comfortable, like his person; seams and buttons were at full stretch. Mr. Mansfield Matunda was a short, tubby African with small hands and feet, a compelling eye and an air of polished toughness natural to the survivor of many a prolonged, tortuous and sharp-fanged struggle on the field of Hapanan politics. In an age when, all over Africa, students were laying aside gowns, pennants and diplomas to become Cabinet Ministers, he ranked as a veteran, able to recall heroic days when the coveted distinction of P.G. for Prison Graduate could still be won.

His ample family was growing up and, as they reached the necessary age, each member was being, as it were, invested in a different ideological bank, to make sure that, however things fell out, at least one Matunda would be on the winning side. While his eldest son was qualifying as a radio mechanic in Moscow, a daughter was learning industrial nutrition in Chicago, another reading law in Allahabad, a younger son was in Peking—no one knew what he was studying—and the next girl on the list was poised between animal husbandry in Dundee, electronics in Hanover and Slavonic cultures in Split. Mr. Matunda's fondness for imperial purple—a rich purple pullover was now stretched across his stomach—had once caused a reporter to liken him to a ripe and mobile plum; the image had caught on with caricaturists and done him a very good turn. Ripe plums are sweet and soft, two adjectives which neither friend nor foe would ever have felt inclined to apply to Mr. Matunda.

"Mr. Chairman, my point is this," he announced. "We hear Chief Faustus is to draw his salary when he is doing no work. What sort of an arrangement is that? The people of Hapana pay him one salary already, as a Chief. Now there are to be two salaries, one of them for no work. That will annoy my people, it will annoy them very much indeed. I think—"

"I don't want to interrupt you, Mr. Matunda," said the Chairman, doing so, "but perhaps we'd better leave the question of Chief Faustus' salary to the Secretariat. If we start on details like that, we'll be here talking for a month before we even start."

"Hear, hear." Support came again from Sir Jeremy Maxwell-

Palmer, sitting at the end of the table with a hearing-aid. People said he wasn't really deaf, but used the aid to play for time when putting through business deals. At any rate, it had gone wrong at some well-chosen moments. Others believed the neat little mechanism to be a tape-recorder in disguise. He was tall, spare and flaxen-haired, and Alex Burton, who understood him to be a widower, had already decided that he would do for Mrs. Tripp.

"Mr. Chairman." The Rev. Zaza's tones were less resonant than his colleague's, more impetuous, but equally fluent. "Mr. Chairman, who is this Chief, to be paid for doing nothing? How has he got onto this Commission? I think the time has come when it is out of date to say that because a man is a hereditary Chief, he is a true representative—"

"You're going to keep me on my toes, gentlemen, I can see that." The Chairman blended a stern inflection with a half-smile at the Rev. Zaza. "I can see that everyone has an opinion of his own. No stooges! Yes, Mrs. Tripp?"

"What about the U.N. nominee?"

"Well, not nominee exactly. We are all appointed, as you know, directly by the Prime Minister. In this case there was to be a short panel of names submitted by the Secretary-General of the United Nations. . . . We are to be joined, I understand, by Dr. Horatio Rumble from the Loan Exchange and Development Agency—LEDA for short. Dr. Rumble is an authority on—let me see, what is it, Hugo? Something very much up our street, but I can't find the paper at the moment."

Hugo Evans was looking down a list. "Co-operatives in Afghanistan—no, that was the Turk. Factory legislation in the Andaman Islands—prostitution in Tibet—the economics of the gutta-percha industry—youth clubs among pastoralist camel-owners—we seem to have been offered a wide variety. Dr. Rumble—ah, yes. On loan from the Fairweather Foundation—of course, that has a lot of irons in the fire. Wide experience, no doubt."

"What of?" Mrs. Tripp inquired.

"It's here somewhere, I expect. He seems to have come to the Fairweather Foundation from the Joint Collegiate Board, where he was

Senior Executive. . . . I'm sorry, sir; if you'll give me a little time, I'll get a short biography drawn up and circulated."

"I think we ought to have it," Mrs. Tripp remarked severely.

"Is this Dr. Rumble also going to draw a salary without having to attend our meetings?" Mansfield Matunda ominously inquired.

"Come, gentlemen—Mrs. Tripp and gentlemen—we are chasing red herrings," the Chairman protested. Alex thought he could detect the merest trace of harassment behind the dark-browed self-assurance of the eminent swan.

Apart from Dr. Rumble and Chief Faustus, all the Commissioners were there. A nine-man Commission—eight-man, rather, and the single lady. Not single, of course; somewhere a Mr. Tripp must be lurking, or have lurked once, but he did not appear.

Mrs. Tripp had been in Parliament long enough not to be a novelty, but not long enough to be an institution. A testing, critical time when only constant effort and ever-whetted skill could keep a Member from slipping into the great pool of nonentity. A time for toiling through dull committees, for cultivating colleagues neither too high nor too low, for injecting into conversation enough critical comment to be thought on the ball, not enough to be suspected of ginger-group leanings. Mrs. Tripp had done well to get herself appointed to this Commission. Had she got on the right side of the Minister? Alex wondered. A friend of Sir Christopher Connor's? A word in the ear of the Chief Whip?

An even greater puzzle was presented by the Vice-Chairman, sitting on Sir Christopher's right. No one, literally, seemed ever to have heard of him before. The Earl of Bagpuse. In *Who's Who,* the entry was short. He was old for this job—nearly seventy: stout and heavy, too. But he looked healthy, as indeed he should be from the outdoor life he evidently led. A landowner, farmer, breeder of domestic animals. President of the Norfolk New Spot Pig Society, Chairman of a committee on artificial insemination, senior judge at the Five Counties Show. . . . It was almost too good to be true, Alex thought, too much in character; as if he had built up the part to conceal some less innocent occupation.

And then this Commission, gathered together to suggest how best the Protectorate of Hapana could be steered into the haven (as all hoped) of full independence. It did not appear that Lord Bagpuse had, at any period of his active life, taken the least speck of interest in any aspect of colonial development, of constitutional change, of the politics of new nations—or of old ones, for that matter. He had stuck to his New Spots and Red Polls in Norfolk, like a sensible man.

Then there were three Hapanans: the absent Chief and the present pair, pointedly sitting apart. Staunch political foes: between them charges of treachery, corruption, vice, sorcery, lechery and fraud volleyed like a whole flock of tennis balls. Did they really hate each other? Or was it shadow-boxing? Alex had no idea; nor had anyone, he supposed. The politics of Hapana were not so much a closed book as a sealed cave, full of goodness knows what vampire bats and secret treasure.

Mr. Mansfield Matunda belonged to the extreme nationalist wing: the People's Peace Party, or Triple-P. He was known as a fire-eater, a rabble-rouser, a white-hater, famous for having ordained that whites were to be yoked in teams to night-soil carts and forced to clean up African slums. His party had boycotted the Commission and offered the Presidency of a Free Hapana to Dr. Nkrumah; but here was Mr. Matunda, jovial as a black Cheryble brother, apparently playing tic-tac-toe, or something of the sort, with Sir Jeremy Maxwell-Palmer, Chairman of Steyn Consolidated who owned, or controlled, everything about Hapana that was worth keeping off the scrap-heap. Was Mansfield Matunda there to undermine from within, to sap the redoubts? Or to prevent a march being stolen on his party by the Rev. Goliath Zaza, who belonged to the rival Forever Forward Group?

"I shan't detain you any more this morning," the Chairman said. "One suggestion, though—my wife and I would be very glad to see you all at an informal supper on Thursday evening. Eight o'clock. The Prime Minister hopes to look in."

Hugo Evans said something in a half-whisper to his Chairman.

"Oh, yes, security," Sir Christopher added. "You know as well as I do the importance of keeping everything we think and say absolutely under our hats. Our meetings will be in private; our papers confidential; even the way our minds move when we start our job, even our speculations, simply must be kept to ourselves. Of course you all know the drill. The Official Secrets Act. . . . Quite a lot of people would find it useful to run a pipe-line into our discussions, as it were. I needn't say more, but rely on your discretion, gentlemen—Mrs. Tripp and gentlemen, I should say."

The Chairman coughed; he was not sure his afterthought hadn't been tactlessly expressed. Really, it was a nuisance about Mrs. Tripp. There had to be women on commissions, he recognized that—at any rate one woman on this; the Prime Minister had insisted. But did the woman have to be Mrs. Tripp? "I'm an old-fashioned sort of bloke, I suppose," Sir Christopher sometimes said, with one of his smiles, and he had grown to count on the reaction: an answering smile of incredulity, a gesture of protest, a half-laugh or a pat on the shoulder.

For Sir Christopher was a Progressive, well known for his enlightened views on capital punishment, nuclear tests, penal reform and the colour bar; he stuck up for teenagers, nuclear disarmers and anti-foxhunters, and his signature was often to be seen on letters to *The Times* condemning *apartheid,* hereditary peerages and the Iberian dictatorships; he was to be seen at first nights (or soon after) of plays by Pinter, Wesker and Ionesco; he was a friend of Mr. Dingle Foot's and professed some irritation with Lord Salisbury, the Beaverbrook press and the BBC. It was for such reasons as these that his appointment as Chairman of the Commission had been welcomed, if with some condescension, by the Left, while at the same time it had not wholly alienated the Right, who had after all chosen him.

Despite all this, he did not like women barristers. He was prejudiced, he frankly admitted, against women who argued, especially if they argued too well; and, while he strongly supported the principle of women in politics, he found himself seldom *en rapport* with those who actually took part.

Mrs. Amelia Tripp, for instance, was a tiresome woman. She talked too much—as women politicians had to, that was his main reason for disliking the breed—and she was too pleased with herself by half. While he admitted her views to be well presented and respected the care she gave to her appearance, he could not feel the least stirring of interest, the least desire to impress. And a woman who did not exert upon him the slightest pull of attraction was a dead loss so far as he was concerned. If this was old-fashioned, well then, he thought, make the most of it: he was not ashamed.

Fortunately, he was so constituted that very few women made no impact at all. His brisk, searching glances had taken in Hugo Evans' P.A., sitting in a corner with her pad. He liked her hair, tawny in colour and growing strongly off her forehead; he admired her sinewy build. She looked intelligent without arrogance, composed without conceit; he must test her voice. In women he hated ugly voices, sloppy dress and exhibitionism. Spoilt, of course—he'd been able to pick and choose. Now, in his gloomier moments, he knew the day was coming when this would no longer be so; sooner or later, young bulls must push out the old; but the old bull was in fighting fettle still and would give the youngsters a run for their money. They could have Mrs. Tripp.

"One other matter, Mr. Chairman," she was saying. "Our terms of reference."

"Yes, Mrs. Tripp?"

"I think we should make it absolutely clear that we're not to be tied down by them so closely that we can't recommend any future arrangements for Hapana that we think fit. We must hear—"

"Mr. Chairman," Mansfield Matunda protested, "our terms of reference are entirely wrong. I don't agree with them. They use the words 'appropriate arrangements.' We do not want our arrangements to be appropriate, we want them to be free. And we do not want the British Government to make them, we want to make them ourselves. We do not agree that colonialist oppressors—"

"Mr. Chairman, this Mr. Matunda does not know what the words mean," the Rev. Zaza said excitedly. "To be appropriate does not mean to be tied down to colonialism. It means that we shall be free to make our own arrangements. For instance, if we wish to come to an arrangement with our neighbours about things like customs duties and trade and animal diseases. Is it not a good thing to have more trade and less animal diseases? Is it not—"

"Animal diseases? Can't get anywhere till that's been tackled, eh?" At the words "animal diseases" Lord Bagpuse, hitherto somewhat comatose, had sprung as suddenly into life as a willing engine in response to the ignition. "Thousands of beasts, I'm told, die of something called *stuklestinck*. Can't make out whether it's a kind of anthrax or one of these deficiency things. Deadly, anyway. Now, my idea is if we call in—"

"Yes, yes, indeed, Lord Bagpuse, you are quite right," the Chairman interrupted. "I don't think we ought at this stage to enter into a discussion about our terms of reference. I promise you we shan't try to stifle anyone. Meanwhile—yes, Sir Jeremy?"

The Chairman looked towards his colleague with a mute appeal. At least Sir Jeremy must know how to keep to the point; his Board, people said, was pretty well to heel. And indeed Sir Jeremy, leaning forward as if to declare a record dividend, did come straight to the point.

"I suggest that we adjourn for coffee," he said.

"I second that," Alex Burton put in quickly.

"An excellent suggestion," the Chairman responded quickly, pushing back his chair. "A cup of coffee, then I think we can adjourn until the day after tomorrow. Mr. Matunda, please give me some advice. As a stranger to your delightful country, I need a few tips. Shall I want a macintosh? And although the climate's tropical I suppose a couple of good sweaters . . ."

The Chairman took Mr. Matunda firmly by the arm. My God, he thought, there's going to be some talk before we're through. These Hapanan orators, *and* Mrs. Tripp. And that idiot Bagpuse, with his crops and beasts. Maxwell-Palmer's an unknown quantity, but he must know the form. Burton—all these university types are self-opinionated, especially Redbrick ones; all trying to live up to Kingsley Amis; he's sure to have theories, cranky ones, too. And this Amercan, heaven knows what he'll be like. Of course it was a shrewd move by the P.M., with the World Bank in the background and the need for loans, and all that feeling at the United Nations. . . . What a circus! The great thing was to get the Commission home and dry before Ascot week.

Alex Burton had spotted the Secretary's P.A. slipping quietly out of the committee room. He caught her at the door.

"Aren't you coming in for coffee?"

"Oh, no thank you, Dr. Burton. I've got these notes to transcribe."

"I should think they'd keep."

"Mr. Evans wants them immediately."

"The first instalment of several million pompous clichés and blinding glimpses of the obvious. Don't they give you nightmares?"

"Their meaning isn't my concern," she said, and left him. She walked neatly and well. Alex went back into the coffee room feeling a little restored. Mrs. Tripp was nibbling a biscuit, her long neck curved towards it like a heron. She was graceful, reasonably decorative, trim, somehow enamelled with that metallic coating—brass for men, enamel for women—all politicians acquired.

"Frankly, I'm not at all happy about our terms of reference, Dr. Burton," she said. "You could drive a coach and horses through them. Something more precise is needed. I had a good many doubts about accepting the Prime Minister's invitation, I must admit; I only hope we shall be able to bring a little *clarity* and common sense to bear. Hapana presents a challenge to our policy . . ."

"Another biscuit, Mrs. Tripp?"

"No, thank you. Tell me, Dr. Burton . . ." She lowered her voice. "Our colleagues—quite a well-balanced team, I should say, but I do think there's a certain *mystery* about one of them. At least about his presence here."

"An emissary from behind the Curtain?"

"Well, hardly that. I was thinking, to be frank, about our Vice-Chairman."

"Ah! An emissary, then, from the Romney Marsh Sheep Breeders' Society."

"You take my point. But why *Hapana* . . . ?"

"Agricultural," Alex said, helping himself to a biscuit. "Peasants, mealies, compost, all that. He'll be able to talk to them as man to man about liver fluke and glanders and they won't notice whether they're getting universal suffrage or a kick in the pants."

"Ah, but you're wrong there." Mrs. Tripp looked crafty. "There *aren't* any livestock. I've found out. Or scarcely any—a few nomadic cattle-owners in the north. Hapana's full of tsetse fly, and floods all over every year; they grow things like rice and tapioca."

"Perhaps Lord Bagpuse is an expert on those, too."

"In Norfolk?"

"This Commission seems to be full of mysteries," Alex agreed.

Chapter 2

"THE WIFE of an ambitious man," Alex Burton was saying, must either be hard, tough and even more ambitious than her husband—a sort of diamond drill—or soft, dreamy, inefficient and protectable, a Madonna image. Then he's got to either satisfy or shelter her—both incentives. Nothing in between."

"Do you think the second sort of woman really exists?" Mrs. Tripp inquired, nibbling a canapé. The room was crowded, and here she was stuck with this rather farouche young man in a tweed jacket, when everyone else was in a tidy dark suit. She edged towards Dick Howard, the Minister for African Affairs, who was talking to the Chairman.

"All women follow the laws of supply and demand. If men want them to exist, they do. It's not a fashionable line at present, but there's always a demand for the Madonna image. A limited but steady seller, like Dundee cakes, encyclopedias and pianos."

"I think generalizations about women are silly. Half the human race . . ."

"Our Chairman, now, has been sensible," Alex continued, paying no attention to his companion's views. "His wife's a diamond drill, I think."

"One shouldn't discuss one's hostess at a party. Besides, we don't know her. I'm glad she's coming to Hapana with us. Social contacts —ah, Sir Christopher. A delightful party! Talk to the Minister? Yes, of course. I was only saying . . ." Mrs. Tripp made off with alacrity in the wake of her host.

Alex looked round the room and found himself next to a youngish individual with a beard: a neatly trimmed, circular black fringe of rather silky hair. The man had thick eyebrows and a dark-complexioned face that reminded Alex of an advertisement for something, he couldn't remember what—detergents, tobacco, gin?

"I'd better introduce myself," this young man said. "The name's Partridge, Stephen Partridge. I'm joining the outfit as P.R.O. As of this afternoon. Got back yesterday from Pakistan. I had to choose between this, and creating a father-figure image of the Consolidated Cocoa Corporation among the West Indians. Thought I'd try this. I've never been to Africa. Hapana *is* in Africa, isn't it?"

"So I believe," Alex agreed.

"Wind of change and all that—right in the fashion. Sir Christopher knows where to go for honey. But no one seems to know where the Vice-Chairman sprang from."

"He's sound on pigs, I believe," Alex remarked. "And he breeds Suffolk Punches."

"Breeds *what?"*

"Suffolk Punches."

Stephen Partridge looked incredulous. "No wonder they picked him. A modern genius! I've got one in my garden at Weybridge. Perhaps he can make it breed."

"One what?"

"A Suffolk Punch."

"That seems an unlikely thing to have in a garden at Weybridge."

"Why?"

"Bulky, for one thing. And expensive on oats."

Stephen Partridge was looking at Alex with a mixture of hostility and doubt. Alex felt the same about Partridge, with an added element of impatience.

"Mine runs on petrol and oil, old boy," the P.R.O. said gently. "You know, chug-chug. It cuts the lawns. Perhaps I could mate it with an Allen-scythe. I must talk to Lord Bagpuse."

"I must get another drink."

"The Chairman's pretty sound on drink, I've heard; no stinting. Interesting chap, the Chairman—briefless Dublin barrister to top-ranking British colonial Governor—a good deal of irony in that, isn't there? He's played his cards well. And now this Commission. . . . New ground for you, too, Dr. Burton? I hear your thesis on the origins of the Royal Prerogative is quite sensational."

"You hear a lot, Partridge. You mean that Pakistan is ringing with my name?"

Stephen Partridge laughed; his red, full lips curled away to reveal shapely teeth that brought to mind thoughts of vampires and garlic. He said:

"I've seen you on television—rather late at night, generally. Who's that talking to the Minister? Ah, Mrs. Tripp."

The Minister for African Affairs was nibbling olives to conceal his irritation; Mrs. Tripp was wasting his time. Her views on the economy of Hapana were of no interest to him whatever; women in politics, in his opinion, were too conscientious by half. The great point about Hapana was to prevent its affairs—always explosive despite the fact (he understood) that most of it was underwater—from erupting at a particularly awkward moment for the Cabinet. This Commission ought to keep things quiet for six months or so—not much, but something in a hard world.

The Minister sighed, and looked round for somewhere to put his olive stone. He didn't envy Connor, with this lot to shepherd round Africa. Well, he'd done his best with the appointments. He'd got, at any rate, one sound man in Maxwell-Palmer; Mrs. Tripp would come into line. Something of a disaster, of course, about that idiot Bagpuse—a bad blob. One hoped the Prime Minister would never get to hear the full story.

Alex Burton, about to detach himself from his bearded companion, glanced round to catch an odd expression on the P.R.O.'s face. Partridge was looking across the crowded room at Mrs. Tripp and for an instant his eyes had narrowed and he had registered some kind of reaction—surprise, animosity, recognition? Just the latter, probably; Mrs. Tripp, M.P., featured as often as she could in newsreels and press photographs, now and then on television. Partridge appeared about to speak, and then checked himself; a murmur emerging from those cherry lips sounded, amid the monkey-chatter, like something Jewish such as Loewenstein.

Just at that moment the Minister escaped and Amelia Tripp, looking round for a new companion, caught sight of Partridge. Alex saw her stiffen like an antelope that "freezes" at the scent of danger. Her nostrils seemed to pinch in. She knew him all right: and did not like what she knew. Then someone came between them and Alex found his hostess by his side.

"Chris tells me that you and he are practically the only Commissioners who don't know all the answers before you start," she remarked, with a confiding smile. "He says it's marvellous to know there's at any rate *one* other amateur—though he's nervous of your erudition, of course. Why do dons and professors look about twenty-five these days? Or is that just one's own advancing age, as with policemen?"

"The pace is too hot for older men," Alex suggested. "They drop out into the more restful, secluded professions like politics and business. . . . Our Chairman's going to need all his famous high voltage, Lady Connor. We have the makings of an unruly tribe."

"Then he'll be in his element. He likes difficulties as dogs like bones. And treats them the same way."

Constance Connor was, Alex understood, the Chairman's second wife. Men who started poor and obscure, and rose in the world, often dropped their first partner somewhere along the line in favour of a helpmeet with a better head for the higher rungs of the ladder. A good-looking woman, inclined towards the statuesque, rather mannered, hard perhaps—it would be difficult, at any rate, to put a finger on a human spring behind her enamelled face of competence and sociability. She was very affable to anyone to whom affability was a duty: this included the Commissioners.

"Everyone nowadays seems to have just flown in from Bulawayo, or been week-ending in Kampala," she added. "I've never even set *foot* in Africa."

"Nor have I."

"We can keep each other company—babes in the jungle. The others obviously know it like their own front gardens. Even Mrs. Tripp, I think, has been to conferences on female circumcision, or it may have been family planning . . ."

"There's Lord Bagpuse."

"Ah! Lord Bagpuse . . ."

An abstracted look, perhaps her substitute for distress, came over Constance Connor's even, handsome features. Her hair-do was immaculate, she wore a plain black dress with pearls and a single, but splendid, diamond ring. She was a woman of about thirty-five; Sir Christopher, fifty-six. When comparatively young he'd won a name as a brilliant barrister, but it was the war that had carried him to eminence and honour in a wider field, first as legal adviser to the Military Government of an Occupied Territory, then on into the fluctuating world of post-war reconstruction and international manoeuvrings. He'd become an expert on the tricky job of hatching colonies into independent states, with sympathy towards the nationalists combined with firmness of timing—a strong man in the midst of a retreat. Sir Christopher Connor had brought to birth, from their colonial womb, two independent states, one of which had so far stayed in the Commonwealth.

A remarkable career—and not one to have been pursued without making enemies. He'd survived an attempted assassination, released from jail two nationalists who'd become Prime Ministers, and weathered several States of Emergency.

A flurry round the door quickly dispelled the slightly sour look that had crossed Lady Connor's face at the mention of the Vice-Chairman.

"Ah, here, I think, is the P.M. We hoped he'd be able to look in, but one never knows when the House is sitting. Forgive me, Dr. Burton, I must do my duty . . ."

The Prime Minister was genial, buoyant and affable. "We all attach the greatest possible importance to the job you've taken on," he told each Commissioner, as Sir Christopher led them up in turn for an introduction. He gave each one a good ten minutes, and his briefing had clearly been thorough.

"I've read some of your papers," he said to Alex, "even if I haven't yet had a chance to get down to your major work on the Royal Prerogative. And, if I may say so, I've very much admired some of your television performances. Should one call them performances, or does that suggest an element of insincerity? If so, I didn't mean it —insincerity is supposed to be *our* métier, of course, our political prerogative."

They both laughed—with insincerity, Alex thought. "I'm awfully grateful to you for taking on this job," the Prime Minister added. "Hapana's rather an obscure, unimportant sort of place, you may feel. But I do assure you that the *principles* involved are vital. Whatever you decide to recommend will have its repercussions all through Africa, indeed all through the world. The Americans are watching carefully, and of course we all know that Big Brother in the Kremlin . . . We think we're very fortunate to have got together such a well-balanced, first-rate team. Having given you the best Chairman in the country, of course we had to look round pretty carefully for people who wouldn't just be yes-men. And we're confident we've found them."

Sir Christopher approached with Lord Bagpuse in tow. The Vice-Chairman was looking hot, flushed, harassed and uncomfortable, like one of his prize bulls confronted by a cattle lorry that was to convey him to a show. He had done some homework on Hapana, but couldn't remember whether it was rice they grew, or sugar-cane, or something he had never heard of called sorghum. Or was it semolina? And he had read something about native customs full of extraordinary words like *matrilineal, siblings, ethnocentrism.*

"I don't believe you've met the Vice-Chairman, Lord Bagpuse," Connor said, in rather flat tones.

"I'm absolutely delighted—" the Prime Minister began on a jovial note, but a glance at Lord Bagpuse caused a look of surprise, followed by one of annoyance, to pass over his distinguished features.

"Lord Bagpuse?" he said, with an air of disbelief.

"Well, this *is* an honour," the Vice-Chairman responded heartily. "Never thought I should be hobnobbing with Prime Ministers and the like, eh? Mind you, we're quite used to Royalty. We always have some Royalty or other at the Five Counties—never miss. The Queen knows a sound Red Poll when she sees one, and of course the Gloucesters' Guernseys always do well. Only hope the younger generation are going to carry on the tradition. Wouldn't do to let it slide, you know. Now I understand that the cattle in Hapana . . ."

Alex drifted out of earshot, wondering what there was about the Vice-Chairman that put everyone off his stroke. As if a strange dog had wandered into a herd of cattle, arousing in the beasts instincts of menace. People seemed reluctant to believe that he was really there. Yet he was harmless enough—too harmless, possibly. One could easily imagine Bagpuse taking a strong line about a New Spot pig with the wrong markings, striking it from the herd book, but not so easily about the affairs of Hapana, and with characters such as Mansfield Matunda—who was at this moment tucking happily into the whisky, beads of sweat on his shining forehead, buttons straining on his barrel-stomach. He greeted Alex with jovial delight.

"You don't know my country, Dr. Burton, I believe?"

"Not yet."

"You'll find it backward—no television, no parking meters, very few swimming pools or public lavatories. But now we have a sewage plan and a lady barrister—you see, we're trying. I think you will enjoy my country. I hear you are very often on the TV?"

"Not often. Now and again I take part in gladiatorial contests among minor scholars in our contemporary area."

Mr. Matunda shook with laughter like a wind-tossed bough. "That is very good. A gladiator, eh? You slay with the tongue. We do the same in Hapana, but we don't get paid for it. Not so well, anyway. I think the TV is good pay. For just a few minutes, I got twenty-five guineas. But that wasn't long enough. How can I explain the politics of Hapana in five minutes?"

"How long would you need?"

Mansfield Matunda looked thoughtful, and shook his head. "At least two days."

"Why? All politics are the same. One lot's in the saddle, the other lot wants to climb up and knock the rider off and take the reins."

Matunda skilfully fielded a full glass from a tray being borne past him by an anxious young man; his quaking laughter shook with mounting force. "Oh, you are humorous," he exclaimed. "Now I have a proposition. Let's go on TV together to explain to the British people the truth about the situation in Hapana. We could cross-talk together, like Burns and Allen. We should make much, much money. Perhaps a hundred pounds?"

"A lot more, if we could do as well as Burns and Allen."

"We'll be modest to start with. To tell the truth, I need the money. My party are very mean with the funds, very mean. I think I.T.V. pay the most."

"They wouldn't have us," Alex pointed out. "It's against the rules. There's the Official Secrets Act for one thing."

"We needn't give away important secrets. At least, not unless they pay us very well. You see, I have a difficulty. The treasurer of my party has been unjustly fined by the colonialist oppressors for some stupid technical offence. He's telegraphed to Moscow, but no answer yet. So can you lend me five pounds?"

Chapter 3

"I EXPECT you've got a couple of spare seats on the plane," Lord Bagpuse remarked to Hugo Evans. The Secretary was toiling late in his office, embattled among documents, as the Commission's departure drew close.

"Plenty of seats; the weight's the trouble. With all our documents and blue-books and equipment, it's going to add up to at least a ton. And now Sir Jeremy insists on tape-recorders. I'd have thought . . ."

"He may want a tape-recorder. I want my wife."

"Your *wife,* Lord Bagpuse?"

"And Lady Connor needs a pal. Someone to go shopping with, see the sights, that sort of thing."

"Accommodation is extremely difficult, you know, in Hapana. And there are no sights. I very much doubt whether . . ." At the last minute to upset everything, create a crisis about accommodation—it was too much!

"I've had a word with the Chairman," Lord Bagpuse added. "He's delighted—in fact, he insists."

"I see." Hugo paused, exuding disapproval; but the Vice-Chairman was showing unexpected spirit.

"But *two* seats, Lord Bagpuse?"

"My wife overflows."

"Overflows?"

"It's these ridiculous little seats they make nowadays. You'd think they were catering for a race of pygmies. They've forgotten what a decent, shapely female figure's like. I've no use for these modern skimpy, scraggy little bundles of bone. Well, then, that's settled, eh? Two seats for my wife. And if there's any trouble, Sir Jeremy must take his tape-recorder on his lap."

Hugo looked with foreboding at the Vice-Chairman's lumbering back. Things were going to be even worse than he'd feared.

The Commissioners were not to fly direct to Umpah, Hapana's capital, for fear of demonstrations, even riots. Instead they were to start work at a mining centre about two hundred miles away in the bush.

Thirty years ago a spiky, featureless and boring kind of vegetation called *momombo* had enveloped thousands of square miles of flat, featureless and boring country without so much as a *kraal* or cattle-track to break the monotony. Underneath this *momombo* and a desiccated soil seething with termites hostile to all forms of husbandry, ores loaded with copper had lain undisturbed since the origins of our planet. Then, all of a sudden, explorers, prospectors and concession-hunters had erupted into this forgotten world. Old treaties with native chiefs, filed for decades in some silver-fishy nook, had been taken out and found to contain clauses surrendering mineral rights to Queen Victoria. (The chiefs had, at the time, supposed that they were formally permitting those of her trusty friends who had come to visit them to dig holes for latrines; however, as the chiefs' heirs did not themselves want the copper, it had scarcely seemed, at this late stage, worth trying to clear up the misunderstanding.)

Now, remote from other human settlements, a mining city prospered in the heart of the bush. Innumerable model bungalows, alike as bricks, straggled under the lea of a low saddle of hill; tall chimneys poked up unexpectedly, belching smoke into a sun-stoked, heat-simmering air.

In course of time the bearded, slouch-hatted prospectors and the mushrooming speculators' companies had been swallowed and digested by Steyn Consolidated, an octopus with brain and heart in handsome skyscrapers with modern décor in London and Johannesburg, and tentacles securely fastened to nickel mines in Canada, gold on the Rand, nitrates in Peru, chromium in Australia, and heaven knows what other minerals in other lands.

Not that one could easily associate Sir Jeremy Maxwell-Palmer, one of its Directors, with anything so sinister and unendearing as an octopus. Sir Jeremy was diffident, almost self-effacing in manner, just as Steyn Consolidated was beneficent, far-sighted and socially-conscious in the conduct of its affairs.

What with financing humanitarian research and bursaries for the brighter children of its innumerable employees in a dozen universities; what with maintaining good relations with progressive nationalist politicians; what with providing generous pensions and schools, hospitals and model houses, recreation halls and sports stadia and polytechnics—what with all this, and so much else besides, you might well have thought that the Directors and higher executives would have no time to spare for the mundane business of extracting metals and making money from their sale. Somehow or other, however, behind the scenes and beneath the surface, the business of the Company was carried on. So it was to be at Shooting Star—so named by a prospector who had observed this phenomenon from his rude camp at the end of the very day on which he had made his historic find—that the work of the Connor Commission was to begin.

One of the few things at Shooting Star which belonged not to the Company but to the Government of Hapana, was the airport: an unworthy gateway to a centre reached by air by practically everyone, from visiting transatlantic tycoons to sturdy tribesmen in search of tax money or the purchase-price for brides. These Hapanans arrived in batches, clutching bundles of charms and cooked cassava roots, from the swamps and distant principalities whence they had been collected in lories by recruiting firms. The treasuries of Hapana were permanently as bare as those of the Company were well stocked; indeed, practically all the Protectorate's revenues were derived from royalties on copper and from taxes on the Company's profits.

A single concrete runway sufficed to receive those modest types of aircraft which met the needs of Shooting Star. Despite attempts if not to conceal, at least not to publicize, the Commission's arrival, an unofficial reception had been prepared for the Commissioners by the

Peoples' Peace Party, led by Mr. Moto Mguu, which numbered Mr. Matunda among its distinguished members.

At one end of the runway a huddle of buildings bunched together as if for company on the fringe of the bush. Separated from this runway by a fence made of two strands of slack barbed wire, slung between posts already half-digested by termites, a group of tattered Hapanans held aloft placards scrawled in stencil ink on the backs of posters which had been pinned to plywood boards. About a dozen hefty black policemen stood with their backs to the small crowd, whose spirit seemed lethargic rather than revolutionary. After a while, a battered limousine with dented wings arrived at full speed, and three well-dressed Hapanans carrying fly-whisks jumped out. One leapt onto the bonnet and started to address the crowd. Several youths broke off a conversation with members of a white-overalled refuelling team standing by a yellow petrol tank, and started to incite the lounging placard-bearers and onlookers to a proper enthusiasm.

"Greetings to our saviour, our leader, our God-given deliverer from the foreign yoke!"

"Comrades, cheer for our freedom-fighter, our hero, our future emperor of Hapana!"

"Freedom! Down with the oppressor! Victory! Moto Mguu!"

"We follow you to hell! Moto Mguu!"

Despite all this hard work by party organizers, the crowd's response was languid. Most of the placard-bearers, hired for sixpence each, belonged to a tribe whose members loathed the tribe of Moto Mguu. They had demanded to be paid in advance, but had lost the argument. The party organizers were senior boys from the secondary school whose voices did not carry far, and whom the placard-holders looked upon as lunatics, probably bewitched. Had it not been for the policemen, the placard-bearers would have advanced upon the speakers to demand their sixpences on the spot. A flurry of rain, brief but heavy, damped everyone's spirits and made the lettering run. Even the journalists, sitting on uncomfortable chairs in a lounge decorated by posters depicting Alpine holidays and advertisements for lemonade, jotted down their pieces with ennui.

Hysterical crowds, shouting for freedom and brandishing matlocks, surrounded the isolated airstrip here thundering support for their leader, the Communist-trained firebrand Moto Mguu, who arrived a few moments before the members of the Connor Commission flew in from London on their desperate eleventh-hour mission to save the key protectorate of Hapana from bloodshed and ruin. I watched them march with banners, cheering to the echo a slashing attack on British rule, while military police, rushed here in armoured cars, linked hands and fixed bayonets in an effort to keep the runway clear as the V.I.P.-laden Viscount . . .

"How do you spell this chap Mguu?" Fleetway Black of the *Clarion* inquired of his colleague, Mervyn Sparks of the *Popular*. "Has it really got a double-*u*?"

"Not a *w,* old boy; two *u*'s."

"Bloody silly name, anyway," Fleetway Black said gloomily. "Bloody silly story. Doesn't anything ever happen here?"

"We could hire some blokes to tear down some banners," Mervyn Sparks suggested. "Bill Bannerman got a splendid riot going in one of these two-by-four countries. Potted a cop in the backside with an air-gun. Then he got some more stories out of the inquiry."

"Jim Stumbletoes started a fire somewhere or other in the local parliament buildings. Half the opposition were tried for treason and he got a peach of a story."

"Hardly worth bothering here," Mervyn Sparks regretted.

"Flat as a dud Cape Canaveral rocket. Get away tonight, with any luck."

"Well, here they are." The roving correspondents stood up and pocketed their pads. Fleetway Black wore a pair of old khaki shorts, Mervyn Sparks a shiny, tight, pepper-and-salt suit to which he was faithful in all countries and climes. The aircraft came to rest, but no one alighted.

"What's holding them up?"

"Could be a hitch . . ."

A note of very cautious hope crept into their voices. They gazed a little more alertly from the open-sided lounge.

"Could be they're waiting for an escort . . ."

"Someone could've been taken ill . . ."

"Probably only nose-powdering."

Hopes of some fatality, faint as they were, soon withered. The hitch was Lady Bagpuse, who had occupied two seats next to the exit and, while she was gathering herself together, plugged the passage like a cork. Endeavouring to unfasten her safety belt, the air hostess had tickled Lady Bagpuse, who had wriggled and strewn her handbag, her knitting, gloves, books and other impedimenta about the aircraft. All these things took time to reassemble in her reticule while Lord Bagpuse, having cunningly retreated to the other end of the aircraft, looked out of the window and pretended to notice nothing wrong. At last the party filed down the steps, adjusting dark glasses as they emerged like creatures from a burrow, feeling the light.

Hapana's Chief Minister, Edmund Butterfield, awaited them at the foot of the steps. The fact that Mr. Butterfield was British, or rather that a Briton was still Chief Minister, was a festering wound on the body politic. Mr. Moto Mguu's People's Peace Party and the Rev. Zaza's Forever Forward Group were, for once, united in their condemnation of this imperialistic arrangement. Unquestionably Mr. Butterfield, colonialist oppressor and capitalist stooge, should relinquish his position without a further day's delay—should have relinquished it long ago—to the leader of the people of Hapana, democratically chosen.

Mr. Butterfield's eagerness to retire on a generous pension to a house at Henley and seats on the boards of at least two large companies exceeded even the eagerness of the Hapanans to get rid of him. The British Government could scarcely wait to relieve itself of an inconvenient, costly and politically dangerous burden. All that remained was to choose Mr. Butterfield's successor.

Unfortunately, this was not as easy as it sounded. Who *was* the leader of the Hapanan people? Mr. Moto Mguu, or the Rev. Goliath Zaza? Mr. Matunda, scheming in the wings, or the General Secretary of the Trade Unions? Who, indeed, *were* the Hapanan people? The powerful Chuma tribe, who backed Moto Mguu; the scarcely less potent Mongu supporters of the Rev. Zaza; or the unprogressive but united Shiwa, who had proclaimed their unswerving determination never to acknowledge either party or person, but to die to the last man for their Paramount Chief and their hallowed, sacred and inviolable agreement with Queen Victoria?

Until such details as these had been settled it seemed impossible to appoint, elect or otherwise determine Mr. Butterfield's successor, and Mr. Butterfield remained a harassed, conscientious, overworked and exceedingly reluctant Chief Minister.

The rain ceased, press cameras clicked, Sir Christopher presented the Commissioners to Mr. Butterfield. Posters and banners were held aloft as the party walked towards the buildings. On each poster was scrawled a substantial essay, too long to be read at a distance of more than two feet or in less than five minutes; but the banners carried briefer messages.

NO TAPIOCA!

NEVER SURRENDER NEVER APPROPRIATE

HAPANA WOMEN ARE NOT FOR YOU SIR CHRIST

FERTILITY AND FREEDOM

The Chairman surveyed these and other legends in a startled silence. Constance Connor, however, looked vastly entertained.

"Why *tapioca,* Mr. Butterfield?"

"It's a long story." The Chief Minister sounded gloomy. "Part of our five-year agricultural plan to boost exports. Our research people went to a lot of trouble, not to mention expense, to breed the right kind of tapioca but then, of course, it got mixed up with politics. The Triple-P spread the story that tapioca causes sterility."

"But surely the leaders . . . Didn't Mr. Mguu get a university degree?"

"I'm afraid Mr. Mguu hasn't been at all co-operative. Several agricultural officers have been attacked, and anyone who tries to plant tapioca now is certain to get beaten up at the very least, burnt alive most likely. Several Better Farmers have been impaled. It's most discouraging."

Defeatism, Sir Christopher noted; a bad sign. Our first task, he thought, must be to raise morale: inject a stiff dose of confidence.

"Our Vice-Chairman is an agriculturalist," he remarked. "I expect he'll be able to talk them round."

"I hope so." Mr. Butterfield did not add that a couple of dozen energetic white experts and several hundred African assistants had been dedicated to nothing else for about five years, so far with extremely meagre results.

Amelia Tripp, meanwhile, was reading the essays on some of the posters. Their holders, delighted to be at last getting some attention, held them up eagerly.

Hapanas Sacred Soil never defeyd by feet of Tyrant. We fight on Beeches Hills Streets Freedom is our Berthrite. One man one vote no taxes no tapioca. Go away Connor we dont want you here. Go back to Sir Roy Welensky. No Bomb tests No Basses no Welensky no Appropriating here. Send Kennedy Mac Salaza Connor Butterfingers Welensky to hell Moto is our Saver. To Hell Sir Christ.

"I think it should be explained that we have nothing to do with Sir Roy Welensky," Mrs. Tripp remarked.

"Or tapioca," Sir Jeremy added.

The placard-holders clustered round Mrs. Tripp like swarming bees, chanting a word obviously potent in their own tongue.

"I suppose that is Hapanan for *freedom,*" Amelia Tripp said.

"It's Hapanan for *sixpence.*" A police officer had come to the rescue, and shooed the placard-holders back with his little cane. They retreated amiably, chanting another refrain in which the words Moto Mguu could be distinguished.

"They seem to be supporters of Mguu's," Amelia Tripp observed.

"They're after his blood. He hasn't paid them. Probably they'll get freedom badges instead."

"They look hungry, poor things." Most of them wore ragged

shirts and very old patched shorts or trousers, the women carried babies on their backs in cotton slings. Their drab, scrubbed, shapeless cotton dresses were clutched by the hem, as often as not, by toddlers with round, startled eyes, running noses and a fawn's timidity.

Amelia Tripp pulled a ten-shilling note from her bag and proffered it to the nearest placard-holder. For a moment there was a startled silence, then an outcry, a forest of stretched hands; and, as it seemed in the wink of an eye, the crowd had vanished like a herd of antelope at the firing of a rifle. Posters and banners lay in the rain-sprinkled dust around the feet of Mrs. Tripp; their holders were in full flight towards the Palm Beach Hotel, where a feast of cow'sfoot stew, mealies and cassava awaited those who reached the goal before either the stew or the cash gave out.

Soon a stream of cars bore away the Commissioners, the secretaries, the P.R.O., the filing clerks, the typists, the office equipment, the baggage; they left the airstrip empty and deserted, an insignificant speck on the bush-clad, heat-baked continent. Even the rain-clouds had gone, yielding to biting sun. There remained only tsetse-flies, the departing police, the special correspondents.

"Not a smell of a story," Fleetway Black complained.

"What's next? Singapore?"

"Or Addis Ababa."

Mervyn Sparks was scribbling on his pad; the hotel had a good bar, he didn't want to waste time on his story once he got there.

> Mrs. Amelia Tripp, M.P., the only woman Commissioner, was rescued by police from a howling mob a few minutes after Connor Commission's aircraft touched down this afternoon. Waving banners demanding freedom, threatening the Commission and appealing to Russia, they broke through a police cordon and only prompt action by a cool-headed, broken-nosed young police officer saved her life. I saw women with babies, young men with sticks, bearded oldsters—men and women from all walks of Hapanan life—worked into a frenzy by Moto Mguu, their god, converge upon her like a swarm of angry buffaloes . . .

Chapter 4

As THE ONLY passable hotel in Shooting Star, the Pig and Whistle was too small to take the whole Commission, a number of its members had, after much heart-searching about protocol, accepted Steyn Consolidated's invitation to enjoy the amenities of a guest-house called the Merry Hippo, maintained for visiting Directors, industrial tycoons and other notables. The rest of the overflow had been billeted on obliging mine employees.

The Merry Hippo lay well away from the dusty town, screened by decorative and flowering trees, amid lawns kept green by sprinklers. It stood on a bluff overlooking a lake created by damming a river for the benefit of a hydro-electric plant.

"Nothing like as large, of course, as Kariba—ours is a *very* poor relation," Sir Jeremy modestly said. "But we're quite proud of it in our small way. Generates fifty thousand kilowatts in three-phase cycles, dam capacity twenty million acre-feet, two hundred thousand acres flooded so far—full compensation paid, of course. Now we're turning the chaps we had to move into fishermen. I must run you out to our training centre one evening; we've got a smoking plant, refrigeration, a school for net-making, a small fertilizer factory . . ."

From the Merry Hippo's windows you could see out across a great sheet of water from which protruded, here and there, the stark, whitened branches of trees drowned by floods. Here in the *momombo* wilderness Steyn Consolidated had established a little world of its own. Out of the bush had arisen a city of some thirty thousand people, from the general manager in his mansion to the miners in their bungaloid townships that looked, from the air, as symmetrical as carefully planted orchards. The regimented lines of square, identical houses, each with its patch of garden, were intersected by ruler-straight roads margined by young trees. These houses had arrived in numbered bits on lorries, and been bolted together like cars on an assembly line. At strategically placed points were schools, free to workers; social centres, a big concrete stadium where twenty thousand spectators could watch football matches and tribal dancing on Saturdays, churches, playing-fields, a technical college where the crudest Mongu or Chuma or Shiwa from the bush could, by means of aptitude tests, be selected to transform himself into a skilled technician.

Now the Company was planning an experimental theatre to be run by an ex-pupil of Brecht's, sending future engineers and managers to non-Communist universities overseas and equipping a centre for research (costing half a million) into the control of deep-level atmospheric dust. Every month each underground worker was weighed, measured, blood-tested, probed, checked for venereal disease and his heart and lungs photographed; as a result the worker's health was ten times better, statistically, than that of the average Hapanan. And the health of his family, too; the Company had created a network of pre-natal clinics, child welfare stations, crèches, infant schools, maternity hospitals. Families were three times larger than the average for Hapana and a new generation of sturdy, healthy, literate and bumptious children was growing up on the mines.

As to the comforts of the guest-house, the Commissioners had no complaints. Each bedroom had its own bath; a corps of soft-footed, well-trained Hapanan servants anticipated every need; meals were served in a handsomely furnished, airy room decorated with murals done by a Hapanan student, depicting the discovery and development of the mine.

The meals themselves showed every sign of excellence without excess. The food was either piping hot or ice-cold, according to its nature; there was a choice of red or white wine. Sir Christopher had to summon all his self-control. He was pledged to reject everything starchy. So was Constance; she had brought supplies of starchless rolls, crispbread and horrid little pills instead of sugar. After their first luncheon, everyone remarked on the excellence of the black coffee.

"I remember my godfather advising me, when I was a briefless barrister," Sir Christopher said, "that when I was bowled over by a glamorous young woman, I should get her to make me an omelette. If she made a good one, she could learn to cook. It's the same with coffee—if it's first-rate, you can be sure the food will be first-rate, too."

Sir Jeremy beamed. "We have it blended specially for us, as a matter of fact. A bit of Costa Rica, a dash of Blue Mountain, the best Kenya, a touch of Mysore. And of course we roast and grind it fresh every day. None of your electric gadgets—roasted on a charcoal brazier and ground in a hand-mill, in small batches—the *personal* touch."

"What a lot of trouble for a little mouthful," Mansfield Matunda remarked, draining the contents of his coffee cup in less than half a gulp.

"A pearl is tiny," the Chairman pointed out. "A wildflower, a wren's egg, even a smile."

The Commissioners ate together in a dining-room with French windows overlooking a lawn with beds of salvia and plumbago, with shady trees and flowering shrubs. In charge of this smooth-running machine was Desmond Slocombe, the general manager: a quiet but forceful man in his late forties, bald as a coot, a pair of horn-rimmed glasses enhancing an air of wisdom and authority. He needed both. Under the mine's crust of high-powered efficiency, volcanoes of disturbance rumbled and hissed.

White miners resented the encroachment of black miners into higher-paid preserves; black miners resented the higher pay and superior conditions of white miners, and demanded immediate Hapanization of all senior posts. Costly machinery had to be guarded night and day against saboteurs; white miners were forbidden access to black miners' places of recreation; a network of telephones connected every sector of the mine and housing estates with a switchboard in the house of the chief security officer; this in turn had a special line to police headquarters, manned all round the clock. Now politicians were striking matches uncomfortably close to this powder magazine. The Triple-P and the F.F.G. were active among Hapanan miners and already several clashes between supporters of the two parties had occurred. Among the whites, members of a Communist cell were infiltrating into the trade unions.

"All in all, not an easy row to hoe," Sir Jeremy concluded, after a brief sketch of the position over a postprandial brandy. "But we've got a first-rate man in Slocombe and a pretty keen staff. Output's going up every year; we're trebling our smelting plant capacity, in the last five years the real value of wages has nearly trebled, thus lowering the differential . . ."

Even Dr. Horatio Rumble of LEDA was impressed.

He had been waiting at the Merry Hippo, having flown in the night before from Beirut, eager for his latest assignment. Amelia Tripp, who found herself next to him at luncheon, decided that he had a nice, kind face—lean and leathery, deeply lined. His friendly dark-brown eyes gazed at his surroundings with an intensity that reminded her of the well-worn gimlet simile. They were framed by thickish rimless glasses, augmented by a pair of clip-on dark lenses. He wore a Palm Beach suit and a dashing tie with mermaids on it, and on his face a slightly worried frown. His manner was courteous, his voice gentle, although perhaps, in large doses, it might bring to mind the whining hum of distant machinery.

"I feel it to be a great privilege, ma'am, to serve on this distinguished body," Dr. Rumble announced. "Our task will be a hard one, but with God's help I feel we shall succeed. The troubled state of Africa, the threat of Communism, the natural impatience of a people gazing at the green pastures of freedom—no wonder, ma'am, the present situation trembles on a knife-edge. On the one side, strife and penury. On the other, progress and hope. I have no doubt, however, as to which side we shall ultimately steer Hapana's ship of state, to anchor in the harbour of progress. There are difficulties, but they are a challenge. I feel sure you agree."

"Yes, indeed," Amelia Tripp agreed.

"I'm happy that we have such wise and well-chosen colleagues.

Yes, indeed. And that among them we have several of the country's leaders, the good Hapanans, to guide us. They will add greatly to our reservoir of wisdom, we shall lean on them heavily. But we have something, also, to offer. You, your ripe experience of British parliamentary democracy, one of the finest flowers of human culture, Mrs. Tripp, if you will permit me to say so. I, for my small part, some experience in the international field."

"In your travels, Dr. Rumble, have you been—"

"Yes, indeed. I've had the privilege of visiting on various missions seventy-eight different countries. That approximates to seventy per cent of the total number of countries in our troubled world. Do you know how many countries this little world of ours is divided into, Mrs. Tripp? How many pens, as it were, into which history has driven the great human family? One hundred and eleven. It is surprising how few people know this simple, basic and supremely important fact. One hundred and eleven. And in nearly all—I would say seventy-five per cent—the plant of progress is firmly rooted. That is an inspiring thought, Mrs. Tripp."

"I suppose so." Dr. Rumble was clearly no quiet American. A feeling of paralysis seemed to be creeping over Amelia.

"We must," Dr. Rumble was continuing, "exempt from this category both Red China and Red Russia. These are large countries, Mrs. Tripp, accommodating many members of the human family. There the plant of progress, far from taking root, has been blasted and scorched by the fires of tyranny. Our task now is to save these innocent Hapanans from the perils of infection by the deadly germ of Communism. That I regard as our sublime challenge. They can be saved, but only if we go right out to reach into their souls and hearts."

"I hardly think that we as a Commission—"

"Colonialism has curdled the milk of human kindness. It has poisoned the wells of action. We must eliminate the last vestiges of colonialism. I was shocked, I must admit, Mrs. Tripp, positively shocked, to see the terrible conditions under which the good people of this British colony are compelled to live—exist, I should say. Why, the women have no nylons. Many of the little children, no shoes.

Thousands of householders have no electricity. In some places, I am told, there are even no latrines. If we are to combat the dynamics of Communism—"

"Dr. Rumble, forgive me if I interrupt, the photographer is waiting. There's to be a group photograph, I'm afraid. We must try to look as if we love each other, at any rate to start with, however much we may feel like murdering each other later on."

Amelia gave the Chairman a look of heart-felt gratitude—almost devotion. With the relief of one just rescued from a particularly barren desert isle, she edged away to sit between Sir Jeremy, congenial despite his suspect tycoonery, and Alex Burton, a bit opinionated and cynical but human, anyway.

"The afternoon to settle in, our first full meeting tomorrow morning and then the week-end to get ourselves organized," had been their instructions. A fleet of the Company's cars waited to convey the curious on a sight-seeing tour of the town. Amelia, still dodging the representative of LEDA—he and the Rev. Goliath Zaza were now locked in conversation—found herself sharing a back seat with Alex.

"Might as well get the lie of the pubs," he remarked.

"We ought to be getting down to our homework, I suppose. That economic survey of Hapanan resources looks interesting, and the memorandum on the tapioca scheme . . ."

"Plenty of time," Alex said firmly.

Not that Shooting Star offered many sights, apart from the great mines and their installations, reserved for an officially conducted tour later on. There was the artificial lake, a viewpoint on the ridge above the town, a public park, a war memorial, a tree planted by the Queen Mother and a clock tower presented by Steyn Consolidated in memory of King George VI. And finally the Pig and Whistle for tea.

"A great place for honeymooners," Mr. Butterfield had explained at luncheon. "I'm sorry it's so full."

"The matrimonial season?" Sir Christopher had inquired.

"No, policemen. Sent up here to look after *you.*"

Mr. Butterfield had sounded distinctly sour. London had insisted on these bodyguards, and each one cost Hapana's Government an extra £5 a day. The health vote would have to be cut again to find the money.

The Pig and Whistle was a rambling, single-storey place built round three sides of a square, with rows of bedrooms like stalls. Creepers festooned with blossom—azure morning glory, orange bignonia, mauve solanum and the glaring, reckless purple of bougainvillea—swathed the posts of a trellis-sheltered patio overlooking a garden dispirited by heat and termites. On it the guests sat at little iron tables having tea. Now that Alex knew what to expect, he could classify without difficulty the healthy, sunburnt young men in open-necked shirts and grey flannels he would otherwise have assumed to be honeymooning grooms awaiting their brides.

On a corner of the patio was displayed a selection of native curios: imitation ivory elephants bought by the gross in Bombay, antelope-hide bags badly made in Omdurman, carved wooden animals and elongated warriors from Nairobi, necklaces of shiny red beans with black caps, the only local product.

Amelia strolled across to inspect the merchandise. African gifts would have to be bought for her daughter, her secretary and a faithful daily. She fingered a bean necklace while three or four eager vendors clustered round.

"You want to watch these fellows. They always try to stick it on." The policeman with a broken nose who had shooed off the placard-bearers at the airport stood beside her; detailed to guard the Commissioners, he felt he might as well protect them from being cheated, which was otherwise certain to happen, as from assault and battery, which was problematical.

"They're called lucky beans, you know; all the honeymooners buy them."

"They're quite attractive," Amelia said.

"Actually, they're deadly poison—one of those vegetable alkaloids. We have a wide selection here. If Hapanans want to do each other in, there's nothing to stop them. Sometimes I wonder why so many stay alive."

"I think one of these necklaces would do for Cynthia. . . . If they were *really* poisonous, surely they wouldn't be so openly sold?"

"It's difficult to keep poison books, you know, in the bush. I'll do the bargaining, if you like."

"That's very kind of you, Mr.—? Inspector, should I say?"

"John Jacey, at your service, ma'am. Superintendent, actually. You ought to get it for three bob."

For three-and-six a string of beans was hers. It encompassed her neck with little to spare. "Chokers, these used to be called," she remarked. "I don't know what they're called nowadays. All the words change. People don't talk about crooners any more—pop singers. But they seem to be the same thing."

"Not altogether." Amelia found Alex Burton by her side. "You find a bit more punch and humour in the Top Twenty these days. But there's a relationship, certainly, in the— Well, this *is* a surprise!"

He and John Jacey were gazing at each other with an air of startled fascination. Simultaneously, each extended a hand.

"King Edward's, Birmingham!"

"Must be twenty-five years!"

"We were half-backs together," Alex recalled. "D'you still play football?"

"No, I gave up all those manly sports years ago. I know I look like a bruiser—" he fingered his broken nose "—but as a matter of fact I broke it chasing a *Charaxes candiope*—that's a kind of butterfly—over a *kopje*. The nose makes me look more ferocious than I am; perhaps that's a good thing for a policeman? I never know."

"Policemen should know their own minds."

"The longer I live, the less I know mine."

Over their pot of tea on the patio, Amelia remarked: "That police officer seems a pleasant young man. D'you think that was true about the butterfly?"

"I shouldn't wonder. He was always a bug-hunter, so far as I remember; and always breaking rules, so obviously destined to enforce them. I, on the other hand, observed them carefully; it was less trouble."

"I hope the reverse doesn't apply."

Neither of them knew that John Jacey was about to acquire an international notoriety as a symbol of imperialist oppression: that as the Broken-nosed Policeman he was shortly to incur the wrath and obloquy of liberal-minded millions, to be scorned by Mr. Krushchev, deplored by the Prime Minister and denounced as a mercenary in the pay of Sir Roy Welensky by the United Nations; that he was to become the cause of several inquiries, reports and lawsuits. For at this moment Fleetway Black's story was being typed out in the *Clarion*'s news-room.

> I saw a tough, fifteen-stone police officer with a broken nose —relic of the boxing ring—beat back an unarmed crowd listening peaceably to their leader behind the barrier. I saw a woman carrying a baby hit repeatedly about the bare legs with his truncheon, amid the screams of terrified children. I saw him strike a little girl with his brawny fist . . .

Chapter 5

Sir Christopher awoke to a mild, golden Sunday morning. Sunlight the colour of fresh honey slanted into his airy bedroom and birds fluted in a nearby pepper tree. Soft, friendly noises came to him from a world outside of hope and promise: the swish of a broom as it languidly caressed garden paths, the rattle of a gardener's barrow, a woman's voice calling to her children. He stretched himself at the open window and gazed over the placid lake reflecting a sky as blue as love-in-a-mist.

Impossible to believe that everything wouldn't go smoothly in such a gentle, sunlit, welcoming land! He had been dreaming of voluptuous sensations on a thick white fur rug; of course, they had been speaking the night before about Lord Curzon and Elinor Glyn. Perhaps Constance . . . ? She was not asleep, but looking rather chalky. He sat beside her on the bed and stroked her hair.

"A glorious morning, poppet."

She opened her eyes. "I had a rotten night. I'm glad I didn't disturb you."

"I'm awfully sorry. I slept like a log." A little worm of guilt began to wriggle. "Overtired?"

"Oh, I don't know. Tummy. I'll stay in bed for breakfast. We haven't anything official today, have we?"

"No, thank God. The others, I hope, will remove themselves to a so-called mountain about fifty miles away. Picnic lunch. I've got a lot of papers to read."

Breakfast in the private sitting-room was delightful: fresh paw-paw with slices of lime, scrambled egg and tomato, crisp bacon, and for once a treat—a little honey on a single slice of toast. Sir Christopher was in the best of humours when Hugo Evans came in from the office opening out of the sitting-room.

"I'm sorry to disturb you—Sunday morning, too. There's been a bit of nonsense. You didn't happen to listen to the local radio last night?"

"God forbid."

"One of our members shot his big mouth and put his feet into it with both hands."

Sir Christopher sighed, pushed aside a light novel, and with little hesitation said:

"Mansfield Matunda?"

"Our fiery particle. How did you guess?"

Sir Christopher smiled a little grimly. "What did he actually say?"

"He revealed details of the great tapioca plot hatched by the neo-imperialists to undermine Hapanan virility. Then he said our own Commission was a fraudulent trick, our members all colonialist stooges and Dr. Rumble an agent of United States imperialists who'd arranged to buy the country from the British and then reintroduce slavery."

"Then how does he account for his own presence on the Commission?"

"He didn't mention that."

Somehow, Sir Christopher didn't feel quite as shocked as he knew he should have been—as he would have been even a week ago. Although they had scarcely been three days out of the United Kingdom, the effects of a different age, clime and tempo had begun to tell. He frowned slightly, recalling his duties.

"You'd better get hold of Matunda, Hugo. I suppose I must ask him to resign."

"And if he refuses?"

They looked blankly at each other.

"He can hardly do that."

"I suppose," Hugo reflected, "if you refuse to accept one rule, there's no particular reason why you should accept another. You can't force his resignation."

"I'll have to talk to him."

"That's another difficulty. He isn't in his room. He hasn't been there all night and no one knows where to find him."

Sir Christopher's expression showed relief rather than anger. Of course he *ought* to be angry at such a disgraceful breach of correct behaviour, but there was something about Matunda that made you forgive him his sins; the twinkle in his eye perhaps, the knowledge that he himself didn't find his conduct in the least reprehensible—just a series of intelligent manoeuvres in the ancient, infinitely variable free-for-all of politics.

"He seems a man of many interests," Sir Christopher observed.

"Slippery as a trout," Hugo agreed. "You wouldn't think he'd once been an acrobat, would you?"

"I wouldn't be surprised."

"In his younger days he got a scholarship to the Spiritual Training College in Buffalo Pans, Idaho, to study divinity, but the money ran out and he toured Latin America as a human thunderbolt, shot by a catapult into a tank full of feathers. That set up his finances again and he went back to college to study International Monetary Adjustments, whatever they are. Meanwhile he'd married the daughter of a Brazilian bullfighter and after that he never looked back."

"So he gave up divinity."

"I think it was always an avenue rather than a goal."

"He seems a resourceful sort of fellow," Sir Christopher remarked.

"Almost too much so, perhaps, for Hapana," Hugo agreed. "The country seems to make up in human resources what it lacks in economic ones. I'll see if I can track him down."

Lady Connor was calling from the bedroom for things with which to do her face.

"Feeling better, poppet?"

"Not much. I'm sorry, Chris, don't let me spoil your day. I'll be all right by tonight, I expect."

"Well . . ." The telephone rang. It was Mr. Butterfield speaking from Umpah.

"You've seen this outburst of Matunda's?"

"I've heard about it."

"I've just had the transcript in. He's dropped every brick it's possible for anyone to drop in Hapana. It's going to spark off a monumental row." The Chief Minister sounded faintly accusing. Sir Christopher's heart sank.

"And another thing. The Minister's been on the blower from London."

"Oh, dear."

"Yes. The Opposition are going to town on this, apparently, in the Commons. As none of them knows anything about it, it's the one thing on which they can all agree. I think you'll be attacked personally."

"Well, I can take it. That seems to be the least of our worries."

"The Minister says for God's sake sort it out somehow. And another thing. Last night Moscow radio put out a full and accurate account of your arrival, but more than that—they had what purported to be a summary of your first meeting yesterday morning. Whether it was correct or not's for you to say, but it sounded convincing. I'm having the transcript sent to you by special messenger."

Sir Christopher was silent for a few moments, this time really taken aback.

"That must mean that someone *inside* the Commission has been—well, indiscreet. Or deliberately spilling the beans . . ."

"Exactly. The Republic of Bonga, you know, is just across the lake. It's stuffed with Russian technicians and Chinese acrobats."

"Troubles never come singly."

"That's what we're paid for, I suppose— though not nearly enough. Then I can assume, Sir Christopher, that you'll give Matunda a piece of your mind?"

"The trouble is, he's disappeared."

"Oh! You mean, bed not slept in?"

"Exactly."

"Try the Palm Beach. He's probably sleeping it off." The telephone clicked.

Sir Christopher returned to the window, but the glory of the morning had gone. Outside he noticed a policeman in khaki walking to and fro at a discreet distance, swishing at shrubs with his cane. What a waste of time! Hapanan politics were mostly shadow-boxing—a form of entertainment, really. Bread and circuses, tapioca and diatribes . . .

But then, this Moscow broadcast: he couldn't get over the feeling that such things were slightly absurd, melodramatic, unreal. Of course, that was quite wrong—these things were happening every day. He had been warned in London to take extra care about security. But why should the Russians take an interest in the Commission? Could one of the Commissioners, or of his senior staff, *really* be a spy? How could the information be passed on? He sighed it; it was the sort of problem he ought to talk over with his Vice-Chairman; how could you discuss anything tricky with *him?*

Lord Bagpuse was thoroughly enjoying the expedition to the distant mountain, even if this was no more than a low, dull, rocky hill surrounded on all sides by *momombo* bush. Local legend had it that an ancient prophetess, nurtured by a cobra, dwelt among the rocks brewing the secret of eternal happiness. Some years before, an American explorer had failed to find the prophetess but succeeded in selling over a million copies of his resulting book, which had been filmed, serialized, translated, condensed, expanded and televised, and finally buried under a new supermarket in Texas as an example of the culture of the nineteen-sixties, together with copies of the *Dallas Times,* the works of Tennessee Williams and a *Time-Life* compendium of modern American art.

The explorer, moreover, had captured from a cave a pair of unusually powerful and intelligent bats. The story of the domestication, training and subsequent love-life of these creatures, who became enthusiastic players on an Irish harp, inspired several more enthralling, copiously illustrated volumes which left the sales of the prophetess in the shade.

Lord Bagpuse had not read them. As the car lurched up a rutted, runnelled track he gazed intensely at the bush, searching for some sign of livestock—even a goat. Nothing caught his eye. A queer country!

The rest of the back of the large motor-car was full of Lady Bagpuse, knitting an enormous pullover.

"It's sure to be hot at the bottom of the mine," she remarked, "and I don't want you to catch a chill when you come up."

"I'm not going down any mines," the Earl firmly decided. "Maxwell-Palmer says there's some decent fishing in the dam or lake or whatever it is. Kind of bass."

"Then you're sure to need a sweater, Freddy."

"You know, Blanche, I've got several already."

"One can never have too many sweaters."

Alex, in another car, had secured a place next to Hugo Evans' Personal Assistant: she had a very fancy name, Thomasina Labouchère. Already he'd discovered that, like many career-girls, she had one personality for her work and quite another for her life out of office hours—or, rather, that when at work her personality was zipped into a sort of space-suit of impersonal efficiency. She could emerge, when off-duty, as gay as a lark, a leg-puller in a gentle, undercover way.

After the party had picnicked under a tree, with a blue prospect below of limitless *momombo,* Alex was able to detach her from the others and to climb farther up the hill, ostensibly to search for interesting plants. None of the plants looked, in fact, in the least interesting, but all alike—bare, spiky and eager to ruin nylons or cling to trouser legs.

"It's not a friendly mountain," Alex remarked.

"No, but superb views."

He took her hand to help her up a steep place. She was warm and lively like a thrush; her tawny hair had fallen over her forehead, she was flushed from the exertion and he took pleasure in the rise and fall of her breasts under a thin flowered blouse, in the throbbing of the pulse in her wrist. She moved with freedom, her mouth had a humorous twist, her voice was delightful—what more could one want on a fine Sunday afternoon?

"Have you done anything like this before?" he asked. "This Commission, I mean?"

"Never. I'm tremendously excited. No doubt Commissions are

really much the same in Hapana as in London, but I can't help feeling as if I were starting off to find Livingstone."

"Today I suppose he'd be a Steyn Consolidated Bishop preaching in an air-conditioned cathedral. Our only lasting achievement in Africa has been to destroy its mystery."

"Don't we carry mystery about with us, just by being human? Take this Commission, for instance . . ."

"Well, we're hardly cloak-and-dagger types."

"No, but can't you detect several little minor mysteries? Nothing much, but—well, intriguing?"

"The presence of Bagpuse is a little unclear."

Thomasina laughed. "To him, I think, as much as to others. Then what's Mr. Matunda doing here? His own party's boycotting and blackguarding the whole Commission."

"I think the explanation's simple. We're getting paid."

"Possibly. Then there's this Dr. Rumble—most unusual, having an American. And he himself seems invisible behind an impenetrable cloud of foundations and departments."

"And is Sir Jeremy's deaf-aid real or bogus?"

"And what's become of Mr. Tripp?"

"And which of Chief Faustus' eight wives is to be asked to our receptions?"

"Full of mysteries," Thomasina agreed.

"You're one yourself," Alex suggested.

"Of course. Not only that, I'm quite different from all the other women you've ever met."

"I can see that."

"Other women don't understand you, but I do."

"There's no need to mock." He took her hand and traced the outline of her fingers with his own, feeling the soft sheath over brittle bone. "Does typing make the tips hard?"

"It doesn't seem to. In my exalted position, I don't type much."

"Have you been married?"

"No. Have you?"

"Yes, but it's over."

"I'm sorry."

For a while they sat in silence, screwing up their eyes to look into the heat-hazed view or watching, by their feet, a beetle with orange stripes scale a rock and vanish into the coarse grass-roots.

"To continue the examination. Why are you here? Where do you come from? What are you looking for? Just to be a competent career-girl? A Chairman's right hand?"

"Mysteries are intriguing, facts are dull."

Alex jumped up impatiently and pulled her after him. "All right, keep your mystery." Taken by surprise, she lost her balance and leant towards him; he brushed aside her hair and kissed her soundly. When he let her go she pulled back, not in anger, but with an odd look of wariness, even of pain.

"Have I offended you? All the same, I shan't apologize."

"It doesn't matter."

"To me it does. You like to keep the two things separate, don't you? Work and play. But they can overlap."

"They can, but it seldom answers."

They started back in single file because of the steepness of the path. "I didn't mean to make a mystery of anything," she added. "There's nothing to make a mystery about. I'm thirty-two. I was born in Liverpool because my father was in the merchant navy. We always seemed to be hard up—the slump, I suppose. My father was lost in a convoy in the war. After the war I messed about in several jobs, then I got into the civil service. Now I've managed to get into a branch that supplies P.A.'s and executive officers to overseas missions and things like this. I'm hoping to travel, which is what I've always wanted. So you see—no mysteries."

"You've told me none of the important things."

At the foot of the track lay a small hotel, a cluster of huts and open-sided lounges and peeling gum-trees that had come together over the years, kept by an easy-going Greek with a great many children. Here they paused for tea. Lord Bagpuse had fallen into conversation with a fat, red-faced man in shorts who was drinking beer and sweating, his air of cheery good-fellowship contradicted by a pair of sharp, beady eyes.

"Can you beat it, only six pairs of tits," Lord Bagpuse was saying as Alex joined them, "and thick in the brisket at that. Rotten type of animal in my opinion. 'I've only judged them on the hook before,' the fellow said when I tackled him. Extraordinary, eh? Laughed till I cried."

"What do you think of the pigs in Hapana, sir?" the fat man inquired.

"Pigs in Hapana? Don't seem to be any pigs at all. Nor cattle, either. Extraordinary country, can't make it out. How can people live without pigs? And all this talk of tapioca. . . . Quite beyond me."

"May I ask your opinion, sir, about the tapioca question?"

"My opinion? Can't bear the stuff myself, but the experts say it grows here, and what's more they can sell it, so they'd better buckle to and grow it, eh? It's for their own good. Can't think what all the fuss is about."

"So you support the pro-tapioca party?"

Something in the fat man's tone warned Alex that Lord Bagpuse was on dangerous ground; but it was no good throwing significant glances at the Vice-Chairman.

"Don't know anything about parties, my boy. Never been a party man myself. I've made two speeches in the Lords, one on otter-hunting, one on cropping horses' ears. Barbaric custom, in my opinion, cropping ears."

"I'm with you there, sir, every time."

"Tapioca, you were saying? So far as I can make out, there's a gang of bolshies in this country out to bamboozle the peasants, or whatever you call 'em, and put 'em off growing this stuff. Well, that's a rotten business, whatever way you look at it. If tapioca's good for them and good for the country, let 'em grow it. Make it compulsory if need be. People made a lot of fuss about compulsory tuberculin testing when it first came in, but we've pretty well wiped out T.B. as a result. But that's just my opinion, and I've only been here a couple of days."

"That's very interesting," the fat man said. "I've enjoyed our chat, Lord Bagpuse."

"Wonder how he knew my name?" Lord Bagpuse mused.

Alex listened with growing dismay. But it was not his business to recall the Chairman's recent and emphatic warnings of the need for discretion. He went in search of the proprietor.

"Can you tell me who that fat man was, who just left?"

"That fat gentleman? That was Mr. Thwaite, sar, a good customer. You like him, sar?"

Somehow the proprietor made it sound as if he was offering Mr. Thwaite for an immoral purpose.

"Is he on the local paper, by any chance?"

"Very much, sar. Sometimes he puts in news of my hotel. Good news, you understand—big people stay here, they like it very much. You like my hotel, sar?"

"Very much, thank you. Mr. Thwaite of the—what's the name of the paper?"

"*Hapana Times.* Very good paper, sar, prints very good news. Riots, murders, robbers, arsons, smashes—everything, you find it there. And good news of my hotel."

"Splendid."

"And Mr. Thwaite, he writes for big papers in London, New York. He is correspondent. My good friend, Mr. Thwaite."

"Better and better." Alex went, reluctantly, in search of Stephen Partridge, to whom he had taken an unreasonable dislike.

"Well, that *has* torn it," Partridge said. "The old half-wit—and after the Chairman's pep-talk on security, too. I'd better get down to Umpah tonight and see what I can do, but to be honest I don't think there's much. Thwaite's got his story, and he'll use it. It's good for half a column in the London dailies."

"I'm really getting quite sorry for Sir Christopher," Alex reflected.

"Well, we've had a nice quiet day," the Vice-Chairman said, as they got into their cars. "To work tomorrow, I suppose." He sighed. "Queer country this. No pigs. No cattle. Can't understand how they carry on."

Chapter 6

"How ON EARTH could I know the fellow was a journalist?" Whenever these Commissioners did anything unpardonable, Sir Christopher reflected, *they* seemed to have a grievance; if anyone had a right to one, surely it was the Chairman.

"You didn't have to know. You just had to keep your mouth shut."

"How can I keep my mouth shut and talk to people? That's what we were told in London—the Minister told me himself. 'Get about and talk to people,' he said. 'Find out their ideas.'" Lord Bagpuse sounded indignant.

"The idea was that *they* should talk to *us*. Not the other way round."

"Oh, well, if you're going to quibble! This fellow asked a couple of straight questions and I gave a straight answer. What's the world coming to, when one gets into trouble for that?"

"My dear chap, you've no experience of politics."

"I didn't mention politics. It was only tapioca. All this fuss about a thing like that! If it grows well, grow it. If it doesn't, don't. That's what I say."

"Your remarks," Sir Christopher said icily, "are fully and forcibly reported in the *Hapana Times*. They're being quoted on the radio in seven languages and in the British and American press. Don't you understand that you played right into the hands of the anti-West, pro-Communist wing of the Peoples' Peace Party? Now they'll brand the Commission as an agent of colonialist oppression, sent to impose tapioca-growing by force. You've probably bust the Commission in pieces before we've even started."

"If the Commission's finished," Bagpuse replied, heaving himself out of the chair, "we'd better all go home. I always thought it was a pretty damn silly thing anyway, to tell the truth."

"You've told enough truth," the Chairman retorted, "and we can't all go home. You should never have joined the Commission if you felt like that."

"I was in two minds, but I thought I might be able to help a bit about livestock and animal diseases and that sort of thing."

The Chairman blew his nose, always a sign of agitation. "You must issue a statement saying you've been misreported."

"But I don't think I have."

"The papers give hard knocks often enough; it won't hurt them to get a little tap in return. I'll get Partridge to prepare a statement for you to sign."

"I shan't sign it if it tells lies."

Sir Christopher got up too, and blew his nose again. But many years ago he had learnt to keep his temper.

"Well, make up your mind when you see it, Bagpuse. You got us into this mess, and you must help to get us out."

"I'll see what I can do," Lord Bagpuse said—much too jauntily, in the Chairman's opinion—and left the room.

"My God, what an outfit!" Sir Christopher sat down again and put his head between his hands. "It only remains, now, for Rumble to drop some colossal clanger. I wish they were all at the bottom of the sea."

Sir Jeremy Maxwell-Palmer came in, to be greeted by the Chairman with unexpected warmth. Sir Jeremy was a great standby. He took things calmly.

"It'll all blow over," he said. "I know Hapana politics. A three days' wonder, then another hare to chase."

But, on the telephone, Butterfield was much less reassuring, and away in London, Dick Howard, the Minister, was working up a head of steam. Fifteen questions were down for him to answer that afternoon in the House. The *Clarion* had plastered its special correspondent's story all over the front page: Connor Commission mobbed at airstrip, woman M.P. attacked, brutal retaliation of Hapana police, women and children injured, broken-nosed officer uses Storm Troop methods on fleeing children. . . . Opposition papers were recalling Sharpeville and Hola Camp: *"Even if sober inquiry should reveal some exaggeration,"* a *Times* leader-writer was dictating, *"this distressing lapse from the high standards we have come to expect of the overseas gendarmerie cannot but play into the hands of Mr. Khrushchev, and affect negotiations now in progress . . ."*

"How's your wife this morning?" Sir Jeremy inquired.

"She's running a bit of a temperature. Overtired, I'm afraid."

"You ought to get her looked at, you know. We're in the tropics, queer kinds of bug about. I can recommend the best doctor in Hapana. He works for us."

Sir Christopher smiled. "The best of everything for Steyn Consolidated? It's rather magnificent. She'll be as right as rain in a day or two. I wouldn't dream of worrying you on such a . . ."

Sir Christopher hesitated. After all, it was Constance who was off-colour; sometimes a sudden change of climate and diet did upset people. And her age . . .

"I'll ring him up, anyway," Sir Jeremy said. "You'll enjoy a talk with him. He's an interesting chap. One of these Central Europeans, I think, originally. He's done some first-rate research on a thing called five-day fever these fellows suffer from. And deficiency diseases. And intestinal parasites."

"He sounds much too high-powered to treat a case of tummy upset. But thank you very much indeed; if Constance doesn't pick up, I'll take you at your word."

Constance was dozing when he looked in just before the meeting; she had a washed-out appearance, and the curtains were drawn.

"I've got a headache," she said wearily, "and no one answers the bell."

"I'll see to that at once. How's the temperature?"

"Oh, nothing much." He took it, and found it to be the same—about a hundred.

"I'm sorry, Chris," she said. "Such a silly way to go on—and you—with such a lot of worries."

Sir Christopher smiled at her tenderly. It was just like Constance, to think of him when she herself was the one to be fussed over. He was a lucky man. She was always thinking of his welfare, his interests—sometimes, ungrateful fellow that he was, he even wished she'd leave them to take care of themselves. Now and again he felt almost like a pawn reached out for by a maestro's hand, a plan hatched by some warring general.

Constance didn't often relax. But her advice, her calculations, her attention to detail, her wide acquaintance in the right quarters—where would he be without them? A devoted wife, indeed! Precious beyond rubies. He must try to care for her as she cared for him.

"Maxwell-Palmer thinks a doctor would be a wise precaution. He's got an ace in that line up his sleeve. Trust Steyn Consolidated to have the best of everything, doctors included. Would you mind?"

"I'll be all right, Chris. You mustn't worry."

"I'd worry less if you were under medical orders."

"We'll see later on, shall we?"

"All right, poppet. Want the curtains back?"

"No, I'll just doze. You must be off to your meeting."

"We'd better make a start, I suppose."

The start was not altogether happy. Matunda was missing. Bagpuse was sulking, Rumble was talking, Chief Faustus not yet arrived. A flow of memoranda was overwhelming everyone except Dr. Rumble, who had started an elaborate filing system of his own.

The first to give evidence were members of the Penumbra District Council, five in number. They were large, black, bulky men in overcoats and sandals, each carrying a fly-whisk in his hand.

"We have all read your memorandum," the Chairman said. "Wouldn't it save time if we questioned the President about it? Which is the President?"

The largest of the Councillors, who had discarded his overcoat to reveal a very tight suit beneath and wore a topee that had once been white, rose with deliberation to his feet. He spoke slowly, in halting English.

"I am the President. I am the President of the Penumbra District Council. First, I tell you the history of my people, the Waguma. You know the great King Chaka and Musuma, his general. Now one day this general came with his *impis* to the country of the Pangani and saw a white bullock there. He said, 'I will slay this bullock and take the liver and—' "

"Forgive me, Mr. President, that's very interesting," the Chairman said, "but our purpose here is to frame a new constitution for Hapana. Isn't all this . . ."

"He said, 'I will slay this bullock, and grind its liver with the sap of the *mugumu* tree to anoint the warriors, and then God will help us conquer all this country.' So he told his councillors to fetch his new spear . . ."

The story went on for ten minutes before Sir Christopher interrupted again.

"Mr. President, we are all very interested in what you have to say, but can you tell us something about the *constitution* of Hapana? Have you considered on what basis the franchise should be framed?"

There was a short silence. The President was not used to being interrupted, and needed time to adjust himself.

"I will consult my council," he said at length. In low, musical voices and stately periods the five Councillors conferred in their own tongue.

"Mr. Chairman, we have their memorandum in front of us," Mrs. Tripp pointed out. "It sets out very clearly their suggestions on the constitutional issues. Franchise, composition of Assembly, bicameral legislature, Council of Ministers, reserved powers, relations with neighbouring territories—it's all here. Can't we question them on it?"

"Go ahead, Mrs. Tripp, by all means."

Amelia Tripp cleared her throat. "Mr. President?" The Councillors continued their conference.

"They do not understand that they can be addressed by a lady," the Rev. Zaza intervened. "I will ask them. Chief, will you open your ears? This lady has a question to ask. In England, she is herself a Chief. She addresses you as an equal. The Chairman is a cousin of the Queen and he is asking you to hear her. Please, madam, now ask your question."

Mrs. Tripp felt embarrassed, like someone forced to repeat to a deaf acquaintance for the third time an observation on the weather.

"You demand in your memorandum," she began, "the immediate introduction of one-man-one-vote. Also a democratically elected Council of Ministers, independence back-dated to last January, and union with Ghana. These are rather sweeping demands, you know. Take universal suffrage, for instance. Do you really want all the *women* to have the vote?"

The faces of the Councillors looked blanker than before. The President coughed, and said: "Madam?"

"Is this what you want? Women voting equally with men?"

"What we ask the Government," one of the other Councillors intervened to say in loud, strong tones, "is for a new market at Kumbula. Five years ago, Mr. Butler the District Commissioner made this promise. A new market, with latrines. Our market now is very little. Too many come, and the people are cheated. The goats can eat the yams because it is without fences. We ask—"

"Yes, yes, but the *franchise,* Councillor. The vote."

The Councillor shook his head. Another of the five cleared his throat and spoke.

"We are needing in Penumbra a new school. Our school is too little and many children come. The teacher's house is falling down. We need . . ."

"It doesn't look as if the Councillors' memorandum is an exact reflection of their views," the Chairman remarked. "Mr. Zaza, perhaps you could interpret? Did they write this memorandum themselves?"

An animated conversation in a Hapanan tongue followed between the Councillors and the Rev. Zaza, who grew quite excited.

"Mr. Chairman," he reported, "these Councillors did not write this paper at all."

"Then who did?"

"Their clerk wrote it. He is an educated man."

"It's a very educated paper. Do they know what it says?"

"The clerk read it to them, but not the same as what is written here. It was about markets, schools, a new road and the price of yams. Then the clerk translated it into English."

"A free translation, evidently. Perhaps we'd better sound them on their real views. Please ask them, Mr. Zaza, if they would like everyone to vote equally, women the same as men."

The question, once translated, appeared to be involved and long, but there was no doubt about their response. With one accord they thundered a single resounding word.

"They say no," Goliath Zaza reported.

"Would they like to see a democratically elected parliament with sovereign powers and no reserved seats?"

The Rev. Zaza looked a little dubious. "That is rather hard to translate. But I will try."

He did so; surprisingly, the question was much briefer. The response was the same, perhaps even more vehement.

"How did you translate it?" the Chairman asked.

"I asked if they wished to be governed by Mr. Mguu," Zaza replied. "They said no."

"But that isn't quite the same thing?"

"But yes, Mr. Chairman, it is. The Triple-P has bribed most of the electors and frightened all the rest by burning down their houses. That is what I have often told Mr. Butterfield. If my party, the Forever Forward Group—"

"I take your point, Mr. Zaza. Well, I'm glad to have cleared that up. I'm not quite sure how we should record their evidence in the minutes, Hugo? Perhaps they would like to submit a revised memorandum? You might explain that to them, Mr. Zaza. I don't know what we should do, I'm sure, without your help."

Two nuns were the next to give evidence. They wished to see more religious instruction in schools, an end to female circumcision and fewer child marriages.

"I'm sure we're all in favour of your proposals," Amelia Tripp said. "For instance, child marriage. But as there's no registration of births, how can you know a girl's age?"

The nuns looked puzzled. They had soft, white, pudgy faces under their coifs, and amiable expressions; one wore pince-nez and was middle-aged, the other had badly fitting dentures and was younger.

"There could be a law passed," said the older nun in a soft, high Irish voice, "to make it wrong for any girl to marry until three years after she was circumcised."

"But you want to do away with female circumcision?"

"Och, yes, and so we do. The Bishop is very strong on that, your Honours."

"Well, then, if the girls *weren't* circumcised . . ."

"It has been a shock to me, I must admit it, quite a shock," Dr. Rumble intervened, "to find this primitive rite being practised in our nuclear age right here in the heart of a British colony, where your British flag has flown for over fifty years. I needn't remind you gentlemen—and lady—of the importance of the home in the progress of the human family. Now if in the heart and centre of the home we have these unfortunate girls to whom the benefits of Christianity and the democratic way of life have not yet been extended . . ."

"You're quite right, Dr. Rumble, but if we could get back to, let's say, the composition of the Central Legislative Assembly . . ."

"Mr. Chairman, it is part of the policy of the Forever Forward Group—"

"Mr. Chairman," said Sir Jeremy, "may I suggest that we adjourn for tea?" Before anyone could speak again, the Chairman was on his feet.

"An excellent suggestion. Thank you, Mother—er—Ursula; thank you, Sister Mary. You've been a great help to us, a great help." He bowed to the witnesses and left the conference room, followed closely by Sir Jeremy.

"The doctor's arrived. I hope you'll allow him to see Lady Connor."

"That's quick work, Jeremy." They had got on to Christian name terms. "And uncommonly kind. It'll cheer her up, anyway. Ask him to join us first, will you, for a cup of tea?"

Thomasina was in the outer office, decoding messages. She looked flushed and hot but still, the Chairman thought, thoroughly ornamental.

"Thick as autumn leaves in Vallombrosa, I suppose," he observed, nodding at the papers on her desk.

"I'm afraid so. Mainly about this so-called airstrip incident and the brutal policeman. There's a rocket from the Prime Minister."

"Well, I must say . . . What about our Vice-Chairman's *gaffe?"*

"Mr. Partridge has prepared this statement for him to sign, saying he was misreported. The tapioca issue is one the people of Hapana themselves must decide. Mr. Partridge thought perhaps you'd want to tackle Lord Bagpuse yourself, Sir Christopher."

"I don't know about *want.* I will. Has anyone found Matunda?"

"Yes, he's been located and brought back to the hotel; Mr. Partridge thinks it's not much good your seeing him before tomorrow morning."

"I bet he's right there."

The girl doesn't flap, thank God, he thought; there's something about her that's level, calming; and yet, in another sense, exciting, too. He wondered if he would pat her on the shoulder, and decided against it; too avuncular. If he made a move, it would be on the adult level of equality. But not, he supposed regretfully, while this Commission lasted; at least not while Constance . . .

"I'm going to have a quick cup and then see my wife," he said. "Let me know if anything urgent comes through."

Chapter 7

Sir Jeremy introduced the doctor with the air of an impresario presenting an entertainer fresh from triumphs in the major European capitals. The doctor was dark, sallow, lightly-built, with deep-set eyes rather close together and a lined, monkeyish, clever face.

Sir Christopher shook hands, then looked more carefully at Steyn Consolidated's medical ace.

"Haven't we met before somewhere? I seem to know your face."

Dr. Godfrey looked back at Sir Christopher with formidable intensity, but did not show any sign of recognition.

"I do not think I have had the honour." He gave a formal little nod that, in a Continental country, would have blossomed into a bow. About his gentle, pleasing voice hung a faint foreign intonation.

"I don't know whether Sir Jeremy warned you, I think you've come on a wild-goose chase. There's really not much wrong with my wife."

"I'm glad of that," said the doctor. "But we're in the tropics, where it's wise to take precautions."

"I understand your profession's made such great strides in tropical medicine that it's now rather healthier for a European here than at home."

When the doctor smiled, he looked more monkeyish than ever; his flesh was stretched tightly over his bones.

"If he takes proper precautions, that is true. There's less time lost on the mines here from malaria and dysentery than from colds and respiratory infections in the U.K. But that's only if no one forgets his little pill. I hope, sir, that all members of your Commission take with regularity their malaria prophylactic."

"My paludrine's on the breakfast table every morning. My wife sees to that."

"I take daraprim on Sundays," Sir Jeremy said.

"I think it's easier to forget a pill if you only have to take it once a week," Amelia Tripp remarked. She looked blooming, Sir Christopher observed; evidently a hot climate suited her. Really she wasn't a bad-looking woman: a good figure, though too long a neck. Her neck now was encircled by her string of black and red lucky beans. Their bright colour set off her grey suit of heavy silk, white blouse and, to show she was in the tropics, red sandals.

"Your local purchase looks very handsome," he remarked, stirred for the first time by a faint, a very faint, desire to please.

Amelia Tripp smiled. "I was glad to be able to find something local to buy. There's not much."

Dr. Godfrey was looking at the necklace. "You know those are called lucky beans? Whether they bring luck or not I can't say, but I know they contain a deadly poison."

"So I've heard," Amelia said. "But I suppose it would have to be extracted by some complicated process to make it effective."

"If you were to swallow those beans, you would be quite safe. But if you were to grind them to a powder, then they would kill you."

Amelia looked slightly alarmed. "You mean that would be enough? Just to grind them up?"

"They have a very tough skin, too tough for the digestive juices, but if they're finely ground the toxins are released. The local people use them to settle old scores—to get rid of redundant wives, or perhaps husbands, there are many uses. But I mustn't give a lecture on native poisons; I'm at your service, Sir Christopher."

"Then we'll go and see my wife immediately." They walked together across the lounge and along a covered way to the bedroom. "Have you been long in Hapana, Doctor?"

"Nearly twenty years."

"Then you know it well."

"Well enough to know that I know nothing. That takes about twenty years to find out."

The medical examination was reassuring.

"I don't think you need add the condition of your wife to your worries. She's overtired, and there's a slight streptococcal infection. I shall send her some tablets, and I think you'll find that in twenty-four hours she'll be herself again."

"That's splendid news."

"Like so many ladies nowadays, she is strict about her diet?"

Sir Christopher smiled. "Well, yes, she takes care of her figure. In fact I have to do the same. No starches, no potatoes, rich sauces, pastry. Ryvita instead of bread, that sort of thing."

"I've told your wife it would be better to relax a little. She could permit herself a slice of toast for breakfast, a little sandwich for tea."

"If you can persuade her, Doctor, I'll salute you. And I'm awfully grateful. I feel it's been an imposition, dragging you here on such a slight pretext."

"The health of a man's wife, Sir Christopher, can never be a little thing."

"Well, no, of course not; you're right there. But it isn't every doctor who's quite so conscientious."

Sir Christopher felt mildly rebuked, and they parted with an almost excessive politeness. Somehow, Sir Christopher didn't feel quite at ease with Godfrey. But Steyn's wouldn't think so highly of him if he wasn't a first-class man.

During the next few days many aspects of Hapanan life that beneath a quiet, even dull, exterior seethed with passions like a nest of termites were brought to the notice of the Commissioners. Before them appeared a great variety of witnesses: Austrian missionaries, Italian sugar-planters, Greek traders, Syrian hoteliers, Irish vets, English botanists, French anthropologists, German foresters, Swiss financiers, Portuguese wine salesmen, Pakistani tailors, all these and many others had something—as a rule a great deal—to say about the future of their adopted land.

Hapanans themselves came in even greater numbers, anxious to impart their views on everything from the marketing of yams to the need for adult literacy campaigns, from the virtues of Mr. Mguu to the devilish plots of Mr. Butterfield and Sir Roy Welensky. For events were moving fast in Hapana. Demands for immediate, back-dated independence submitted to the United Nations had won enthusiastic support from the Afro-Asian bloc. A delegation from the Triple-P had been received with honours in Moscow and given an ovation at the ballet, while some of the Rev. Zaza's central committee had been publicly embraced in Peking.

"It is of the utmost importance," the Prime Minister cabled to the Chairman, "that you complete your deliberations with the greatest possible dispatch." "We're all hoping that you'll be able to push ahead as fast as you possibly can," Mr. Butterfield said on the telephone, adding, "The situation really is a little tricky, I'm afraid."

"I know the schedule's tight enough already, Hugo," the Chairman told his Secretary, "but we must give the screw another twist if we can."

The Commission started earlier and sat later; typists tapped and mimeographed in shifts throughout the night; memoranda flowed from the machines like rivers in the rainy season; even Dr. Rumble, who could be heard pacing his room and dictating observations into a tape-recorder most of the night, found the files slipping away out of his control.

Tired or not, the Chairman always worked late. Any Commissioner wishing to consult him could find him in his private office until about seven o'clock. Hugo and Thomasina filtered messages and callers through an outer office; after dinner one or the other, sometimes both, resumed the struggle to keep abreast of the paper-work flood.

Just before seven, Alex found Thomasina there on her own, looking harassed. He asked:

"Can I see the Chairman for about five minutes? But if it's too late I can wait till tomorrow."

"Tomorrow's going to be chaotic. For one thing, we've just heard that Chief Faustus is to arrive."

"Will that cause much chaos?"

"It's not just the arrival of our missing Commissioner. The Paramount's his cousin and is coming too, with a troop of retainers. There's to be a buffet lunch in a marquee on the lawn."

"That'll make a change."

"There's a flap on about security. The Shiwan miners, it seems, want to greet their Paramount with a mock battle, but it mightn't be mock—they're feuding with a secret sect of religious fanatics called the *Sulu Sita*. It's led by a bearded prophet who goes about in skins and thinks he's a reincarnation of St. George. And now some of the white miners want to tar and feather all the Commissioners and hand everything over to Dr. Verword. So Superintendent Jacey's got his hands full. About seeing the Chairman—could he wait? The doctor's with him now."

"He's not ill, is he?"

"Not really, but he's tired, and Lady Connor talked him into seeing Dr. Godfrey, much against his will. I'm glad: I like Dr. Godfrey." Thomasina was billeted on the doctor and his wife.

The telephone rang, and Thomasina dealt with it. She was tired, too. They all were. Days were long, nights sultry, thunderclouds were gathering to bring in the rainy season. At this time of year tempers were apt to be on edge.

"Take a day off on Sunday," Alex said. "We'll get hold of a boat and explore the lake."

"Too much work."

Alex went across to sit on the edge of her desk and reach out for her hand.

"It's warm; you're human. Break out of the paper prison you've built."

"*I* haven't built it." She neither removed her hand, nor returned his pressure. "The doctor's taking a long time. I hope there's nothing wrong with Sir Christopher."

"You sound maternal."

She smiled, too gently for his liking. "The iron hand's there, all right. I wouldn't like to get in his way. But he's fun to work for."

"A couple of careerists. Like calls to like."

"Aren't we all? Ah, they're finishing."

The door opened and Dr. Godfrey appeared in the doorway. Alex saw the Chairman standing beside a polished mahogany table lit by a small chandelier exactly overhead. The swan look was evident—an angry swan. They were aggressive birds, Alex recollected; once when he'd been sitting in a punt, a swan had snatched a ham sandwich out of his hand. Swans broke people's legs with their wings. The Chairman looked as if he'd gladly break someone's leg, perhaps Dr. Godfrey's, and the doctor himself appeared a little flushed, even agitated. He shut the door, however, gently, and smiled at Thomasina.

"You'll turn into a patient yourself if you continue working at this pressure," he remarked. "Now Lady Connor wants me to see her, I think."

"I'm to ask you to go straight along to her room."

Alex nodded to Thomasina and walked with Dr. Godfrey into a roofed-in patio that formed the entrance lobby to the guest-house. The floor was made of Spanish tiles, the patio had a fountain and a small lily-pond in the centre and potted plants all round. It smelt ripe, moist, of growth and water. Goldfish glinted in the pond. Opposite the front door was an arch through which you proceeded, down a few steps, into a lounge furnished with comfortable sofas, armchairs and writing-tables. On one side a French window gave onto a small, open patio shaded by a trellis smothered in bougainvillea, where you could sit at ease over drinks; on the other side lay the parquet-floored dining-room, hung with scenes from Livingstone's last journey by the artist Baines.

From this dining-room a covered way led along one wing of the guest-house to an all-electric kitchen at the other end. Three doors gave onto this narrow veranda: those of the Bagpuses' room, of Amelia's, and of the Chairman's suite, into which his private office opened at the back. Dr. Rumble, the Rev. Zaza and Alex occupied rooms in the other wing.

Alex left the doctor near the Chairman's door and joined Amelia as she emerged from her bedroom changed for dinner, in a neat black silk cocktail dress, wearing her red beans. She looked strained and rather wan.

"I hope *you're* not wilting, too," he said. "First Lady Connor, now the Chairman—we shall be like those ten green bottles hanging on a wall."

"There's nothing wrong with me."

Before joining their colleagues in the lounge, they took a turn on the lawn. Daylight lingered just a little in a dark-blue western sky, the stars were soft still and tentative, not diamond-hard as they would become. The silent lake, with its gaunt dead tree-limbs raised as if in desperate prayer, lay below, gunmetal-grey, stretching towards invisible hills. A mild curiosity to know more about Amelia stirred in Alex's mind.

"Forgive my asking, Mrs. Tripp, but you've a daughter, haven't you? Are you a widow, by any chance?"

"My daughter's sixteen. No, I'm not a widow; I divorced my husband some years ago."

"No offence, I hope."

"None. And your married status?"

"Similar to yours: I had a wife, we parted, and I think we're divorced. I'm not quite sure. She's in Canada somewhere."

"Oh. Whereabouts?"

"Toronto, probably. D'you know Canada?"

"No, not at all. But there are certain points about its constitutional development we ought to look into. For instance, their handling of minorities . . ."

"Meanwhile, how about a drink?"

"Perhaps a little sherry."

"By the way," Alex added casually, "where did you run across our friend Partridge?"

"Partridge? I've never seen him in my life before this Commission."

A less emphatic reply would have rolled off his mind like a raindrop on a windowpane; as it was, the raindrop made a little impact, and his thoughts went back to the Chairman's London party when a look had passed between Partridge and Amelia that had left neither at ease.

"He said something about recognizing you."

"He did? When?"

"Oh, I don't know. I may have got it wrong."

"One of you has. Of course, I meet a lot of people, you know, and one can't remember everyone. I suppose I might have run across him at some meeting or other."

"Probably."

She should have said that, Alex thought, at the start: now it looked too much like recanting. Perhaps Partridge had worked for some rival politician, or been mixed up in Amelia's domestic upsets—an old flame, even? Hardly likely. Anyway, it was no business of his.

All the same, something bothered Alex. What was it that Partridge had muttered when he'd first caught sight of her? Something to do with music, opera. Something Jewish. Lohengrin? No. Rosencrantz and Guildenstern? No. Lewin? No. Steinbeck? Sweet and low. Cannery Row, mice and men, Okies . . .

"Loewenstein." He said it, involuntarily, half-aloud, and then heard, as it were, a dead silence. Amelia had halted in her tracks. Turning his head, he saw in a half-darkness, half-pierced by a long shaft of light from the open windows, that she was standing like someone in a *tableau vivant,* her fingers on her red beans, her lips parted, her face chalk-white.

"You—what—" She checked herself and stirred as if life was flowing back into numbed limbs, a stunned heart.

"It's getting cold. The dew at this time of night. . . . I'm going in."

They walked together to the open French windows. Desmond Slocombe came towards her, his bald head shining in the diffused, indirect light.

"Now, what will you drink, Mrs. Tripp?"

"Whisky, please," she said.

Chapter 8

The Company had prepared with its usual efficiency to welcome the Paramount Chief of the Shiwa. The reception was to be small and private, on the Merry Hippo's lawn; the Shiwa's own proposals to hold it in the stadium with twenty thousand guests had been turned down.

This was, in fact, the third or fourth occasion on which plans to greet the Paramount had been made. To predict his exact movements was always tricky. Custom as ancient as the ancestors themselves forbade the Paramount to cross the river bounding his territory until his body was conveyed in a funeral barge for burial in a sacred mountain—in fact a low mound, for the Shiwaland was absolutely flat. When the Shiwas had been, despite their protests, incorporated into the Protectorate of Hapana, this custom had been gradually modified, and now the Paramount could make occasional visits to the outside world, provided certain forms were observed.

His barge had first to be caulked with the fat of a white ram and decorated with cowries taken from the waistband of a virgin. The paddlers had to drink the infusions of certain rare herbs, and the Paramount himself must wear anklets made from the hide of a pregnant antelope and sacrifice a black bullock. The journey could take place only during the moon's last quarter, provided no bees had swarmed near the Paramount's palace, and that none of his wives had given birth to twins.

All this made it rather difficult to hit off an appointed date, such as the opening of the Legislative Assembly. The last time preparations had been made to receive the Paramount in Umpah he had been obliged to cancel his visit, the status of the girl whose waistband had supplied the cowries having turned out to be equivocal.

On this occasion, other difficulties had arisen whose nature remained obscure. It might be that the right herbs had not been in season, or that the bees had swarmed. As time went on Mr. Butterfield grew nervous that Chief Faustus would never be able to take his place on the Commission. The moon was waning; by Monday it would be too far gone, and if the Paramount had not come by Sunday, Chief Faustus would assuredly have to wait at least another month.

On Saturday morning Mr. Slocombe's Rolls-Royce and two gaily painted lorries were waiting by the river to convey the Shiwan party from their barge to the feast on the lawn. All was well: with a burst of song and flourish of paddles the royal barge arrived, propelled, as tradition insisted, by members of the Ancestral Council, who were also the Paramount's Ministers of Finance, Health, Education, Trade and Commerce, and the like. When the Rolls-Royce swept up to the guest-house it spewed forth a remarkable number of stalwart, lusty, dusky men, some of whom, vigorous as athletes, must have been nearing eighty. All but one sank to their knees, clapped, and intoned a chant of victory. The tall, lean, grey-haired Paramount strode onto the lawn with the air of a king walking on cloth of gold, clasping a sacred staff of office. He wore an ordinary suit and a straw boater adorned with a black ostrich feather plume. The old Chief's deeply scored face, his dark parchment-like skin, the sharpness of his obsidian-bright eyes, his air of dignity and command, all these impressed the Commissioners.

A knot of Shiwans gathered on the lawn knelt and clapped their hands. Each of the Ancestral Councillors had slipped on a handsome scarlet gown. They looked, Alex thought, like a moving bed of gigantic, black-centred scarlet cannas. Three short, sharp bellows, the traditional welcome for a warrior chief after victory, shook the air.

"I am honored, Chief, to meet you," Sir Christopher said. The Paramount bowed.

"Very happy."

The Paramount spoke only a few words of English, but they were gentle ones.

Gowns billowing, staffs thudding, feet tramping to the rhythm of clapping, the party strode into the marquee where, at a long trestle table, the feast had been spread. Two bullocks had been killed as a foundation, half a dozen sheep had been roasted and dismembered, fowls, platters of rice, whole roasted mealies, sorghum, millet, plantains, yams and piles of boiled cassava loaded the table. There was even tapioca: the Paramont had come down firmly on the side of this cereal, thus alienating even further, if possible, Moto Mguu and other leaders of the Triple-P, who were in any case strongly anti-traditional. On a separate table stood the beer, guarded by non-Shiwan waiters armed with openers, and charged with the difficult task of operating a rough kind of rationing system.

Chief Faustus was younger than the Paramount and lacked his authority, but he, too, was lean and tall and full of dignity. He wore a tidy flannel suit and, like the others, a scarlet robe faced with purple.

"It's the gown of Master of Arts at the University College of Llandudno," Edmund Butterfield explained. "One of the Paramount's nephews was there and they all liked the get-up so much it was adopted as a royal uniform."

The appetites of the Ancestral Councillors proved fully equal to the challenge set them by the cooks. Piles of food sank and vanished like snow before an April thaw. Soon dishes were empty, the trestle table bare. Drained, too, were the beer bottles; and, as empties accumulated, spirits rose. Strong, resonant voices filled the marquee with flowing periods in the Shiwan tongue. Chants of victory burst from deep throats and from the broad chests of healthy, well-fed, satisfied men.

"They've done it again, I'm afraid," Desmond Slocombe remarked to Alex in gloomy tones.

"Done what?"

"Got at the brandy."

Each Councillor was half-filling his glass with brandy and topping it with beer. Brandy bottles were circulating from hand to hand, laughter and song were shaking the air of the marquee like a gusty gale. A harassed canteen manager appeared, to withdraw the waiters and replace them by police constables in plain clothes. Alex saw John Jacey mingling with the throng, also out of uniform.

"I don't know how this happened," Slocombe said. "Everything was locked up. The trouble is that if the Paramount gives *any* Shiwan an order, that Shiwan is absolutely bound to obey, on pain of impalement. And one can't send *every* Shiwan on the place off for the day. If I may suggest it, Sir Christopher, I think if you were to slip away . . ."

The Paramount was seated on a leopard-skin thrown over a chair. Sir Christopher thanked him for entrusting Chief Faustus to the Commission.

"Very happy," boomed the Paramount.

"His Highness," translated the interpreter, "wishes you long life, good health and good crops, and may your wife be as fertile as the queen of the white ants."

"I wish him the same."

"He says also, will you tell the English Queen of his love and loyalty. The Shiwa people suck her breasts, they are her children and she must not desert them, because of the treaty between her and the Paramount."

"She will be glad to hear of the loyalty of the Shiwa people."

The Paramount rose, a fine sight in his robe and plumes, and lifted his glass.

"Queen Victoria!"

More brandy had mysteriously appeared and the marquee rang to the cries of "Queen Victoria!", followed by the royal salute. Mr. Butterfield, the Chairman and the rest of the Commissioners weaved a way among heated bodies out of the marquee, into the calm and quiet of the guest-house.

"Whew! It's a bit overpowering."

"Normally, they go on like that for two or three days," Butterfield explained. "I'm afraid they think us terrible unmannerly, to close the party down after a few hours."

"The Paramount's impressive," Sir Christopher said.

"Yes, he's a splendid old man. Of course he's a bit hazy on certain points. For instance, nothing will convince him that Queen Victoria isn't still on the throne. I've tried to hammer home that it's a different Queen now, but the Paramount suspects us all of hedging on the treaty."

"One would think that photographs, for instance, of Princess Anne and Prince Andrew . . ."

"Yes, but of course they all think Queen Victoria's a remarkable woman, and that's merely taken as another proof."

It was all very different, Sir Christopher reflected, from the last Commission he'd sat on, to inquire into the revision of superannuation schemes for local government officials.

The noise from the marquee was like the thunder of a distant, or perhaps not-so-distant, crushing mill at the mine. Sounds of horny, naked feet, pounding in unison with the rhythm of a Shiwan victory dance, thudded with a blunt piston-stroke through the afternoon air. At intervals a roar of triumph from lusty male throats, resonant and full of menace as the grunt of hunting lions, recalled past classic victories and slaughters. Against his will, Alex found his breath quickening, his heartbeats accelerating and his thoughts scattering like a flock of startled birds, disturbed by unsuspected, hitherto imprisoned, emotions.

The party went on until six o'clock, when all the brandy and the last shreds of bullock had gone. The Paramount shook hands in dignified splendour, swaying a little but still on his feet.

"They're not going to paddle back tonight, surely?" Sir Christopher inquired. On either side of him stood Mansfield Matunda and Sir Jeremy, representing the Commission, come to say good-bye.

"Oh, yes, they *must* paddle back," Mansfield replied. "If anyone should drop his paddle, he must pay a fine of one hundred goats. If he slips and falls, he will be impaled."

"Surely those are things of the past!"

"No one has been able to find the last Minister of Public Works. One day he fell over backwards in the barge, the next day he disappeared."

Chief Faustus stood with the Commissioners, divested of his scarlet robe and looking dispirited. It was, indeed, a new, strange world into which he was about to plunge.

"It has been an honour, Chief, to meet you," Sir Christopher said to the Paramount.

"Very happy."

"I wish I could feel as sure of that as you." For the interpreter's benefit, the Chairman added: "Don't bother to translate. Just say I'll take his message to the Queen."

Catching the word, the Chief raised one hand aloft and cried, "Queen Victoria!" His Cabinet and attendants echoed the words with a mighty shout, climbed into their waiting lorry and vanished into the *momombo*.

"Well, Chief Faustus," Sir Christopher said, "we're looking forward to our work together, and I hope you'll enjoy working with us."

"Very happy."

"There's a lot of reading to be done, I'm afraid. You'll find a great big pile of memoranda in your room."

"Very happy."

"We'll meet at dinner, then."

The Chief bowed with courtesy, belched, and withdrew to his quarters, where piles of fat O.H.M.S. envelopes were stacked on every table and chair. He drank half a gallon of water, lay on his bed and went to sleep.

Chapter 9

"You look worried," Alex said. He had come to offer to the Chairman some observations on Hapana's balance of payments and foreign exchange, but the Chairman was preoccupied. It was after seven o'clock, the day's work was not yet done.

"Frankly, I am," Sir Christopher agreed. "Not so much about the work of the Commission, but all this security trouble. . . . Hapana seems to be a mass of double-dealing and intrigue. As bad as fifteenth-century Italy."

"Minus the Medicis and Michelangelo."

"Alas, yes. You're a level-headed sort of fellow, Alex—if I may call you that. In fact, speaking quite frankly, I look on you and Jeremy as the only two really sensible, reliable people I've got."

"There's the Vice-Chairman."

Sir Christopher gave Alex a look. "On pigs, certainly. Unfortunately we haven't much to do with pigs." He hesitated, fiddling with a paper-clip. "There's what's known in the jargon of these matters as a leak. Someone's feeding stuff into the pipeline at our end. It reaches Moscow by way of the Republic of Bonga just across the lake. The radio station there sends it on. I can never get used to this kind of spy-stuff—it seems to be a thing that can't really happen. But obviously it does."

"I don't quite see what use our dark secrets can be to the Muscovites."

"It's partly a question of prestige. Supporting the Russian legend of omnipotence, of knowing all that goes on. And of course it *is* one up to them, we must admit. And gives our Commission a pretty bad mark at home. I can tell you, I've had some sharp comments."

"I suppose we're all under suspicion."

The Chairman nodded. "That's the position, roughly. Nine Commissioners—seven, I really don't think they suspect me, and our friend the Chief has only just come. Then there's Hugo and Miss Labouchère. The typists can be eliminated, the work's all split up and they never go to meetings. Nine in all."

"And Partridge? He sits in most of the time."

"Yes, of course, Partridge . . ."

"If I'm a suspect, as I must be, why do you talk like this to me?"

"As you can guess, there's been a pretty thorough check on everyone. No skeletons fell out of your cupboard, not even a party ticket as an undergraduate."

"That must apply to most of my colleagues. I can't believe we've *all* got sinister pasts."

"In fact, only one of us. At least, that the cloak-and-dagger boys have so far unearthed."

"Then doesn't that solve it?"

"It may. Or it may not. I've got the unpleasant job, very shortly, of tackling the individual concerned."

"So we must expect a resignation."

"I don't know," Sir Christopher said. His lightness of touch had gone from him, he was clearly a worried man. "Say you've been involved in the past—years ago. And perhaps involuntarily, even then. You've made a completely new start, new career, new name. You've succeeded. You're doing well. Would you, for any consideration whatever, risk going back into the trap again? Wouldn't you keep clear at any cost?"

"If I could," Alex agreed. "There's the question of blackmail."

"Yes, of course. But if someone tried that game, and you went straight to the authorities, you'd be absolutely safe. I'm assuming you're an intelligent person."

"He could have lost his nerve."

Sir Christopher sighed. "You're taking the same view as the security boys. Perhaps it's the right one. Anyway, I shall have to take the plunge. It won't be easy."

Alex was puzzled. Sir Christopher had no doubt reached a point where he needed to talk to someone, but why choose himself? Why not Sir Jeremy? Perhaps he *had* spoken to Sir Jeremy. Why not the Vice-Chairman? Well, perhaps that was obvious. Or was he trying to convey some sort of warning?

"Isn't there one rather obvious candidate?" Alex suggested. "After all, the Triple-P is openly dickering with Moscow. And I doubt if our friend Mansfield would look at passing information on as anything more than an act of courtesy to a friend."

The Chairman smiled. "You know, I've really got quite attached to our colleague. I don't put that forward as a reason for trusting him. He's the obvious candidate, as you say. But he's not the one I've got to interview."

"No?"

"I don't say he isn't being watched. We all are. But our own security officer, anyway, seems pretty satisfied. I suppose Matunda's just *too* indiscreet."

"You mean the other side doesn't trust him either? I daresay they've got a point there."

"I'm afraid the only reason we can more or less eliminate him is that he's never been approached. Then, of course, there's Zaza. So far his party's kept clear of outside entanglements, despite that foray to Peking. Now he's got mixed up with a very queer bunch of religious fanatics called the *Sulu Sita*. Literally, I'm told that's the six keys, or locks, but no one really knows what it means."

"Something Biblical?"

"Possibly. I'm telling you all this because I really do need your help. You're an observant sort of chap. I want you to keep your eyes and ears open and let me know, if you will, if anything crops up that strikes you as a bit, well, unusual, suggestive—any line at all. You know what I mean."

"A sort of unpaid spy."

Sir Christopher sighed. "I was afraid you'd say that. I don't want to suggest you turn snooper. It's just that if you're in the picture, you can use your own judgement as to whether anything occurs that needs looking into. We all want to get this leak plugged."

Alex rubbed his fingers through his thick, untidy hair and pondered. He was careless about his clothes; his collar was too big, his loosely-woven tie on one side. The Chairman was right, of course; it was irritating, how often he *was* right. Alex got out of the chair.

"All right, I'll more or less co-operate, although I don't like it."

"Believe me, I don't like it either. It's just one of those things."

"I'm putting my money on Dr. Rumble," Alex said. "He's always sounding off about colonialism. I expect he wraps the minutes up in an avocado pear and sends them off on the head of one of the oppressed."

Sir Christopher smiled. "The information would be rather long-winded. Now, how about a drink?"

"Thanks very much, Sir Christopher—"

"I think you might drop the *Sir.*"

"Well, thanks very much. I won't, though; I've got a date for dinner."

"Another time, then. I hope you're coming on this fishing trip tomorrow? I'm looking forward to a Sunday off, I must say."

"I'll be there."

"And now, I suppose, I must tackle this unpleasant business." The Chairman gathered up some loose papers and put them in a folder. "Might as well get it over. Thanks, Alex, for your help. Well, understanding." He smiled a dismissal. No wonder, Alex thought, he had people eating out of his hand. In the last colony he'd governed, now an independent state, he'd been known as the Snake-Charmer.

Alex was dining with John Jacey at the Pig and Whistle: a chance to get away, even for an hour or two, from his fellow Commissioners. Inevitably, they all talked shop. Not that he was likely to escape that with Jacey, who was at once startled, appalled and entertained by the world-wide fame that had so unexpectedly come to him, or at least to his broken nose. It was dying down in the press, but still rumbling on locally. He'd been cross-questioned by everyone from the Commissioner of Police to the Chief Minister. Now, on the insistence of the Opposition at Westminster, there was to be a full-scale inquiry.

The Commission had lost its news value for the time being, and Jacey was able to pursue in comparative peace his job of guarding it from its numerous and vociferous enemies. Comparative only, Alex understood; threats to behead, impale, hang, shoot and dismember the Commissioners were received almost daily from younger and more ebullient Hapanans. Threats merely to ostracize, boycott and deport them, to set them to work planting tapioca or to enslave them to Mr. Mguu, came from the older, more sober elements. Only that morning, Alex learnt, the police had removed from tree-trunks in the garden crudely scrawled posters proposing to turn Mr. Matunda and the Rev. Zaza into fertilizer for the tapioca plantations, and suggesting that Sir Christopher should be dropped over the Pacific instead of a megaton bomb.

"It was the work of the girls from the Little Sisters of the Immaculate Conception," Jacey had explained. "Just high spirits, of course."

Alex anticipated hearing more about it all at dinner. On his way out he looked into the lounge for a quick drink with some of his fellow Commissioners. Chief Faustus was sitting beside Lady Bagpuse, watching with fascination her needlewoman's skill. She was making a design of fishes, in cross-stitch, on a square of canvas. Already she had extracted from the Chief a remarkable amount of information about his four wives, his twenty-seven children (nineteen at school) and his domestic life generally.

"I'm sure your second wife would find the cross-stitch very useful, Chief," she said, "now that she's getting so close to her time. Her ninth, you say? She's the one with twins?"

The Chief nodded. His proud grin was delightful.

"I'm sure she would find it restful to have a piece of work on hand. It's such a good excuse to sit down. One can't do cross-stitch standing up, or not very easily."

"Yes, madam."

"Not that she can get much time to sit down. She's the one, isn't she, who's done so well this year with her tapioca?"

"Very happy."

Dr. Rumble, who was allowing himself a small sherry, looked up at this, his spectacles gleaming.

"I wonder, Dr. Burton, if you have been as distressed as I have been—yes, I may say it, so truly distressed—to find the manual toil of the fields actually performed by *women,* down here in this British colony? It is indeed a painful sight to see these good wives and mothers toiling in the sun for a bare pittance, their little babies out in all weathers, a prey to exposure and disease. According to Article One Hundred and Thirty-two of the Protocol of Aix-les-Bains on the employment of female labour, the nations of the world have pledged themselves—"

"I can't make out whether we're to tackle these bass tomorrow with live bait or a spinner," Lord Bagpuse interrupted. "Everyone seems to think differently. What's your opinion, Burton?"

"I should think we'd better try both."

"Looking forward to a day's fishing, I must say, though it's out of a boat. Get a bit cramped, I daresay."

". . . eliminate progressively this survival of the dark ages and liberate women for the inspiring work of caring for and training in the arts of life the coming generation . . ."

"It sounds to me, Chief, as if your senior wife had a touch of lumbago. She must be very careful; I was laid up once with lumbago for the best part of a month, and just before the Five Counties too, the year Freddy won the Red Poll championship. You must come and see our Red Polls, Chief, and our Norfolk New Spots. I know they'd interest you, and your eldest son who's studying at the agricultural institute."

"Very happy."

One of the stewards entered with a note on a tray, looked round and approached Lord Bagpuse, who took it with an air of surprise.

"Whoever can be writing notes at this time of night?" A distressing thought came to him. "Hope it's not a telegram from home. I've been a little worried about the last report on Marquis of Monterey. Could be erysipelas."

Lord Bagpuse read the note, frowned, and heaved himself out of his chair.

"The Chairman wants to see me. Can't get used to the late hours they keep here. I'll take my drink along with me." He bore his glass away.

"It must be such a comfort to Sir Christopher to be able to consult Freddy about everything," Lady Bagpuse remarked, completing the tail of a fish. "He's always so calm and sensible. Nowadays it isn't very fashionable to be sensible, but it's a great help all the same. Don't you agree, Chief? If you won't think I'm being too personal, I knew as soon as I met you that you were another just like Freddy—a really *sensible* man."

Chapter 10

"If I had a son," Alex remarked, "I'd bring him up to be a mining magnate. Of course, the mine would have to own a lake or two, with fish in them. Seems a passable existence."

"I've got three boys," said John Jacey. "I *had* thought of a shipping line or two, but perhaps you have to be a Greek for that."

They lay at ease in the shade of a tree on a small island. Lunch awaited them in plastic containers, one-man-one-box, each box neatly labelled with a Commissioner's name. Individual tastes had been previously consulted: some Commissioners liked eggs, some preferred ham to tongue, others didn't eat lettuce. Baskets of fruit were separate, the beer came in a container holding crushed ice. Stewards spread rugs, set out chairs, distributed the luncheon boxes, opened the beer and then withdrew. Two launches were moored to a tree-stump in the shade: one had brought the Commissioners, the second had followed with stewards and luncheon.

The three Hapanan Commissioners, not being fishermen, had chosen other ways to relax on Sunday. The other six Commissioners were there, together with Hugo and Thomasina. Desmond Slocombe was in charge, with Jacey as the bodyguard. Constance Connor and Blanche Bagpuse had stayed quietly at home.

"Not very sporting, these lake fish," Lord Bagpuse complained.

"Why *should* a fish be sporting?" Alex inquired. "All it asks is to be left alone."

"Well, take a salmon, now. He'll give you a damn good fight."

"Is that sporting, or merely futile?"

"It's instinctive," Sir Jeremy said. "Nothing wants to die."

"What about these Hapanan fish, then? Fatalists?"

"Lazy," Jacey suggested.

"Piscine stoics," Alex persisted.

"Don't know what you're talking about," Bagpuse said a little testily. "They don't fight, that's all. Life's too easy for them; all the food they want without having to work for it."

"You think that saps their morale?"

"Naturally. Same with people. If life's made too easy, no one's going to bother. Why should they?"

"Wasn't life easy for you, Lord Bagpuse?" Alex inquired.

"Not a bit of it. My old father saw to that. Up at seven every morning, winter or summer, and into a cold bath. Six of the best if I blotted my prep till I went to Eton, never had a bob to call my own till I was twenty-one. The old school, my father was. It's all different now. I'm going to eat my sandwiches in the launch, it's more comfortable. Ants here."

"I'll come with you," Slocombe said, picking up a couple of sandwich boxes. "I'd like you to talk to the captain of the launch. One of our first Hapanans to be trained in navigation, now the Commodore of our little fleet. We're planning a small line of launches to link the fishing settlements we hope will . . ."

Alex watched Lord Bagpuse's large retreating back with some puzzlement. Since his talk with the Chairman, he had felt disgruntled. It went against the grain to pry into others' business. He was a live-and-let-live man, and he had not in fact done any prying, but the conversation had disturbed his detachment. And if his surmises about Lord Bagpuse had any substance, the Vice-Chairman should at least have shown signs of uneasiness. Neither the hunted nor the hunter could walk calmly and indifferently through the forest, and a sense of strain could seldom be wholly concealed. But old Bagpuse was going on as if he hadn't a care in the world.

"I hope I shall be half as fit as Freddy when I'm his age," the Chairman remarked, starting on his luncheon. So far he'd been unusually silent, his self-confident urbanity impaired. The sense of strain, in his case, was not being wholly concealed. "A case of clear conscience, I suppose." Was there, Alex wondered, a note of irony there?

"A good constitution," Sir Jeremy suggested.

"Doesn't the one affect the other?"

"You mean a bad conscience gives one rheumatism or flat feet or colds in the head?"

"Ulcers, perhaps. But let's find a more cheerful topic of conversation. Have you any wild animals for us on this island, Jeremy? Here we are in Africa and so far I haven't even seen a mosquito, let alone an elephant."

"There are some monkeys, I believe."

"And ants," Amelia pointed out. "As Lord Bagpuse said. I suppose the food attracts them."

Sir Christopher was extracting chicken's breast from his sandwiches and discarding brown bread, out of consideration for his figure. Within a few minutes hundreds of ants, alerted in some mysterious fashion, were bearing away tiny crumbs into the grass, to some hide-out presumably. Within an hour or two, every speck would be gone.

Amelia Tripp was not eating sandwiches either; her box contained no carbohydrates, just chicken, egg and tomatoes, and she was only nibbling at these. She had the look of one who hadn't slept soundly, with something pressing like a growth on her mind. Alex bit enjoyably into his soft, well-buttered brown-bread sardine sandwiches, glad that he didn't have to worry about his figure—or at any rate didn't worry. If he did get a bit paunchy, what would it matter? There was no one he wanted to please.

For once Dr. Rumble was relaxing, telling them about his Midwestern childhood. His father had been a minister of religion, his mother had baked the best corn muffins in Dogwood Creek, and he was one of ten children and had gone to work at fifteen. Thomasina looked up, caught Alex's eye and winked. He felt suddenly gay, and gobbled up two more sandwiches. As soon as lunch was over he'd suggest going to look for monkeys.

Before he had time to make a move, Sir Jeremy was rounding up the party for another go at the fish. "Bagpuse is anxious to be up and at 'em," he said, "and I'd like to show you some work we're doing on the destruction of a water-weed that's giving trouble. So if you're feeling rested . . . ?"

Alex made his way forward to sit in the bows of the launch, armed with a pair of binoculars. The afternoon's heat was raging and under the awning it was sweltering and stuffy; in the bows there was always a bit of a breeze. He passed Lord Bagpuse, and saw at once that he was unwell. Under his weathered ruddiness he had gone a grey, pasty colour and was breathing oddly.

"Are you all right?" Alex asked.

"Feeling the heat a bit, I suppose. Probably a touch of the sun. I'll just . . ."

Lord Bagpuse bent forward to a doubled-up position, retching and shuddering. Alex took him by the shoulder and helped him to the side of the launch. He leant over and was painfully sick. Sir Jeremy supported him on the other side.

"You'll be better in a moment," he said. "Lie down on these cushions; it's the heat, I expect."

"Better now," Lord Bagpuse gasped. "Damn silly. Apologize."

"Don't talk nonsense," Sir Jeremy said, "and lie down."

They settled Lord Bagpuse on some cushions on the bottom of the launch, but he had not recovered. He was shivering, and breathing jerkily, and spasms of pain gripped his stomach. Once or twice these were so severe that he let out a groan.

"We must get back immediately," Sir Christopher said, in deep concern. "The sooner we get hold of that doctor of yours, Jeremy, the better. I don't like the look of this at all."

"Sometimes, you know, people do get these short, sharp attacks in the tropics—some bug. As a rule it goes as quickly as it comes. He may be perfectly all right by the time we get home."

Lord Bagpuse did, indeed, appear to improve when the launch got under way. He lay quietly with his eyes closed. The diesel engine throbbed, the water swished away from the bows as the boat headed at its fastest speed for the jetty. The launch had been built for leisure rather than dispatch, but it did the best it could. No one spoke much.

Thomasina was sitting by the sick man and, unobtrusively, Jacey moved over to her side. Now and then Thomasina wiped the sweating, contorted face with her handkerchief. Another spasm of retching and pain shook the Vice-Chairman's bulk. He looked as pathetic, lying at the mercy of something dreadful and unknown, as a stranded whale. The pain seemed to subside, his breathing grew quick and shallow and he opened his eyes. Jacey took his wrist gently to feel his pulse.

"Blanchie," he muttered. "Blanchie. Never did want—" He broke off. Thomasina took his other hand. "Tell Percy—tell . . ." He stirred again, his mind was clouding over. Suddenly he half sat up and said loudly: "Soviet Ambassador. Give him . . . Can't wait . . ." His voice faded, a little froth trickled from his mouth and his face, the colour of dough, was sweating and twitching. Alex saw the lips move and bent over him. So far as he could make out, Lord Bagpuse's last words were "Marquis of Monterey." Then the Vice-Chairman lay still and did not writhe any more.

They sat in stunned silence for a few moments. The chugging of the engine, the swish of water against the bows, the squawk of a bird, the Chairman blowing his nose—these and other small sounds became suddenly magnified. Gently, Thomasina put the hand of the bulky, quiet man on his chest and released her grip. The hand lay motionless. Thomasina was as white as one of the egrets they were passing, perched on dead trees.

"So quickly . . ."

Alex got up and walked over to Sir Christopher in the bows.

"Alex, is he going to be all right?"

"It's over."

"You don't mean . . . ?"

Alex nodded.

"But that's impossible! Only twenty minutes ago he was sitting there talking. . . . There *must* be a mistake."

"I wish there was." Despite the heat, Alex felt cold. He looked across at Slocombe. "How soon can you get the doctor, do you suppose?"

"If he's at home, in fifteen minutes, once we get there. This is absolutely appalling . . ."

"You had lunch together," Alex said. "What did he have? Did he leave any of it?"

Slocombe looked round the launch hopelessly, as if trying to find a way out of a cage. "We each had our box of sandwiches. You remember, everyone had a separate box. I think he ate everything. I can't remember—I wasn't noticing." Slocombe frowned, he looked dazed from shock. "Yes, I do remember now—he said something about damned wafers, he liked good honest wholemeal bread, and then he threw what he didn't want into the water. Make the fish rise, he said—lazy blighters. I don't think there was much over, though. The box must be somewhere about . . ."

"Are you suggesting he was poisoned?" The Chairman's voice was sharp, incredulous.

"This attack came on quite soon after lunch. And it doesn't look to me like a stroke or anything."

"It could be heat-stroke, I should think," Slocombe said doubtfully. "I've never actually seen a case. But he'd been complaining of the heat. And he's a heavy man."

Alex shook his head. "The pains in his stomach . . ."

"The less said the better at this stage," Sir Christopher ruled. "If only Lady Bagpuse had been here!"

Amelia came forward, walking stiffly, to sit near the Chairman. Everyone moved carefully—almost, Alex thought, like people who are a little drunk and don't want to give themselves away.

"I simply can't take it in," she said blankly. "So full of vitality. . . . Did he say anything at the end?"

"He did say something rather strange. He mentioned the Soviet Ambassador."

There was a dead silence, broken tersely by Sir Christopher.

"I don't think we should discuss this tragedy any further. Superintendent Jacey's here. For the moment, the matter's in his hands."

Jacey had found a rug and thrown it over the recumbent figure. Then he'd taken Thomasina to a seat in the stern and made her comfortable with cushions: she was badly shaken. Now he was searching for something on the floor of the launch. Slocombe beckoned him over.

"I'll go for the doctor when we get in. There's nothing else, is there, we can do?"

"I want to get hold of the plastic box the sandwiches were in."

"Both boxes were collected by one of the stewards, and taken to the other launch."

"Where I suppose the stewards will wash them out?"

"I should think it's been done by now," Slocombe agreed.

"Lord Bagpuse didn't make any comments when he was eating his meal?"

"Only about preferring wholemeal bread."

"How did you get hold of the sandwich boxes?"

"The stewards carried them to the picnic place and then we each took our own. Every box had a name on it, you know. People liked different things."

"But Lord Bagpuse got wafers?"

"I don't know what he meant by wafers—crispbread, probably. Oh, yes, I see . . ."

"All right. There's nothing more to be done for the moment."

Sir Christopher had taken out his binoculars and was training them on a bird perching on a dead tree.

"A handsome bird, the fish-eagle," he remarked. Alex glanced at him. The Chairman's face was set and strained. Alex said:

"A disturbing cry."

"Yes. Can one tell a male from a female? Have a look."

"Not by the plumage, I think." Alex leant forward to take the binoculars. A speck of white under the chair in which Sir Christopher was sitting caught his eye. He leant down and picked it up. It was a small square of paper and on it was written, in neat writing, *The Chairman*. He handed it to Sir Christopher.

"Yours?"

"I suppose so. Where did it come from?"

Jacey took it from the Chairman's hand. "It's the label off your box of sandwiches."

"But I ate mine on the island."

"And Lord Bagpuse ate his here."

"You mean . . . ?"

Jacey didn't answer. Alex broke the silence in a flat voice. "The boxes got switched."

Chapter 11

"THE ONLY THING we can be reasonably sure of is that Lord Bagpuse ate the wrong sandwiches," John Jacey said. "And that's only speculation," added the Commissioner of Police. "I suppose, Sir Christopher, you're *quite* sure you've no recollection . . ."

"I've been over it in my mind again and again," Sir Christopher said, "and I can only suppose I just didn't glance at the slip of paper on the sandwich box. One of the stewards handed it to me—I think I was looking round at the time to see if I could spot any monkeys. And, of course, the sandwiches were made with bread; I see your point. The ones I *should* have got were made with crispbread. And so the wretched Bagpuse—it hardly bears thinking about. He took the wrong box and died in my place."

"So far it's mere speculation," Colonel Cottrell repeated. He had the pared, timbery appearance of the military campaigner of the old school, and his greying moustache stood out a little from his lip as if in perpetual protest at the world's disorder. One of his legs had been stiffened by an honourable wound. He had been kept on because his post was so soon to be Hapanized that it had not seemed worth while replacing him by a younger, more up-and-coming man who would only have to be abolished in a year or two, at a heavy cost in compensation. Colonel Cottrell, nearly due to retire, could be abolished without extra expense. Already a promising young cousin of Mr. Mguu's was being groomed for the job by means of six months' attachment to the Bethnal Green divisional headquarters plus a Polytechnic course in adult literacy.

Summoned, at half an hour's notice on Sunday afternoon, to the scene of the disaster, Colonel Cottrell sat next morning in Sir Christopher's office, appalled by the horrors that all too plainly lay ahead: world publicity, interference by everyone from the British Prime Minister downwards, heaven only knew what international complications. He thought with wistful, lonely-hearted longing of the simple forms of inquiry he had pursued on the Northern Frontier of Kenya, in the Aden Protectorate, in the Trucial Oman.

Desmond Slocombe was no less distressed. Lord Bagpuse had died in the Company's launch, while the Company's guest, apparently from eating the Company's sandwiches handed to him, to crown it all, by the Company's Managing Director. The Company's image so carefully built up over the years—this would be shattered by a single disaster. And it was he who had organized the sandwiches.

Edmund Butterfield was nearly as dismayed. The politics of Hapana were like a powder-barrel, a drum of high-octane fuel. This calamity might well be the spark. Poor old Bagpuse had been a fool to meddle in the tapioca war: now Matunda might accuse Zaza of complicity, Zaza retaliate, Mguu intervene, and the next thing anyone knew there'd be riots, shooting, United Nations resolutions, inquiries, the lot. Worst of all, perhaps, the date of independence postponed: that fat Abolition of Office payment, that house at Henley, that seat on the Board, receding into the distance. . . . No wonder Butterfield looked glum.

Sir Christopher, the only one threatened with murder, was much the calmest of the four men.

"Those sandwiches, Slocombe," Colonel Cottrell said. "They were prepared the night before on your orders and left all night in the refrigerator?"

"Yes—they keep quite fresh in plastic boxes, you know."

"So any of the staff could have got at them in the night?"

"Well, of course, they're supposed to lock the kitchen door."

"Who's supposed to?"

"The cook—Annunciation. An absolutely trustworthy chap."

"So far as you know. You don't, I suppose, know his political views?"

"No, I'm afraid I don't," Slocombe agreed.

"You're not suggesting, surely," Sir Christopher said, "that there's a *political* motive?"

"It's much too early to suggest anything yet. But this is a political Commission, you know. And a damned political country. There've been dozens of threats against your personal safety. Up to now we haven't taken them all that seriously—we get so much of it. Of course we laid on detectives and guards and Jacey here in charge. Not good enough, apparently. So now we've got to consider very seriously the possibility that it's a political crime."

"That opens up an enormous field," Sir Christopher said glumly.

"Exactly."

"I suppose there's no doubt, Colonel Cottrell, about the cause of poor Bagpuse's death?"

"There's every doubt about *everything* so far," the Police Commissioner answered testily. "All supposition. 'Multiple lesions of the gastric organs and intestinal tract accompained by numerous submucous haemorrhages'—that's what Godfrey's report says. 'No toxic principle can be isolated and the symptoms are similar to those of an acute sudden infection from staphylococcus or a virulent bacillus.' So there you are. *Could* be a perfectly natural sudden infection, not foul play at all."

"But Dr. Godfrey doesn't think so," Butterfield pointed out.

"No, he doesn't; he's had too much experience of these native poisons. Comes across them all the time. So do we. The devil of it is there's never any *proof*. None of these vegetable poisons leaves traces that can be spotted in the labs."

"If things like that grew in England," Sir Christopher reflected, rubbing his chin, "my goodness, the homicide rate . . ."

"All our scientific skill, and we've got to give the witch doctors best when it comes to a simple, everyday poison anyone can dig up from the bush. There's one, for instance, the women use to commit suicide; they simply insert some powdered root into their vagina—"

"We'd better stick to the point," Butterfield said brusquely. "Godfrey thinks it was poison, and Dr. Furneaux from the Government hospital agrees. They did the P-M together. And Lord Bagpuse had shown no signs, I take it, of anything wrong until after he'd eaten the sandwiches." Sir Christopher nodded.

"He was certainly in his usual robust health right up to the time he walked off with the luncheon box in his hand."

"Godfrey thinks it was poison," Colonel Cottrell agreed, "though he can't tell *what* poison. Might have been any one of half a dozen, he says. Well, then, assuming it was, it comes to this, Sir Christopher —do you know of anyone who's anxious to put you out of the way?"

Sir Christopher looked startled, and then ran a hand over his smooth, dark hair. "Stupid of me, isn't it—I hadn't quite looked at it like that before." He smiled in a deprecating way. "I suppose there may be quite a few, in one way or another, but I just can't imagine anyone getting to the point of putting poison in a sandwich. It's such a deliberate, calculated, cruel kind of thing."

"Well, it's done every day in this country by the locals," the Police Commissioner said, "without blinking an eyelid."

"It may be a political crime," Butterfield said, "as Cottrell seems inclined to think—one of Mguu's extremists, for instance, determined to wreck the Commission. Or, I suppose, it could be an act of personal vengeance or fear."

"Fear?" Sir Christopher frowned.

"One of your Commissioners, Sir Christopher, was about to be called on to resign. You've spoken to the individual concerned?"

Sir Christopher's frown deepened. "Yes, I have."

Colonel Cottrell sat up even more stiffly in his chair and his moustache seemed to bristle. "I must ask you to put me fully in the picture, Sir Christopher. This is the first I've heard of any trouble with your own colleagues. It may put quite a different complexion on things."

"It's merely the latest development of what you know already," Sir Christopher said soothingly. "The security situation, I mean. The leak."

"Well, I must say, sir, if you've discovered who the agent is, I think I might have been informed." The Colonel was turning brick-red, his eyes had become more prominent.

Sir Christopher held up a hand. "No, no, Colonel Cottrell, we're going too fast. I don't know who the agent is. You know we asked London to make a thorough probe into the record of everyone connected with this Commission. They sent us some information about one of our members they'd failed to unearth before. It looked bad on the surface—previous complicity in a very dubious affair."

"And you told this man your suspicions?"

"I did."

"And asked him to resign?"

Sir Christopher shook his head. "I wasn't quite convinced. I'm not still. The suspect put up a good case. As you know, someone's getting information away regularly and it comes back smartly to us on the Moscow radio."

"By way of Bonga, and those Russian technicians."

"Presumably. Well, I'm going to give out a special announcement to the Commission just before we adjourn this afternoon, and I'm going to make a special point of secrecy. Our suspect has agreed not to be there, and won't have access to this information. If it comes back to us, just the same, on Moscow radio, then it's at least a tenable thesis that this particular Commissioner is blameless."

"Supposition again," Colonel Cottrell said disgustedly.

"I know; but what else can be done? I'm just not satisfied we're on the right line."

The Commissioner of Police did not look mollified. "I should be obliged," he said, "if you will at least let me know the name of this suspect."

"I don't want to do that yet."

"If you'll forgive my speaking plainly, sir," Colonel Cottrell retorted, "It's your *duty* to inform me. This man has a strong motive for the crime. If he's a spy, he's not only a blackguard but he's being threatened with exposure. You spoke to him last night, you say?"

"Yes, I did."

"And the very next day an attempt was made to poison you."

"Yes, it looks bad, I agree," Sir Christopher said. He was worried. "And I suppose . . . Will you give me another twenty-four hours?"

Colonel Cottrell shrugged his shoulders. "If you're satisfied that you're doing your duty to assist my officers by holding back vital information for twenty-four hours, I've nothing further to say."

Butterfield intervened. "Nothing to be gained by getting hot under the collar about all this. I'm sure Sir Christopher realizes the importance of following up every lead—after all, it's his life that's in danger. But we've got to watch our step, you know. As soon as this news breaks we'll have the press on top of us like vultures round a kill. Does anyone else know your suspect's identity, Sir Christopher?"

"Only our Secretary—and Miss Labouchère, she knows everything. And of course our P.R.O. Until last night. But then . . ."

"Yes?"

"I felt I really had to tell my Vice-Chairman."

There was a pause, loaded with feeling. Butterfield broke it. "So Lord Bagpuse knew?"

"Yes—and while it's a question now of *de mortuis,* one couldn't be *absolutely* sure of his discretion. But I felt I really couldn't spring it on him publicly, as it were."

"This puts a new complexion on it altogether," Colonel Cottrell repeated.

"In other words," added Butterfield, "Lord Bagpuse could have been the intended victim after all."

"But he ate my sandwiches," Sir Christopher objected.

"We're getting nowhere with all this," Colonel Cottrell said, still smarting. "There's been a murder—at least we must assume it's one—and it's the duty of the Force over which I have the honour to preside to prosecute inquiries. We shall do just that. And the more help we're given, the better we'll get on. Meanwhile, what I'd like to know from Sir Christopher is this. Do you intend to go on with the work of the Commission? Or will you all return to the U.K.?"

Colonel Cottrell left little doubt as to which alternative seemed to him the most desirable. The flicker of a smile passed over Sir Christopher's worried face.

"I've not yet consulted my colleagues," he said, "and the decision must be made by the Commission as a whole. But, as you may know, I've already consulted the Secretary of State. He entirely endorses my own view."

"Which is?"

"We carry on, of course. And I'll be very surprised if my colleagues think differently. We still have our job to do."

"You realize, of course," Butterfield said, "that there's a big personal risk?"

"Perhaps we'd better adopt the medieval system, and try every dish on a taster." Sir Christopher glanced at Desmond Slocombe. "Do you suppose Steyn Consolidated could supply a hungry but reliable cat?"

The others looked blank, plainly regarding Sir Christopher's levity as in bad taste. Perhaps it was, he admitted to himself, but better misplaced flippancy than solemn gloom. He knew perfectly well that Cottrell and Butterfield, and probably Slocombe, nourished an ardent, if slender, hope that the Commission would pack up and go.

"I promise I'll take all the care I possibly can not to get myself poisoned," he said.

"We'll look after that cook," promised Colonel Cottrell.

"I'd stake every penny I've got on his reliability," Slocombe protested.

"All the same, it won't do him any harm to be pulled in for a bit. I'll see that one of our mess cooks replaces him."

Slocombe looked horrified. "Oh, dear," said Sir Christopher.

The Police Commissioner's moustache really did bristle this time. "The fact that Sir Christopher's life is in danger may be of less interest to you gentlemen than getting your fancy meals, but I've got my duty to do just as you have. I'm afraid, Slocombe, you'll have to rough it on a mess cook."

"There's one other question to be settled," Butterfield put in hastily, "and that's the terms of the official communiqué."

"I think, if we possibly can, at this stage, we should avoid all mention of foul play," the Chairman suggested. "We've absolutely no proof, after all."

"Then we'll issue a communiqué to the effect that Lord Bagpuse died following a brief illness caused by a tropical infection and that he's being buried today. Despite the deep distress of the Commission and the Government of Hapana, et cetera, the Commission will continue its duties according to plan. Right?"

"That seems the best arrangement," Sir Christopher agreed. His voice was sober, his expression thoughtful. The implications, Jacey thought, were coming home to him. If Lady Connor dug in her toes, would the Commission be able to carry on with quite such a stiff upper lip as the Chairman intended? Jacey rose to go.

"If you'll excuse me, sir, I think I should be checking up on Sergeant Chisanga. I thought in the initial stages he'd get on better on his own."

In the doorway he almost collided with a large, agitated figure who swept past him as he stepped aside. It was Lady Bagpuse, her face streaked with grief and the lees of tears. Her hair was wispy and her dress unpressed, one stocking was awry.

"Sir Christopher, I *must* speak to you!" She was trying hard to keep her voice under control. It wavered, but didn't break. "I've been waiting for nearly an hour, and your secretary—"

Sir Christopher leapt to his feet, overcome with dismay. "My dear Lady Bagpuse, I can't possibly say how sorry—I had no idea—"

"It was my fault," said Butterfield. "I've been keeping Sir Christopher. I'm going now. Lady Bagpuse, you know the very deepest sympathy of the whole Government of Hapana . . . This dreadful tragedy . . ."

"You needn't go," Lady Bagpuse said. "What I've got to say isn't secret. My husband's got to be avenged, Sir Christopher. He was a good man, and he shouldn't have died."

"He was one of the very best men I've met in a long career." Sir Christopher's voice was impressive and sincere. "And he shouldn't have died. I'll never forgive myself for not having realized, at that picnic, that he was overdoing things—the hot sun, the stuffy launch, and then one of those devilish sudden tropical infections—"

"Infection my foot," Lady Bagpuse said, with a distant echo of her husband's delivery. "Freddy was murdered."

"My dear Lady Bagpuse, there isn't a shred of proof—"

"I don't need proof," Lady Bagpuse retorted. "I *know*."

Chapter 12

JACEY TURNED to his right out of the Chairman's suite and walked a few paces along the covered way into the all-electric kitchen. Although it was a light, airy, gaily painted room full of gadgets and fitted with the sort of units you saw in windows in Regent Street, it was nearly always deserted. The real business took place in a shed out at the back saturated and blackened by smoke from an old-fashioned Dover stove. The only window was generally stuffed up by a dirty sack, the interior was dark, richly smelly and always packed with people getting in each other's way.

The stove was littered with large saucepans, blackened outside (and inside as well, no doubt, if you could see) and bubbling with mysterious brews. Tea was always on tap, served in tin mugs, thick with sugar and strong as the kick of a mule. Children darted about in the interstices of adults. It was here that elegant meals were, by some ineluctable mystery, created out of queerly severed, bleeding hunks of meat, out of vegetables stored in tattered baskets, out of eggs kept in old kettles and from other, less identifiable raw materials. The all-electric kitchen served as a sort of staging post on the way to the dining-room. It was much too cold and bleak and clean to feel at home in, and therefore to inspire any good work.

The cook was called Annunciation because he was a Portuguese citizen who, although a native Hapanan, had learnt the culinary art in Mozambique. He was a stalwart, savage-looking man with a wispy Chinese kind of moustache and heavy-lidded eyes. Normally, his dress consisted of a torn football jersey and a grubby pair of shorts, but when he appeared in the electric kitchen to carve a ham he could look resplendent in a white apron and chef's cap. Among his possessions were many well-fed children, an illustrated Bible, a profusion of lurid pictures of martyrs in various stages of transfixion and dismemberment, and two crumbling but heroic lorries with which he ran a transport business on the side. He got drunk regularly every Saturday night. It seemed to Jacey unlikely that he would be embroiled in Hapanan politics, but you never knew; he might be one of the caucus of the Triple-P in his spare moments, or Zaza's brother-in-law.

Sergeant Chisanga was sitting in the kitchen on an upturned bucket drinking tea, deep in conversation in some Hapanan tongue. He was gathering plenty of news. From an especially potent magician over the border, he learnt, Moto Mguu had lately obtained medicines that ensured certain and complete success in the next elections. The plan was now to call a general strike and seize the Government as soon as the tapioca was harvested. Party funds were flowing in satisfactorily and Mguu's Youth League was dealing effectively with the dwindling opposition, whose more obstinate members had been found stuffed head-first down latrines, burnt to cinders in their huts or floating on the lake like papyrus.

Of even greater interest was the progress of the personal sub-war between Mguu and Matunda. Most people had expected Matunda to be dead by now, so fearful had been Mguu's threats of retaliation for Matunda's defiance of his leader's orders in joining the Connor Commission. But Mansfield Matunda was no fool. He was in debt to one of Mguu's fathers-in-law, and, if he died, all chances of the debt's repayment would die with him. And he had managed to convince his leader that a prompt, full supply of inside information about the Commission would be of value to the Triple-P, if only to prevent a march being stolen on the party by the Rev. Zaza.

Indeed, such information, Sergeant Chisanga learnt, was taken regularly across the lake in small packages by a family of fishermen, and delivered to a stranger on the other side. When the Sergeant inquired as to who gave the fishermen these packages in the first place,

Annunciation shrugged his shoulders and said that it was one of the Europeans.

Just when it looked as if the Triple-P must carry all before it, something unexpected had occurred. A Prophet had appeared, speaking with the voice of a mighty warrior of old who slew monsters called dragons. This spirit, through the Prophet, had announced Mguu to be the embodiment of a crane, a bird famous for its treachery and its hatred towards the Chuma people, who supported Mguu and the Triple P.

Many years ago, a crane had entered into possession of a Chuma chief who had, in consequence, led his warriors to total disaster in a gorge where the Mongu tribe had surrounded and exterminated them. Could this treacherous crane really have seized the tongue of Mguu, their leader? If so, they were undone. No wonder, among the Chuma, doubts were rife.

And now the Prophet had announced a new purification rite to remove that uncleanliness with which all men, sooner or later, became contaminated, especially when they worked in the mines. It was well known that older, traditional forms of purification lacked strength to expel the contamination of the mines; new ills needed new remedies.

To obtain them, a man must first join the new society, the *Sulu Sita,* meaning *Six Keys*. In return for an oath of allegiance to the Prophet and a fee of ten shillings, they received the rite of baptism and a green robe with a white cross sewn on to the back, and were required to grow beards and give up cigarettes. Rumour had it that the latest recruit was the Rev. Goliath Zaza.

Sergeant Chisanga's sympathies lay with Moto Mguu, who was counter-attacking by means of a story that the Prophet was the offspring of Zaza's mother and a man-eating ogre with five buttocks, and that his baptismal rite was even more lethal than tapioca to male virility.

With all this enthralling news to talk about, Sergeant Chisanga found it hard to maintain his interest in the death of a fat European the previous afternoon. Still, he had his duty, and he was famous as a conscientious man. After his third cup of tea, he addressed himself to Annunciation.

"This white man who died yesterday, the fat man: the Europeans are saying he ate medicine in the sandwiches you made."

Annunciation was busy stirring an enormous pot full of bones, skin and mysterious vegetables. "Europeans talk like guinea-fowl," he replied loftily. "Chk-chk-chk-chk-chk. Why should I put medicine in the sandwiches of a fat European?"

"Perhaps the medicine was put there by one of your enemies. When did you make those sandwiches, important cook?"

"I made them after I had cooked dinner for the Europeans. Eeeeee, how they eat! Like elephants or rabbits. Do I not work all day and nearly all night, for a few miserable shillings? No one works as hard as I do for so little pay."

"Yes, they do," Chisanga contradicted. "In the police force I have to work all day and all night also, and my pay is absurd, for my work needs brains and cleverness and bravery and skill. After you had made the sandwiches, what did you do with them?"

"I put them in the fridge."

"Very well. Did you lock it?"

Annunciation threw back his head and roared with laughter. His Chinese moustaches shook in the gale.

"Are you so ignorant, policeman, that you do not know that fridges do not have keys? They have doors that go clk clk. But no keys. Ho, ho! Even the small children of kitchen-boys know that."

"Do you think I don't know about the doors of fridges?" Chisanga cried indignantly. "When I am a Superintendent, which will be very soon indeed, I shall have three fridges of my own while you are still stirring potatoes in a pot. Perhaps, if you behave well, you shall cook *my* meals."

Annunciation waved his ladle over his head and made a dash for Sergeant Chisanga, who jumped up with agility and dodged behind a sack of greens. Everyone laughed until the air shook. A great deal of vituperation and cross-talk occurred before everything settled down again and Annunciation loudly declared that he would answer no more impudent questions from the bastard son of a leprous beggar and a diseased hyena.

"You will have to answer them," Chisanga warned, "because white policeman will lock you into the jail if you don't."

"That would be a holiday, after cooking night and day for a herd of elephants and getting pestered by tsetse-flies in trousers in between."

"Did you lock the room in which the fridge is kept, ignorant cook?"

"Do you think this place is full of thieves? Besides, I was busy. That night my son Joshua was ill. He had a fever, a dangerous fever, and the doctor came."

"Perhaps he had eaten food cooked by his father," Chisanga said, and was rewarded by a shout of laughter.

"Is that the manners of policemen, to laugh when they hear about a child's illness?"

"I did not laugh at the illness," Chisanga said, somewhat abashed. "Is the child better?"

"Yes, the doctor came and gave him medicine. Also, I am a Christian, and prayed to God who sent him strength to drive out the fever."

"I am glad," said Chisanga. "Do you think an enemy of this fat white man put medicine into the sandwiches?"

"How do I know? Many people touched the sandwiches after I made them. Perhaps Slocombe put in medicine."

"Why should he do that?"

"He came here several times to talk about these sandwiches as if they were very important, and then he marked the boxes with bits of paper. He has not done that before. Why was he so interested in these sandwiches?"

Chisanga nodded sagely. "Yes, why? I will find out."

"The fat white man had a very fat wife," Annunciation volunteered, "even fatter than he was. She looks fertile, though she is too old now for child-bearing. She talks a great deal to that Shiwa Chief. Perhaps that Chief killed her husband, so as to take the fat white woman to his village."

This was a good joke, and everyone was laughing when John Jacey edged through a crowded doorway into the dark, delicious-smelling fug. The Sergeant grinned and continued his conversation; detectives, when engaged in profitable talk, didn't spoil it by springing up to salute. Besides, the Superintendent was soon to be Hapanized and Sergeant Chisanga was to inherit the job. By rights, it was almost time for Jacey to start saluting *him*.

Chisanga bore his superior no ill will, but looked forward with natural impatience to the day when he would take over the job. He might even visit the Superintendent when he went to England. He had put his name down for a crash course and expected to be there quite soon, feeding on meat every day, riding in trains that burrowed into the earth like honey-badgers, drinking tea with the Queen and seeing the naked white girls he had heard about who stood quite still like herons and were pink all over. Some people said they were made of soap, but a cousin who had been to England on a crash course in trade unions swore they were real, and that one of them had sneezed and twitched all over.

As soon as Jacey entered, the atmosphere changed. No one objected to his presence, but it was like a draught of cold air. Nevertheless, he showed that he could joke, too.

"Well, Chisanga," he asked, "have you got the handcuffs on anyone yet?"

Chisanga grinned. "Not yet, but I have been thinking that this cook wears no bangles, although he is a rich man."

"Go away, policeman, I am busy," Annunciation snapped. He was kneading fat in a bowl of flour. How could you make pastry, Jacey wondered, in this football scrum and a temperature of at least a hundred? Nevertheless, he'd heard that Annunciation's pastry was excellent.

"Come along, Chisanga, we've got work to do," he said. "Where's the steward who handed round the sandwich boxes at the picnic yesterday? I want to speak to him."

Chapter 13

Jacey found two of the stewards in the all-electric kitchen cleaning silver and grinding coffee. Ranged among the units were two large refrigerators. Perfunctorily, Jacey examined them—he hardly expected to find clues among the eggs and milk and things in plastic bags. They did themselves proud, he thought, these Commissioners —or, rather, Steyn Consolidated did them proud.

"Where are the boxes," he asked, "that had the sandwiches in them?"

One of the stewards abandoned his silver cleaning and opened the door of a formica-faced cabinet. Inside were stacked a number of empty plastic boxes.

"And you washed these out after the Europeans had eaten?"

"Yes, we washed them out completely."

"What happened to the food left inside?"

"The food? We threw it into the water."

"It wouldn't be wrong to eat food that had been left over. It would be sensible. Are you sure none of the stewards ate anything?"

The silver-cleaner shook his head. "We weren't hungry. Besides, we're not dogs to eat the scraps of other people's meals."

Jacey felt snubbed, and gazed morosely at the plastic boxes. Was it worth taking them for laboratory examination? Almost certainly not; still, he supposed that any outside chance, even ten thousand to one, couldn't be ignored. "Find something to put them in," he instructed.

Chisanga made no better progress with the other steward. The full boxes had been put into a hamper, taken to the launch and unpacked there, and the steward had seen no one interfering with them. Only Mr. Slocombe, who'd been in charge.

Jacey sighed, gazing through the open door to the sun-flooded veranda. Everything outside looked bright, smiling, restful and at ease. Sunbirds quavered over glowing salvias and mombresias, a wagtail picked its way across a green lawn. The trees slept in the heat. It was mid-morning by now. No one seemed to be stirring in the main body of the Merry Hippo, it was impossible to imagine anything wrong.

A nice case, Jacey thought bitterly. Anyone could have walked into the all-electric kitchen at any time during the night or early morning, taken the boxes from the fridge and slipped in the poison, unobserved and undisturbed. Anyone could dig a deadly poison from the bush at any time, or strip a few leaves from one of half a dozen trees or shrubs, or pluck a few beans or pods, or buy them for a shilling. He remembered the necklace Mrs. Tripp had bought. She could have poisoned Bagpuse as easy as falling off a log. The wonder was that anyone stayed alive in this country.

A flicker of colour caught his eye, over by a buddleia. In an instant he was alert as a pointer. A brilliant peacock blue with black and russet markings: not only the colour, but the shape—not one of the local standbys. He stepped into the sunlight and advanced cautiously towards the buddleia. His walk became a stalk, silent, careful, above all steady, without jerkiness. His sharp eyes searched the bush and then he saw it, resting on a twig with its wings closed.

Alas, no net. Could he manage with a handkerchief? Too risky—even if he trapped it, the wings would crush. He'd have to let it go and come back with the apparatus. The insect rose and fluttered away. Jacey's heart gave a little jump. Yes, it *was* a *Cosmolyce boeticus*. He'd never seen a specimen in this region before.

The butterfly vanished, twinkling on the air like a tossed jewel, the embodiment of joy and gaiety. The sun warmed it, the colours shone, it danced to find a mate or to sip honey. Jacey sighed; how much more pleasant to pursue the butterfly than this tangled mystery, so much less beautiful. He turned and, to his embarrassment, saw Alex Burton looking at him with a sardonic grin, his hair tousled, his hands in his pockets.

"After big game again," he said. "No more broken bones, I hope." Jacey could think of no excuse.

"You caught me out this time. Come and talk to me."

"I can offer you a pint of the Company's iced beer."

The lounge was empty and they sat down. A steward came, took the order and returned with the beer.

"Everyone's gone to the funeral but you," Jacey remarked, a question in his voice.

"Beer, sunshine and contemplation are more in my line."

They sat in silence for a few moments, their thoughts idling, savouring the cold, sharp flavour of the beer and the feel of sunshine on their backs.

"Your contemplation," Jacey ventured. "Any end-products?"

Alex shook his head. "Only the obvious. I think someone got the wrong man. But Lady Bagpuse doesn't. She's got a theory. More than you have, probably."

Jacey agreed. "To do with pigs?"

"And Poles. A quagmire of passion, violence and intrigue bubbles only just under the surface of the pig breeder's world. It's rather fascinating."

"It's a far cry from Shooting Star."

"There's a new breed of Iron Curtain pig, it seems, for which the Russians—although actually it's Polish—claim the most exaggerated virtues. A fabulous conversion ratio. A sort of Sputnik among pigs."

"The virtues of *that* weren't exaggerated."

"True. A group of British breeders—traitors or pioneers according to your point of view—want to introduce some of these porcine Sputniks to revolutionize the British pig industry. Old Bagpuse was the leader of the opposition."

"No red pigs for British styes?"

"I daresay that was at the bottom of it. The reason he gave was disease. No red germs to pollute British pigs. Also, I suppose, a lot of British breeders would be ruined if the Sputniks lived up to their reputation."

"This is a nice fairy tale, Alex, but I *am* supposed to be investigating a murder."

"You'll get it from the widow in generous doses, so you might as well hear the outline. Bagpuse was convinced this was all a deep-laid Russian plot. British pigs have no immunity to certain diseases rife on the Continent. If Polish Sputnik pigs brought in any one of these diseases, our bacon industry might be virtually wiped out. A body-blow to our economy, a big cold war defeat. Clever."

"It sounds as if she's convinced *you*."

"Almost anything's possible these days. However, that's not all. Bagpuse lost the first round and some Polish pigs were actually imported, but on condition they spent three months in quarantine at the docks. Before a month was up they were all dead."

"Sabotage?" Jacey inquired, interested in spite of himself.

"That's what the Poles claim, of course. The British breeders say it was a disease the pigs brought with them. The vets, like doctors, disagree. There's quite a row going on. Bagpuse versus the Soviet and the Polish embassies and so on. He was convinced they were out for his blood. Literally."

"Are you trying to suggest that Bagpuse's last words, or nearly last words anyway, were an attempt to tell us he'd been poisoned by the Soviet Ambassador?"

"I'm not, but Lady Bagpuse is."

"And one of the stewards or cooks, or perhaps one of your fellow Commissioners, is an agent of the Soviet pig breeders, I suppose? Really, Alex, for a supposedly level-headed type—"

"I'm only warning you what's coming. She says she's known all along Bagpuse was risking his life for the pig breeders of Britain. And I think she's got a suspect, too, for the role of Soviet agent."

"Is she *quite* round the bend, d'you think?"

"She's suffering from shock. I don't suppose they've been apart for over forty years. It's knocked her endways, poor old thing. Curiously enough the only person who seems able to comfort her is Chief Faustus. You'd think with so many wives . . . But I suppose he and Bagpuse were the same type in some ways. He was actually crying."

"They'll be back soon from the funeral," Jacey said. "I must get on my way."

But as he drained his beer the first of the returning cars drove up and Jacey changed his mind. This would be an opportunity to see some of the other Commissioners while Chisanga, he hoped, picked up more gossip. Whether the gossip would be passed on, however, was another matter. For if this really was a Triple-P job, Chisanga would say nothing. Too risky. Even if Chisanga wasn't a Triple-P supporter already, he'd have to become one when the Triple-P formed the Government and the Government ran the police.

Amelia Tripp came into the lounge. She looked pale, washed-out and drawn, as if she hadn't slept for good reasons.

"You didn't come to the funeral," she said accusingly to Alex.

"No. I should have, I know."

"They got it over quickly, thank goodness. Of course, this Commission must go on, but sometimes I feel as if there's some ghastly fate or curse or something hanging over it. I suppose it's just nerves."

"Sit down and have a drink," Alex suggested.

"I think I will." She took the window seat and looked at Jacey. "There's something I want to tell you. It may mean nothing, but it may . . . First of all I thought I wouldn't say anthing. I'm getting so muddled up I may have made some silly mistake. Lord Bagpuse *was* poisoned, wasn't he?"

"He may have been, or he may not." Jacey offered her a cigarette. "Officially, as you know, it was a sudden tropical infection. That could be true."

Amelia Tripp fitted the cigarette into her holder and Jacey observed that her hands were shaky. "You remember those lucky beans you helped me buy at the Pig and Whistle?"

Jacey nodded. The seed of the creeper *Abrus precatorius,* found all over the *momombo* bush, and containing a toxin called abrin that could kill a man in twenty minutes. It could have killed Lord Bagpuse. But why pick on one particular necklace when the beans were to be found in profusion all over the country?

Amelia Tripp drew deeply on her cigarette and said: "It's disappeared."

Jacey looked at her with awakened interest. "Stolen?"

"I think so."

"When?"

"On Saturday night."

Amelia hadn't slept at all well that night, she said—nothing new. She had some sleeping pills but tried not to use them very often, and hadn't done so then. At last she had tired of tossing on her bed; the night was fine and starlit, warm as toast, so she'd put on a wrap and gone out, leaving the door ajar. This was about midnight, or soon after.

"Where did you go?" Jacey asked.

"Down towards the lake. There's a footpath that leads down beyond the garden to the road. I saw one of the guards on the way." She glanced at Jacey with a smile that made her face look less haggard. "He was asleep."

"They have to keep their strength up. How long did you prowl about for?"

"Half an hour, I should think. When I got back I still felt restless and decided to take a pill after all. They live in a small drawer at the bottom of the mirror on the dressing-table, where I put my odds and ends. That's where the beads were. At least I'm almost sure they were. Anyway, I noticed they'd gone."

"Had you worn them that day? On the Saturday?"

"Yes, I had. I left them on the dressing-table when I changed for dinner and popped them into the drawer just before I went to bed."

"You're really sure of that?"

Amelia rubbed her forehead with her fingers. "I *think* I'm sure. I mean, I'm sure I am, but sometimes I'm wrong even when I'm sure. You know what I mean? And just lately I haven't been sleeping well and one's memory can play tricks . . ."

"If you're right," Jacey said, "no one could have taken the beans while you were in bed because you didn't sleep. Correct?"

Amelia nodded.

"Someone must have seen you go out, sneaked into your room and taken them while you were strolling in the garden?"

Amelia looked at him. "But who on earth would want to? And

why? Who'd have been about at that time of night, except the guards?"

"Would you mind if I searched your room?"

"You don't trust my word?"

"I have to check on things."

"I've wondered myself if I could have done something idiotic with the necklace, left it in a pocket or let it fall into a shoe, so probably that would be the best thing."

"No time like the present, if you agree."

Amelia's door was the middle one opening off the covered way that led from the lounge to the electric kitchen. On one side was Lady Bagpuse, on the other the Connors. Amelia's was a pleasant, sunny, well-furnished apartment, done in lilac and primrose, with its own bathroom. On the dressing-table stood a photograph of a long-faced, pony-tailed teen-age girl, another of an elderly woman, and one of a man in uniform. A bowl of honeysuckle adorned the table.

"Will this embarrass you?" Jacey asked. "I have to pry into everything."

"I've nothing to conceal, Superintendent. All the same I don't think I'll watch you. I'll go for a stroll."

Alex went with her and they paced the lawn, keeping as much as possible to the shade of the abrizzia trees. The lounge was filling up as car-loads of Commissioners and staff returned from the funeral and made for the iced drinks before lunch.

"I don't feel like talking to the others at the moment," Amelia said. "This is upsetting, you know. I suppose there may be some perfectly simple explanation. But otherwise it means . . ."

"That Bagpuse was poisoned with your beans," Alex said bluntly. "That's a long shot. There are heaps of other poisons quite easy to get hold of in this country, with the same sort of symptoms. That is if he really *was* poisoned."

"He must have been, don't you think? And why else should anyone take that necklace—the very night before? It was worth three-and-six."

"Perhaps it'll turn up." Alex tried to sound reassuring. He was afraid Amelia might be going to crack, and one hysterical woman at a time was one too many. "You didn't see or hear anything on your prowl that could possibly connect?"

She shook her head. "Quiet as the grave. After I got back to bed, though, not long after—"

"Yes?"

"I think I heard a car start up and drive away."

"From the Merry Hippo?"

"No, it was further off. Towards the lake. But of course it might have been merely going along the road. I might not have heard it until it reached that bit of road below here." She pointed towards the lake; the road to the town of Shooting Star ran parallel to the water and about two hundred yards below the guest-house garden.

"The sooner we get our work done and get home," Alex said abruptly, "the better for everyone."

Amelia nodded. "I feel that strongly, too. And the political situation here is getting tenser. There may be trouble any time, it seems. . . . The Commission meets this afternoon, but unless I feel better I shan't go. I've got a headache."

"I'd go if I were you," Alex said. "Occupy your mind."

"Well, I'll see." She walked off towards the lounge.

Chapter 14

"ANY LUCK?" Alex found Jacey completing his search. Everything was back neatly in place, there was no outward sign of disturbance.

"Nothing. No lucky beans, no incriminating documents, no secret microfilms, not even any dirty postcards. You know Mrs. Tripp. Was she speaking the truth?"

"I'm not sure, John. She's badly rattled. She's a bit of an enigma, is our Amelia."

"Well, there are several possibilites." He ticked them off on three fingers. "Someone really did steal her beans and used them to poison Bagpuse. Either on purpose, or in mistake for Connor. Someone stole the beans as a blind, to confuse the issue or throw suspicion on Mrs. Tripp. Or no one stole the beans and Mrs. Tripp poisoned Bagpuse and is trying to throw us off the scent."

"No reason for her to poison Bagpuse, is there? You mean she was trying to poison Sir Christopher."

"It's possible."

"M'm." Alex scratched his head. "In that case . . . No hidden microfilms?"

"None."

Jacey pulled the door to after him and they stood for a moment in the open passage-way. On Saturday night, round about midnight or early on the Sunday morning, if Amelia Tripp wasn't lying, someone had stood in the darkness near this spot and seen her leave her room with the door ajar and cross the lawn. Why had this individual been standing here? He couldn't have foretold Amelia's midnight prowl. The whole thing must have come to him on impulse, on the spur of the moment. He must have known about her lucky bean necklace. Well, everyone even remotely connected with the Commission could have known that, and seen it. The idea must have come suddenly to him that here was his chance.

He took the necklace from her dressing-table. He came back to the veranda. Then, the sandwiches—ten or fifteen paces to the unlocked kitchen, to the refrigerator. He must have known the sandwiches were there.

He must have known that each of the party was to have his own box. Slocombe had gone round the day before asking everyone what he fancied, so all the Commissioners knew the drill; and, of course, so did the staff. Might as well have put it out on the radio, Jacey thought.

Then, somehow, this lurker in the shadows must have crushed the beans. How? A faint smell of coffee came to Jacey's nostrils. That sort of thing had happened to him before—the brain gave a leap in the dark and fooled the senses. A queer trick. With a little grunt he strode along and into the kitchen.

There was the coffee mill, screwed tightly on to a shelf. He detached it, looked round, seized a tea-cloth, wrapped up the coffee mill and tucked it under one arm. Probably a waste of time—it had been in use that morning, thirty-six hours had gone by, they'd have washed and wiped it. Even if his idea was right, no traces of crushed bean would be likely to remain, but one couldn't neglect the least possibility. A minute, invisible grain of powder could conceivably be nestling in some interstice. One of the stewards watched him as if hypnotized, his mouth slightly open. More lunacy! He was speechless as Jacey vanished with his booty. Then he shook his head slowly and went on putting the silver on a tray.

Alex stood for a while on the veranda, watching the quivering wings of a bronze-plumed sunbird and pondering the same questions. Who had been lurking in the shadows on Saturday night? If, indeed, there had been anyone? Was Amelia inventing it all? Lady Bagpuse came towards him, walking slowly with her head bent. No longer like a billowing, square-rigged ship, she moved now without spring or confidence, like a heavy broken-down cart-horse. Alex stood to one side, but she stopped and said: "Can you spare a few moments, Dr. Burton? I've something I'd like to say."

"Of course."

She led the way into the bedroom next to Amelia's. Freddy's brushes lay on the dressing-table; his suits, no doubt, were in the cupboard, his shaving kit in the bathroom next door. A handbook of the Country Gentleman's Association lay on the table where he must have put it down, next to a heap of knitting. A pullover, perhaps, that would never now be worn.

"Please sit down," she said in a flat voice. "I won't keep you long. I'm flying home, you know, tomorrow. Mr. Evans has arranged it. He's been very kind. He and the Chief . . . They were the same sort, you know. The Chief and Freddy."

"It's the best thing you can do, go home. There'll be a lot to see to."

She nodded. "Yes, a lot. You see, the fight must go on. Freddy gave his life for it, for his country. I must do what I can."

Alex didn't often feel embarrassed, but he did now. "No one can be certain, you know, that your husband didn't die naturally."

"*I* can be certain. You see, I saw the man who killed him."

"You did *what,* Lady Bagpuse?" Now she really has, he thought, gone round the bend.

"You think Freddy's death has driven me out of my mind. And it's to a certain person's interests to spread the story that I'm off my head. I'm not, you know. He'll give himself away sooner or later. They always do."

"I really think, Lady Bagpuse, it would be better if—"

"You don't believe me either, but you'll see. They had to get Freddy out of the way. So long as he was there, he stood like a rock. He had so much courage, you see. And such great influence. So they had to get him out of the way."

She was gesticulating with her hands, and had a wild look in her eye. "Would you like a glass of water?" Alex asked.

"I saw him walk across the lawn as bold as brass. The light was quite strong enough to see clearly. He'd been getting at the sandwiches, of course."

"Who are you talking about, Lady Bagpuse?"

"The man who killed Freddy."

"Yes, but—if you actually *did* see someone, you'd better tell me who."

"Of course he isn't English. You can't expect the same standards. He took in everyone—Freddy never suspected for a moment he was in their pay. He even took in the Prime Minister. He must have been in their pay all along."

"In whose pay, Lady Bagpuse?"

"The Russians. It's jealousy, of course. They may be able to launch a Sputnik but they can't—they never will—breed a first-rate New Spot boar."

There was a knock on the door and Lady Connor came in, and smiled at Alex. "I've come to collect Lady Bagpuse for luncheon. Chris says shall we have a quiet bite together in our sitting-room, Blanche?"

"I'd rather not, thank you."

"Of course we quite understand," Lady Connor said in the kind of voice used to humour invalids. "I'll get them to bring you a tray in here. Just a little soup and vegetables: you must eat *something,* you know."

The worry had marked Constance Connor, too. Her face was looking shadowed and lined under its make-up.

"Chris has been asking for you, Dr. Burton," she added. "Could you come along and see him now? If I were you, Blanche, I'd stay here and refuse to see anyone. The press are pouring in, I believe. So are the telegrams. One from the Prime Minister, Dick Howard of course, and Lord Salisbury—I daresay you'd like to see some of them, my dear." Lady Bagpuse shook her head.

"She's bowled over," Alex remarked to Lady Connor, shutting the door behind them both.

"Yes, it's very awkward," Lady Connor agreed. "She's got some extraordinary delusions. If she talks to any of the reporters it'll be a nightmare. Chris is worried stiff."

Of course Lady Bagpuse was mad, Alex reflected. But *had* she seen a man in the moonlight? Or imagined one? After all, there had been someone there—unless both Amelia and Lady Bagpuse had invented him.

All the old girl had actually said about the lurker in the shadows was that he wasn't English. Who did that suggest? Rumble? Godfrey? Or, of course, *any* African. Zaza, Matunda, even Faustus. That scarcely narrowed the field. If it came to that, Connor was mainly Irish. Surely she couldn't have suggested . . . ? Anyway, it was all a persecution mania.

Alex found the Chairman unperturbed, at least outwardly. But the strain was there: he was smoking more, he'd grown a little fidgety, he blew his nose a good deal. His office was inundated with papers and Thomasina came in with more. Her smile at Alex was preoccupied and yet, for a moment, it made a feeling of euphoria replace his gloom.

"Another batch, I'm afraid. The President of the Royal Agricultural Society, the Council of the Norfolk New Spot Society, the Chairman of the County Council, the Lord Lieutenant, the Bishop of Norwich. Shall I send off the stock answer?"

Sir Christopher glanced through them. "Well, yes, but ring the changes a bit—nothing perfunctory. He had a lot of friends, poor devil."

"So far the press has swallowed our story," Thomasina added, "but there's a note of scepticism in the *Clarion* and Fleetway Black is on the way."

"We must try to keep him away from Lady Bagpuse, that's all. Now, Alex, sit down. We're meeting this afternoon and I want to put you in the picture about this ugly business of our unplugged leak. I'm going to set a kind of trap for X, the traitor in our midst."

Alex said: "I thought you knew who he—or she—was."

"The security people say they do, but they can't prove it. This trap, so-called, won't provide proof but it could be a pointer. The suspect's going to stay away and I'm going to make an announcement . . ." He explained about the trap.

"There are at least two obvious loopholes," Alex pointed out.

"I know. X may pick up the information by other means, despite not having been at the meeting. That's if we're right about X. Or X may be at the meeting but see through our little stratagem and withhold his daily bulletin. That's if we're wrong about X. So this can't prove anything. It may help, that's all."

"We all discuss these things among ourselves. What's to prevent X from hearing the news over drinks after the meeting?"

"Only my appeal. I shall give it to them hot and strong about the absolute necessity of discussing nothing with anyone. I'd be awfully grateful for your help on this, I really would. Try and shut them up if they *do* start talking."

"One might as well try and shut up the Victoria Falls."

Sir Christopher sighed and leant back in his chair. "I suppose this disaster has upset us all the more than we care to admit. I can't quite digest the fact that Freddy Bagpuse's unpleasant end was almost certainly meant for me. A sort of guilt. He was as obstinate as a mule and not all that bright, but if there's ever a Last Judgement he'll stride through the golden gates in a blaze of glory while I'm down in the pit with the howling devils."

"I expect he had fewer temptations."

"That might well be true: a man who's got to make his own way in the world can't, or at any rate doesn't, always keep his hands clean. Bagpuse, of course, wouldn't have got far in the law or politics but I'm pretty sure he'd have kept his hands spotless, even if that meant no money stuck to them. Do you know why he was appointed to this Commission in the first place?"

"I've often wondered. We all have."

"Now he's dead, I'll tell you—in strict confidence. It was a blunder in the Cabinet office."

"Well, now," Alex said.

"You've heard of Ford Bayford?"

"The expert on constitutional law?" Alex lay back in his chair and roared with laughter. "That's too good to be true."

"The Prime Minister has appalling handwriting and he's always scribbling notes on slips of paper. This particular note travelled down the line and some bright individual translated *Ford Bayford* into *Lord Bagpuse*. A letter went out before the mistake was discovered and you can imagine the rumpus. But it was too late then and so we got our Freddy."

"And so he got poisoned in the wilds of Africa."

"Queer, isn't it. Blind chance? The hand of fate? Either way, I can't help feeling to blame." Sir Christopher got up with his usual agility, smiled at Alex and added: "Anyway, it's nice to know I can count on your help."

"I don't quite know what direction it can take."

"General moral support. And—well—keep your eyes and ears open. They're both pretty sharp."

"You'd better keep one eye on yourself," Alex advised.

Sir Christopher laughed. "I'm doing that all right. So are half the security forces of Hapana. Poor Butterfield, I don't blame him, but our security's becoming an obsession. Is anyone's life worth so much fuss? I doubt it. Not mine, certainly."

This was the kind of remark that irritated Alex, because it called for an obvious reply. So he didn't make it. Instead he said:

"I suppose the only thing that saves us all is that we don't get our deserts."

Sir Christopher gave him a curious look—one that disturbed him. It was the look of a man in distress to a man in safety, an appeal to strength from weakness, a signal from the drowning to a watcher on dry land. Or was that all imagination? In a moment, the look was gone, but the Chairman's voice was sombre.

"Sooner or later the bill comes in for being saved. It can be a heavy one . . . Fate? Or blind chance? Will one ever know?"

How tired he looks, Alex thought, in this strong clear light of day flooding through the open window, making the dark and labyrinthine secrets of a poisoner seem impossible, hallucinatory, remote.

"'All discord, harmony not understood; All partial evil, universal good,'" he quoted.

"Well, I wonder," the Chairman said, and added in a matter-of-fact tone: "Thanks a lot, Alex, for your help, past and to come—you're a great comfort, you know, to a harassed Chairman. Now I must go and deal with poor old Blanche Bagpuse, I suppose. It's broken her up completely. And Constance—I'm worried, too, about her. She's none too strong. Ah, well . . . See you this afternoon."

Alex walked thoughtfully towards the excellent luncheon he knew would await him. What had the Chairman wanted—sympathy, reassurance, a human touch? Well, natural enough. Even for someone as tough as Sir Christopher—as courageous, too—it couldn't be pleasant to know oneself the quarry of a poisoner who'd just missed his pounce. To know and yet not quite to know—and to expect another attempt. And to search for the reason. All the same, why pick for sympathy on him, on Alex? Why not on Maxwell-Palmer, so much closer to Connor's age and outlook, cut out to be his natural ally?

Alex could think of only one reason, but it seemed so unlikely that he put it out of his mind.

Chapter 15

THE COMMISSION met at three o'clock in the board-room, round a handsome mahogany table. Everything gleamed: polished wood, clean white blotting-pads, an inkstand opposite the Chairman, a parquet floor, silver cups on the mantelpiece. Outside, two armed Hapanan constables and a holstered Inspector could be seen walking to and fro. On the Chairman's right sat a stranger: a thin, sunburnt man with a small moustache who bore the stamp, indefinable but plain, of a man in authority in the open air.

"I've called you together," the Chairman said, "to settle our future plans. I know that in spite of this dreadful disaster we all think it our duty to carry on with our inquiry. Now before we—"

"One word, Mr. Chairman." Dr. Rumble held up a hand with the gesture of a bishop about to bless his flock. "I hope you'll allow me to pay a very brief tribute to our colleague. Although Lord Bagpuse belonged to the British aristocracy, a section of the human family which, I hope I may say without offence, has in the past soiled its hands with colonialism; although a member of that *corps d'élite*, throughout our short acquaintance I found him the soul of courtesy, a kind and generous colleague with whom it was a privilege—I say a privilege—to serve. I am sure I speak for us all when I say—"

"Dr. Rumble, your generous words exactly hit off what we're all feeling. Now, before we—"

"—it was with a shock of genuine distress that I—"

"—plan our next move, there is something I must say." Sir Christopher glared and the effect, in one generally so disarming, made Dr. Rumble clear his throat; this momentary hesitation undid him. The Chairman pressed on. "We're two short, incidentally. Sir Jeremy asks us to excuse him; something urgent has cropped up at the mine. And Mrs. Tripp, unfortunately, is a bit under the weather."

The Rev. Zaza leant forward and frowned, his lean, thin face puzzled and eager, his spectacles misty. "Mrs. Tripp is under *who?*" he inquired.

"An expression of ours, Mr. Zaza, meaning *indisposed*. Off colour."

"Ah! Off colour," he echoed darkly.

"Mr. Chairman, I think it is a very terrible admission that we can have a member of this Commission who is off colour. If someone is off colour, they should not come to Hapana. They should stay in their own country where they can be with white people only. This is the homeland of the people of Hapana and their colour—"

"Now, now, Mr. Matunda, you're pulling my leg," the Chairman said sharply. "You know the English language as well as I do. *Off colour* means *ill*. Not very ill, just slightly."

"Mr. Chairman, in view of the treacherous nature of this tropical climate, I hope that the very best medical attention—"

"I can assure you, Dr. Rumble, that if there's the least suspicion of anything more serious than a headache—"

"I do not know why Dr. Rumble should say such things about our climate in Hapana," the Rev. Zaza said excitedly. "It is a very good climate indeed. It is healthy for our children. The crops grow to perfection, there are big yields of mealies, of cassava, of groundnuts, there are—"

"Gentlemen, gentlemen, for Heaven's sake let's keep to the point," Sir Christopher entreated. "Out of respect to the dead . . . and you'll all have noticed that we have a guest this afternoon. This is Mr. Hook. Mr. Hook is the Commissioner of the south-eastern province, where we're due to go next week to take evidence. He has some disturbing news for us, gentlemen."

"Let him proceed to speak, then," Mansfield Matunda said majestically.

Mr. Hook cleared his throat and proceeded in dry, wooden tones which made Alex think of a door-hinge in need of oil.

"Well, the thing is, gentlemen, we're having a spot of bother. Some of these agitator fellows have come down from Umpah and there's a subversive society calling itself the *Sulu Sita*—means *six keys* literally, we don't know why—who are stirring up a lot of trouble. Mainly among the half-educated, half-baked lads, you know. The older men are steady, but the security system's stretched to the full. In view of this, I've had to recommend—"

The Rev. Zaza was waving an agitated arm and beginning to splutter.

"Mr. Chairman, Mr. Chairman, this gentleman is quite wrong. The *Sulu Sita* are respectable religious men who want only to purify sinners, like John the Baptist who purified sins in the river of Jordan. The men of this society—"

"Mr. Chairman, Mr. Zaza does not know what he is talking of," Matunda proclaimed in tones at once lofty and rotund. "These men are very wicked, they are pretending to make people clean but really they are taking away their money. They are colonialist stooges who are feathering nests—"

"Mr. Chairman, what is this about feathered nests? The men of *Sulu Sita* have no nests, they give away everything to help sinners. It is Moto Mguu who builds nests for himself and for his friends, Moto Mguu who plucks the feathers of the poor people—"

"Gentlemen, please! Do let's keep to the point." The Chairman sounded desperate. "Mr. Hook, please continue."

"As I was saying, this subversive society is giving us a lot of trouble. It practises the most disgusting rites. It—"

"Disgusting rites?" Dr. Rumble queried with a note of hope.

"Tck, tck, tck," clicked Chief Faustus.

"That is lie!" cried the Rev. Zaza. "St. John the Baptist—"

"Now, Mr. Hook has touched upon a most interesting matter," Dr. Rumble intoned. "It has long been a hobby of mine to study the many and divergent ways in which the members of the human family employ physical means towards spiritual ends. There are, for instance, the Yogi practices in India. There are the flagellants of certain Amero-Indian tribes. If Mr. Hook would give us some examples—"

"Now, please, Dr. Rumble, this is *not* a lecture on anthropology," the Chairman entreated. "Will you be good enough to let Mr. Hook say what he has to say?"

"I should appreciate it if Mr. Hook would give us just one example."

"They purify the body and cleanse the soul," the Rev. Zaza said firmly. Mr. Hook looked at him sardonically, and observed:

"Most of them are unmentionable, but they start off by giving each initiate an enema."

"That is to purify the body," Zaza confirmed.

"Well, they rook the bloke ten bob, when he could get it done for nothing at the hospital. That ten bob goes into party funds to spread the trouble. It's all a racket, if you ask me. But anyway—"

Matunda, Zaza and Rumble were talking at once. Alex caught the eye of Thomasina, who was sitting back with her notebook, and winked. The Chairman had to pound the table to restore an order that was clearly not destined to endure.

"Really, gentlemen, I don't know what's the matter with us all today. I must ask Mr. Hook to forgive this display. And I hope he'll forgive me if I tell you from the Chair the gist of his communication. It's this. Owing to troubles in the south-eastern province, however caused—" he glared at Matunda and Zaza— "the security people can't cope with all of us as well. So our trip to that area is postponed. This means rearranging our schedule—a headache for our Secretary. He's working it out now." Sir Christopher smiled at Hugo Evans. "There's one more point."

"Are we to assume, then, Mr. Chairman," Mansfield said with a note of menace, "that this subversive and blasphemous society has driven out the Hapana police force? Is there no law and order in the south-eastern province? If that is so, then the Government has failed in its duty and should hand over at once to the majority party of Mr. Mguu, who is quite well able to enforce—"

"Please let me finish, Mr. Matunda," the Chairman insisted. "And I must ask you all to pay particular attention to this. What I've just said simply *must* be kept to ourselves. If it were to get out, there'd be a first-class political row. We might even be recalled. So I must ask you—no, I'm afraid on this occasion I must become the heavy Chairman and *instruct* you—not to breathe a word. We mustn't even talk about it among ourselves. You all know the old saying, walls have ears. Unfortunately it's often true. Now, is that absolutely clear?"

Mansfield Matunda bowed his head. "I do not give away secret things. It is to others you must speak." He glared at Zaza, who still looked furious and began:

"The Holy Ghost—"

"We really must leave the Holy Ghost out of our discussions. I think that's everything, isn't it, Hugo? Then we can adjourn until tomorrow morning. And please do remember what I've just said. Thank you, Mr. Hook. Thank you, gentlemen."

The trap was set, Alex thought, such as it was; of course, everyone *would* talk, despite the Chairman's entreaties. And *two* absent Commissioners—which was the intended, which the accidental absentee? Alex wanted to discuss it all with Thomasina—or, perhaps, to talk of something different and much more enjoyable. He managed to intercept her as they left the board-room and secure a promise that she'd dine with him at the Pig and Whistle that evening.

At seven o'clock he was at the Godfreys' to collect her. He hadn't met Mrs. Godfrey before. A bit of a battle-axe, Thomasina had described her: older than her husband, rather gruff, but good-hearted, forthright, competent. She went in for pot plants like African violets and gloxinias and made miniature gardens, using a long pair of tweezers, in narrow-necked jars and objects like old coaching lanterns. The delicacy and skill of the work contrasted with her heavy, almost masculine appearance, her thick sensible shoes and solid shoulders and plain cotton frocks. Her father had been a missionary; the two Godfrey children were away at boarding-school.

"Come and sit you down," she said in bass tones. "Gin-and-tonic? Dubonnet? Sherry? Paul's out as usual, but he'll be back any time. I don't blame you for wanting to get away from Slocombe Abbey—that's what we call the Merry Hippo—for an evening. Must be grim, cooped up there after your spot of bother. Only hope there isn't more to come. Well, cheer-o."

The drinks she poured were generous. The lake lay below them like a vast grey plain full of mystery and shadows. Islands faded into clots of darkness, lights winked here and there from the shore. On the veranda, a plant resembling ivy twined its tendrils round a trellis screen. The furniture was modern in design and strewn with bright cushions. Pot plants and miniature gardens stood on a series of steps and shelves, illuminated by Japanese lanterns.

While they sipped their drinks, Mrs. Godfrey talked about the mine and its queer, closed community. Thirty or forty thousand people derived their livelihood from a few holes in the ground and from lumps of rock gouged out of them by unbelievably complex, efficient and expensive machines. All servants to a blind cause, she suggested, like those Egyptian slaves who built the Pyramids. But theirs was a gilded bondage. In their air-conditioned, ultra-modern bungalows, many of the miners' wives had two giant refrigerators: the first for food, the second for cosmetics, which might otherwise turn greasy in the hot weather.

"All the same, my husband loves it here," she said. "He's only got to put in for some expensive piece of new equipment and out it comes. Whereas poor Dr. Furneaux—he's the Government doctor—has to argue for five years and then he doesn't get it."

"Copper's easier to extract than taxes, I suppose."

"Paul gave up a splendid practice to come here. He was in Cairo, making a packet by prescribing slimming diets and lifting faces of enormously fat black-marketeers' wives. One day he walked out of his consulting-room, just like that, and never went back. He'd had enough. Now he's blissfully happy, he'll never leave. He has everything he wants."

"And you?"

"Oh, I belong here. I'm Hapana born. I don't say everything's perfect, mind you, at Shooting Star—too much damned social nonsense for one thing. Bridge and cocktail parties and elevenses, that sort of thing."

"It sounds like hell to me," Thomasina remarked.

"You'd be surprised how much time my plants take. It's a constant fight against every known and unknown disease. And Paul takes me out on tour sometimes, that's what I really like. Here he is, at last."

Godfrey shook hands with the slight formality which, with his even slighter accent, was the only suggestion of his Continental origin. He wore a spotted bow tie and managed to look cool and dapper even at the end of a hot, sultry day.

"It's quite a performance to get into one's own house," he remarked, helping himself to a whisky. "Security guards everywhere. I was challenged twice and the second fellow brandished a gun in my face."

"They searched the house after Miss Labouchère had gone this morning," Mrs. Godfrey said.

"I hope they didn't damage any plants?"

"No, but they locked the loo. It was very awkward."

"Indeed, yes. Did they give a reason?"

"They looked in the cistern, for a bomb I suppose, and then they locked Miss Labouchère's room and the bathroom, and the loo as well, and took away the key."

"Very thorough," Dr. Godfrey said dryly.

"Luckily I was out all day. They came back and unlocked it after tea."

"It's a distressing time," the doctor commented. "I must express my condolences, Dr. Burton, and profound regrets. An abominable tragedy."

"I saw him die," Alex said bluntly. "You're certain, I suppose, it *was* poison?"

Godfrey twirled his drink in his glass and watched the bubbles rise and vanish. His wife went out to change, remarking that she was hot and sticky after playing golf, and Thomasina followed her.

"It's impossible to be certain of anything," Godfrey at last answered. "Dr. Furneaux, who did the autopsy with me, agrees. There's always the possibility of a very sudden multiple infection. Lord Bagpuse wasn't young, and could have built up no immunity to these tropical micro-organisms. At the same time the condition of the organs was perfectly consistent with the action of one of our local alkaloidal vegetable poisons."

"Lucky beans, for instance?"

"Perhaps. It's impossible to isolate any toxic principle in the organs, you know. Or, rather, I should say that no one has yet succeeded in doing so. Let me fill your glass."

"I must be going, if I can get hold of my girl. Thanks for the drink."

"We find Miss Labouchère a charming guest. Please permit me to drop you at the Pig and Whistle in my car, which can fetch you when your little tête-à-tête is over."

"I wouldn't dream of putting you to all that trouble," Alex said, thinking that this polite formality was catching.

"I have to go out anyway before dinner. As a matter of fact, I promised to call on your colleague, Mrs. Tripp, and on Lady Connor."

The telephone rang, and Godfrey went out to deal with it. In a few moments Thomasina appeared, not changed but *freshened,* he thought the word was—fresh indeed, and so desirable his heart jumped like a bird in the hand. Ridiculous and infuriating, at the age of nearly forty and in face of all those resolutions never to be caught again. He felt as drained of free will as a squeezed lemon—and full of sap as a flowering tree. He took Thomasina's arm: soft, warm and electrifying.

"Come on, let's go," he said.

Chapter 16

"You look at home here," Alex commented. Thomasina's hair was the colour of golden bronze dahlias and any defects there might be in her appearance were left in hiding by tactful lighting. "You also look stunning."

She smiled her thanks. "It's a job to keep up with the standards of an African mining camp these days."

"One still needs gold dust to pay for the drinks."

A feature of the Pig and Whistle was the so-called veranda grill built around a shallow pond adorned by water-lilies. The pond was inhabited by frogs whose throaty cackles blended oddly with sentimental music from long-playing records. It was all so romantic, and Thomasina so exciting, that Alex felt himself sinking into a lamentable kind of emotional syrup. But Thomasina said:

"I can't help worrying about those frogs."

"They seem quite happy."

"Haven't you heard about the crocodile?"

"What crocodile?"

"There are too many frogs, so they've put a baby crocodile into the pond. It's only about a foot long but it's growing rapidly and eating up the frogs. Every night the frog chorus diminishes a little. It's awfully sinister."

Alex glanced at the pond. Now it appeared to him no longer a gentle, fairy-tale kind of pond with its glinting reflections, its soft plopping sounds, its graceful water-lilies, but a pit of menace full of sudden death and secret, predatory murder. Symbolic, somehow, of life in Hapana where few things were as they seemed. Symbolic, too, of the Commission? A bunch of frogs—they croaked enough, certainly—waiting to be gobbled up by a prowling crocodile?

"They don't know what's coming to them," he said.

"Like us?"

"I didn't say so." Across the white-clothed table she looked suddenly so vulnerable that he exclaimed: "Let's get out of here for a day or two. We could fly to Salisbury or Nairobi for the week-end."

She looked at him with raised eyebrows. "Is that a proposition?"

"Certainly."

"It's very kind, but would Sir Christopher approve?"

"The hell with Sir Christopher."

"Tut, tut."

"I really mean it. We could find a game-park and forget our troubles among the lions and elephants."

Thomasina was resting her chin on her intertwined fingers, with her head a little on one side, looking highly amused.

"Girls like me have to work for our living. We aren't employed as lion-watching companions for lecherous historians."

"There are no other girls like you."

"Thank you, but that's not the view of the Civil Service Commissioners. I'd get the sack in five minutes if I vanished for the week-end with one of the bosses."

" 'The ruling passion, be it what it will,' " Alex quoted. " 'The ruling passion conquers reason still.' "

"Really, this is a most extraordinary conversation," Thomasina said primly. "I'm going to change it. That was quite a good sauce with the fish, but I think it might have been improved by a dash of anchovy. Or does that indicate a coarse palate? Ground almonds would be more subtle. What do you think?"

Alex regarded her with a mixture of reproach and admiration. Hardhearted, but she knew how to cook. "Surely anchovy's too strong for any fish more rewarding than frozen Icelandic cod—" He broke off because, over his shoulder, she was watching a party settling itself at a nearby table. Mansfield Matunda was among them, flanked by two men who sat down with a perfunctory air and accepted enormous menu cards from the waiter.

"Oh, dear, it's started," Thomasina said. "Fleetway Black and Mervyn Sparks. It was bound to happen, but it won't make poor Stephen's life any easier."

"Poor Stephen gets paid for it," Alex said shortly.

"I don't believe you appreciate Stephen Partridge."

"I'd appreciate his job. He never seems to do anything."

"He has to cope with those gentlemen over there," Thomasina said.

"With singular lack of success."

Thomasina sighed. "We shall have to change the conversation again. Have you seen this?"

She handed him a sheet of paper she had found in her bag when delving for a cigarette. "I shouldn't have kept it, really—it was part of the confidential waste. The Vice-Chairman's doodles. But I'm glad I did, now. It'll be a sort of reminder."

Alex unfolded the paper to be confronted by a mass of pigs in all postures and sizes and drawn, it was clear, with love as well as expert knowledge: surprisingly well drawn, in fact.

"A secret code, obviously. On its way to Bonga."

He felt resentful: first the press reporters, now this page of pigs, had dragged their thoughts back to their troubles. Perhaps this was inevitable. Disaster was too fresh to be pushed out of mind, even for one evening amid the potted palms and chilled hock and soft music. He surrendered.

"Tell me one thing, Thomasina. You've got a tape-recorder in the office, haven't you?"

"Yes, a portable transistor. Why?"

"Can anyone borrow it?"

"Any of the Commissioners could."

"And *has* anyone?"

Thomasina frowned in thought. "You haven't, have you? Dr. Rumble's got his own. So has Sir Jeremy. Mrs. Tripp—yes, she took it once or twice, I think. I don't imagine our friend Mansfield has borrowed it, or Mr. Zaza, but I don't know for certain. Hugo might have lent it to someone. Why?"

"I just wondered." Alex sounded gruff; the fact was, the evening was half-spoiled now they'd got back to these mind-teasing questions. "Let's go and get some coffee."

Mansfield waved jovially as they passed and plucked at Alex's arm with a compact, determined hand.

"Ah, my colleague Dr. Burton," he exclaimed. "Meet my friends of the English newspapers. Gentlemen, this is the wisest of our members because he says very little. Therefore he must think a lot."

Mansfield looked satisfied, like a financier completing a take-over bid—or a small, fat crocodile gobbling up a bellyful of frogs? Alex was disappointed that he'd not yet produced his Brazilian wife; but she was very busy, Mansfield had said, arranging for the sale of a new line of unguents and potions throughout the Protectorate and the Republic of Bonga. "A blend," Mansfield had proudly explained, "between some of our traditional Hapanan herbs and remedies—the ashes of nightjars for one, and monkeys' kidneys—and your scientific European drugs. A compromise, eh, Dr. Burton? Isn't that what you British always recommend?"

"You've heard what is being said about us?" he now inquired.

"Invented by you?"

Mansfield shook all over with laughter, crinkling up his mobile face until his eyes vanished. It was hard to imagine him as a human thunderbolt, into a pit of feathers.

"That's very good! No, it's quite true. It's about that gang of ruffians, the *Sulu Sita*. They mean to seize all us Commissioners to give us their special baptism, to make us purified. They aren't nice people, they don't respect law and order."

"Not like the Triple-P, for instance?"

Mansfield quaked with renewed laughter. "That's right, you understand! Moto Mguu's a very, very peaceful man. He doesn't like violence."

"Not even against tapioca-growers?"

"That's different. That's colonialism. Everyone must resist colonialism by all means, it's a sacred duty. Isn't that right, Mr. Black?"

But his two companions were intent on the menu.

"I'll finish with a *bombe surprise,"* said Mervyn Sparks.

"Ah, Hapana is full of surprises," Mansfield agreed. "Even bombs. In our struggle with colonialism . . ." But Alex gave a friendly wave and walked on.

When, in the car going home, he put his arm around Thomasina, she let him kiss her ear and neck and then her lips without protest but also without passion, or at least anything to match his own. It was dark and warm in the car and the least exertion made the flesh sticky. And the driver made Alex feel self-conscious. Africans, he'd been told, never kissed. He supposed it was all or nothing with them.

Drinks stood ready on the Godfreys' veranda and Alex helped them both to brandy-and-soda. Thomasina looked tousled and irresistible. He hadn't the least wish to resist, but she wasn't inviting; he caught a look of wariness in her eye.

"Thomasina, you're not a child. You know I want you badly. Let me stay."

"Here, in this house? You know it's ridiculous. You shouldn't ask."

"I have, though. I'm still serious. You see—"

Alex muffled her renewed protests with kisses and felt a distinct weakening of resistance. Blood drummed in his ears, a little flame of victory sprang up inside.

"You can't—" she began.

"But I can!"

A little later he drew back and said: "I'll go if you want me to." They were both breathing fast and she looked so uncertain, torn between the need he had at last aroused in her and what he supposed were her scruples, that he laughed. But she said slowly:

"Yes, you'd better go."

"You *want* me to?"

"You must!"

"Because you don't think much of me?"

"It's not that. It's—"

"Where's your room?"

"No, you can't—"

"It's got a bed, hasn't it?"

"You're very crude!"

"Don't let's waste time."

He took her hand and almost pulled her from the veranda, laughing because he believed he was tugging her in the direction she really did want to go. They were in the passage, then beside a door with his hand on the knob. "This one?"

"Yes, but—no, don't go in—it's madness, they'll hear—"

He opened the door, drew her into the darkness and kissed her without restraint. The whole length of her warm body was pressed against his and he believed her resistance to be ended. As he softly spoke his first endearments an alien sound caught his ear, harsh as a flint in a slipper. It wasn't loud but it was in the room, and human. Somewhere in the dark bedroom was another human being.

Alex jumped away from Thomasina and groped for the light switch. His hands moved like frozen sausages and he could all but feel a blade pierce his back. As the light sprang on he whipped round to see a man lying on the bed, or, rather, in the act of sliding off it: a man fully clad and with a sheepish expression on his bearded face. Alex was convulsed by an alien and ungovernable fury that bowled him over like a gale demolishing a shallow-rooted tree. He lunged out and sent Stephen Partridge sprawling back onto the bed.

The thwack hurt Alex's fist but gave him perhaps the most satisfactory sensation he'd ever had, apart from making love. Partridge sat up clasping his face, blood already oozing onto his fingers. Alex glared at him with exultation. That had fixed Partridge. If the man would only get up he'd do it again.

For a moment he'd even forgotten Thomasina, but now he turned to glare at her and his anger blazed up again.

She'd played the prude, the prissy secretary, she'd half come-hithered him and then cheated; he'd even wondered about her virginity; and here she was with a man waiting on her own bed. A flood of obscene abuse almost choked him, he raised his hands as if to strike her and then saw her flinch. Dropping his hands, he turned to see Partridge mopping his nose with a bloody handkerchief. In tones of withering contempt he said: "Poor Stephen!" and marched out of the room. His hands and knees were shaking as he went down the veranda steps to the car, with its patient driver.

"A fine night, sir," the driver said, politely holding open the door. His name was Jacob.

"Very fine. Sorry to have kept you late." His own voice sounded thick and heavy in his ears.

Jacob laughed. "I drive for doctor, sir. Late, early, all the same. When doctor needs me, here I am." He sounded proud of his loyalty.

As Alex leant back in the soothing, solitary darkness, sanity and calm gradually returned. With it came amazement at the emotional storm that had just bowled him over. If he'd had a weapon on him he'd have killed Partridge, undoubtedly. The implications were terrifying. Gorillas, jungle-prowling panthers, all of us, he thought, under a very brittle skin. Non-violence—a sham, the worst kind of hypocrisy.

His rage against Thomasina very quickly subsided into a ridiculous, even maudlin, reproachful sorrow. He'd lain at her feet the heavens' embroidered cloths and she'd kicked them aside in favour, of all things, of that sneaking little tenth-rate journalist with the manners of a lout and the guts of a wood-louse. Of all people, Partridge. A smart-alec little tyke, a splinter of worm-chewed driftwood: Partridge, to be Thomasina's lover, making free with her body, enjoying her bed. It was monstrous and intolerable. The only redeeming feature of the whole evening was the clonk he'd landed on Partridge. He wished he could drive back and go and finish off the little skunk.

Alone in his bedroom, Alex had to face the bitter fact that his advances had been rejected. Well, that had happened innumerable times before to millions of people. He could take her or leave her. He'd leave her with pleasure to the intolerable Stephen, and good luck to them. Thomasina had at least been right about one thing: this kind of extra-mural sport was a profound mistake. Added to everything else he'd been a bloody fool.

He began to undress. And still he couldn't stop thinking about

Thomasina. He'd desired her and he still did. He cursed obscenely, threw his jacket over a chair and looked for his nail file. Earlier in the day, he'd chipped a fingernail.

As soon as he opened the drawer, he saw that something had been shifted. While he dressed carelessly, he kept his personal possessions under strict control. Ties, handkerchiefs, scissors, combs, studs, matches, nose-spray—everything lived in its correct place and in its proper drawer. The changes in position were slight but they were there.

He'd left a spare wallet in a drawer, with his yellow fever certificate, passport and other indispensable papers. Pulling it out, he checked the contents. They were all right, so far as he could remember. Nothing seemed to have been stolen. Either an over-zealous houseboy had tidied up, or his room had been searched. He climbed morosely into his pyjamas but knew he couldn't sleep, so he put on his dressing-gown and went out to get some air.

It was about half-past twelve, the night was dark and he could see little except dim shapes of bushes which might conceal anything—guards, agents, informers, go-betweens, murderers. All the guest-house windows were dark, too. He went in and flashed his torch around the sitting-room in search of whisky, but careful houseboys had taken away all the drinks, cleared out ash-trays, puffed up cushions like house-proud wives. Not even a drink!

On his disgruntled way back to bed he passed Dr. Rumble's window. As he came abreast of it he saw the flicker of a light inside. The light glimmered, vanished, flashed again. Dr. Rumble getting out of bed? Machine-like as the LEDA emissary was, running on platitudes like a truck on diesel oil, he couldn't be immune from calls of nature. But then why didn't he switch on the bedside light?

Alex paused, reflecting on the absurd state his nerves had got into, to query the behaviour of a man who got out of bed in the night. But then his things *had* been handled; almost certainly his room had been searched. He tiptoed round to the door of Rumble's room, very softly turned the handle and pushed.

And then he hesitated. This was no affair of his. A coldness went down his spine as he thought of murder and he started to pull the door gently to. Let sleeping dogs lie. The light in the room went out, and simultaneously Alex felt the prick of shame. Not only a rejected lover, but a plain funk. He pushed the door sharply open and his torch thrust a beam into the darkness. It picked out an arm and the sleek gleam of metal. He ducked, the torch lost its target, everything froze into silence. Two men holding torches, one of them armed, confronted each other in darkness. A voice gently said:

"Chisanga?"

Alex stepped forward, found the switch and flooded the room with light. John Jacey stood by the dressing-table with an automatic pistol in his hand.

"Well, fancy seeing you," he said. Alex looked round; the bed was empty and untouched. The room was full of folders, envelopes of memoranda, box files and stationery.

"Where's Rumble?"

"Just what I'd like to know. My blokes are supposed to watch every inch of this place but he's sneaked out somehow. And what brings you here?"

"Curiosity. I saw a light." Alex sat on the bed. "Did you search my room?"

"Chisanga did. Evidently not very well, or you wouldn't have known."

"Any luck?"

Jacey shook his head. "Still hoping for those dirty postcards. Though I expect Chisanga would have kept them."

"What are you looking for?"

"Anything I can find."

"Such as microfilms or lengths of tape?"

"Those, too," Jacey conceded.

"Anything here?"

Jacey nodded towards three or four empty cigarette packs on the dressing-table. "I found those in a drawer."

"They hardly seem incriminating."

"Rumble smokes cheroots, doesn't he?"

Alex thought. "Yes, he does. I've never seen him with a cigarette. Still . . ."

"He might use them for collecting seeds or old razor blades or sweet wrappings or something. Or he might just have a mania for accumulating empty cigarette packs. Still . . ."

Alex picked one up. It had contained a common brand of cigarette made for the Hapana market. For some reason Alex sniffed it, inhaling an aroma of cheap tobacco and, beyond and underneath that, some other and more penetrating smell. He handed it to Jacey.

"Pretty poor tobacco."

Jacey sniffed it, too. Then he stiffened and pressed the empty pack to his nose.

"There's something else," Alex suggested.

"Something fishy." Jacey wrapped the pack carefully in a clean handkerchief and put it in his pocket.

Chapter 17

For a man who knew a quick-witted poisoner to be after him the Chairman, Alex considered, was standing up well. Under their heavy, swan-like brows the eyes were tired, but his manner was still urbane, patient, salted with humour. The rest of the Commissioners, even Sir Jeremy, were subdued. Especially Amelia: her thinness was becoming scrawny, she looked a stranger to a good night's sleep. Zaza was strained and edgy, the Chief silent, Rumble preoccupied and only Mansfield Matunda robustly unchanged.

Colonel Cottrell raised no one's spirits. At the Chairman's invitation, he addressed them on security. They were to become virtual prisoners in the guest-house, it seemed. No one was to eat or drink anything that hadn't been examined, checked and supervised. To go off and buy a bar of chocolate in the town would be a heinous crime.

Even their medicines were suspect. Cottrell made them hand in all their aspirins, laxatives, anti-malarial pills—anything that had been lying about in their rooms. Dr. Furneaux was to issue them with new, sealed supplies from Government stores and these they were to keep, at all costs, under lock and key. Every time they went out they were to notify Jacey and supply an Estimated Time of Return. The only satisfaction Alex was able to extract from the meeting was the absence of Partridge. Normally, he sat at a little table on his own, making notes and looking bored.

"What's happened to our P.R.O.?" Alex inquired of Hugo in the coffee break.

"He had a bit of an accident last night. Slipped in the mud and bashed his face against a rock or something, but he's functioning, after a fashion. Trying to keep the gentlemen of the press at bay."

"I'd expected to see them swarming all over the place this morning."

"These security precautions are a blessing in disguise. Of course the correspondents are in hot pursuit of Lady Bagpuse. We've had to postpone her air passage for a few days. She's indisposed." His tone was drier than ever.

"You mean you're keeping her incommunicado?"

"Medical advice. As Dr. Furneaux says, she's better under light sedation for the next few days."

Slipped in the mud, Alex thought. Let's hope some of it sticks.

Things got even worse after the coffee break. A delegation of eager Mongu ladies from the Kazembi Better Living Group, dressed in home-knitted cardigans, protested at length about the price of eggs, a plague of caterpillars and a two-headed calf resulting from artificial insemination.

"Most unfortunate," the Chairman commiserated, "but perhaps not quite our pigeon. Now, have you given any thought to the question of universal suffrage?"

The president nodded vigorously. "Oh, yes, we have."

"You have?" the Chairman sounded surprised. "And your conclusions?"

"That is what we have. We do not want it any longer."

"Universal suffrage?"

"Universal." She threw her arms out wide.

"Surely only those with an annual income in excess of a hundred and twenty pounds a year or immovable property—"

"Our suffrage is universal! Among all our women! We feed the hens, we look for eggs, we clean them, we take them to markets and there is no one to buy them. We want these suffrages to finish! To finish now!"

Next came a Mrs. Ruby Grubb, relict of the Keeper of an Ethnological Museum, with a paper on cannibalism, human sacrifice, ritual murders and bestiality among the Chuma which, despite all the Chairman's charm, entreaties and finally bullying, she read from beginning to end. It took forty-five minutes. A Greek tobacco-buyer, three Hapanan schoolmasters and the Charcoal-Burners' Trade Union occupied the Commission until half past one. When it at last adjourned the Chairman said:

"Can you spare me a few minutes after lunch, Alex? I'm anxious for your moral support."

"I'm in no condition to support anyone."

"We can lean on each other. I'll expect you at half past two."

Alex caught a glimpse of Thomasina getting into one of the Company's cars. His anger had abated but he still felt a hollow, painful, savage ache whenever he thought about her, and he'd been thinking about her all the morning, unbeguiled by eggs and cannibals. He sat next to Amelia at luncheon.

"How's the headache?"

"Better, thanks. Only now I can't take an aspirin without wondering . . . Not that I'm likely to have been marked down as a victim. Poor Lady Bagpuse is half out of her mind."

"She was heading that way yesterday."

"Persecution mania, I suppose. Hugo Evans is having a dreadful time trying to prevent her finding out that all those newspaper correspondents are here. I can't believe she really could have recognized anyone in the dark, but she *thinks* she did and makes no bones about saying so. If the press gets hold of that . . ."

"She made a lot of accusations yesterday, but all she said about the guilty party was that he wasn't English. That opens up a wide field."

"Wasn't English? But he is, surely?"

"Who is?"

Amelia lowered her voice until Alex had almost to touch her head with his own. "She's accusing Sir Christopher."

"Oh, dear," Alex said.

"She looks on him as Irish, I suppose. Yes, it's all *most* unfortunate. Even if Sir Christopher did stroll out to get a breath of fresh air, that hardly proves he poisoned his Vice-Chairman's sandwiches. But with the press nosing round like bloodhounds for a story . . ."

"I can see why our Secretary's worried."

"Poor Lady Bagpuse is rather like an unexploded bomb. The only person now who can soothe her is Chief Faustus. He thinks Queen Victoria will find her another husband even larger than the old."

At half past two Alex heard a car drive up to the front—Thomasina returning. To avoid meeting her in the office, he decided to reach Sir Christopher through the private suite. Lady Connor opened the door. She was looking washed-out, the skin under her eyes almost violet.

"I'll let him know you've come," she said. "I think he's on the line to Umpah at the moment."

"Doesn't he ever relax?"

"Not in Hapana. I shall be thankful when we all get home. If we all do."

"Isn't that unduly morbid?"

"Well, Freddy Bagpuse won't, will he? And now poor Blanche . . . I don't think this is a good climate for women. Mrs. Tripp looks poorly, and I feel like a piece of chewed string. I suppose it's all right for the young and tough, like that Labouchère girl. An affected name, isn't it?"

Alex was surprised at the bitchy edge to her tone. "I suppose it's one of those things one can't help," he remarked.

"If it's really her own."

"Don't you think so?"

"Oh, I suppose it is; only it's the sort of name that *sounds* made up. I don't know anything about her, except that she's a competent secretary. If perhaps a little too big for her boots, or casuals should I say. Can I offer you some coffee?"

Alex declined. "Then I'll tell Chris." Through a half-open door the Chairman summoned him.

"That was Butterfield," he said. "Well, it looks as if the security people were right after all. Not conclusive, of course, and I still don't really believe . . . but I daresay I'm wrong."

"You mean the trap worked?"

"It seems to have. Nothing from Moscow radio, so far, about the south-eastern province. Cottrell's spoiling for action and Butterfield's taking a strong line, too—after all, he's ultimately responsible. So I'm afraid . . ."

"There'll have to be a showdown."

"I hate this sort of thing. Frankly, that's why I asked you to come. Moral support, as I said."

Alex found himself watching the door into the outer office and hoping that Thomasina wouldn't come through. Childish, of course. But humiliation was a childish emotion. And had Lady Connor got some notion that Thomasina and Sir Christopher . . . ? Just how adolescent can you be, at rising forty? Perhaps it was the climate. Everyone blamed that. He was relieved when the Chairman vanished for a moment into his outer office, instead of summoning Thomasina or Hugo, and returned to say:

"Cottrell and Jacey are on their way. I'll be thankful when this is over. You've heard about poor Blanche Bagpuse?"

"A bit unhinged," Alex ventured.

"I suppose so. First there was that rigmarole about pigs, and now she thinks she saw me loitering with intent to do in my own Vice-Chairman at about one o'clock at night. In fact I *didn't* go into the garden in the small hours of Sunday morning but I can't prove it, and I don't suppose any of us could either. Could you?"

"Certainly not."

"And even if I had, it scarcely proves that I stuffed poor Freddy's sandwiches with poison. Or my own, actually, which makes even less sense. That change of boxes *must* have been an accident. It's terrifying, isn't it—the little skips and jumps of sheer chance, all quite unpredictable, that decide one's destiny."

"'All chance, direction which thou canst not see,'" Alex quoted.

"I'm afraid that's wishful thinking. . . . Blanche is another complication. She won't see Godfrey, you know, because she says he's a foreigner, and I don't think poor old Furneaux's much good. She ought to fly home at once to get proper medical attention, but as things are now we just daren't let her go."

Colonel Cottrell came in, with Jacey just behind him, looking purposeful. The prospect of action, even if only of a sedentary kind, had charged his manner with zest.

"We've got it pretty well buttoned up now, I think," he said. "Pity we can't make an arrest. I don't like this kind of cat-and-mouse business, but there it is."

"Certainly there's no question of an arrest."

"Not under the Official Secrets Act, but the more serious charge might come up later. Give a man enough rope, you know . . ."

Alex, exchanging nods with Jacey, asked: "Any more butterflies lately?"

"Too busy chasing rainbows."

There was a half-hearted knock at the door. The four inquisitors were seated in a semicircle behind the desk; in front of it stood an empty armchair. Jacey opened the door.

Chapter 18

Amelia Tripp looked at the four men for a moment without moving. She had gone very pale. Then she fumbled in her handbag for a cigarette and stuffed it into her holder with unsteady hands. Alex lit it for her.

"I'm sorry to disturb your rest," the Chairman said. For once, he could not wholly conceal his uneasiness. "I think we'd better get this over. Sit down, do."

"Am I expected to assist the police with their inquiries?"

"That's just about what it comes to, I'm afraid. This isn't going to be pleasant for any of us. In fact it's about the most distasteful thing I've ever had to do in my life. I can only suggest we get it over as quickly as possible and I'll ask Colonel Cottrell to carry on from here."

Amelia was inhaling and her fingers gripped the holder as if it had been a rope suspending her over a precipice. Colonel Cottrell cleared his throat.

"Please understand, Mrs. Tripp, I'm not framing a charge. I'm merely laying some facts before you and then it'll be up to you to decide your best course of action."

"Thank you."

"I don't think I need beat about the bush. As a result of inquiries made in London and in Canada, we know that your correct married name is Loewenstein and that your husband was convicted in the Canadian courts in 1945 on several charges of breach of the Official

Secrets Act—in plain language, supplying information to the enemy."

He paused, but Amelia didn't reply. She was gazing intently at the floor, white as a water-lily, holding herself together by a visible effort.

"You were implicated as one of his accomplices; but he got you out of the country, with your infant daughter, a few hours before the arrests were made. You were traced to London but after that you managed to disappear. The war was ending, the counter-espionage services were overloaded and, to be quite frank, the Canadian authorities couldn't be sure of a conviction. So it was dropped. In fact, you got away with it—that time. You changed your name and later on you went into politics and reappeared as Mrs. Tripp, M.P."

At this second pause Amelia looked up and said: "Now do we get a burst of music and my old schoolteacher hobbling in? 'This Is Your Life'—Eamonn Andrews does it better."

Colonel Cottrell frowned, but Alex found her attempt to be facetious merely pathetic.

"You don't deny any of this?"

"Tripp was my mother's name."

"Right. The security people slipped up badly when they came to vet the names put forward for this Commission. Your tracks must have been covered very well. So we come to the present situation."

"Yes, but I—"

"You are supplying regular bulletins about the work of the Commission to the radio station in the Republic of Bonga, who in turn transmit them to Moscow."

Amelia leant forward and gripped the edge of the desk and said: "That's an absolute lie! I've got nothing to do with it, I've had absolutely nothing to do with all that for sixteen years! Don't you see I'd be mad to get mixed up in it again? After I'd got clear—made a new life—my whole future—"

"I'm not concerned with your motives, madam," the Colonel said in his most distant tone. "Whether you were foolish or not is no concern of mine. I daresay you had no choice. The point's plain enough, you've been selling secrets to the enemy."

"It's a complete lie. And you've no proof."

"That isn't correct either. We've a number of facts which, taken together, are sufficiently incriminating, in my opinion, to justify an arrest."

"Then why don't you make one?"

"Because the decision isn't in my hands."

"And am I to know these so-called facts?"

"Since I'm not bringing a charge, there's no need for me to disclose them. But I can tell you this. On the night of Saturday, or early Sunday morning, when you took your midnight stroll, you were seen and followed."

"In that case you know my stroll was perfectly innocent."

"You walked down to where a footpath coming up from the road enters the garden."

"Very likely I did."

"Just where path and garden meet there's the stump of an old tree."

"Well?"

"Shortly after you'd walked back to the guest-house, an African came up that path and took something out of the base of the old stump, and made off back down the path towards the lake. The package he took from the stump contained a length of tape."

Amelia was having trouble in controlling the shaking of her hands. "All that has nothing to do with me. You're accusing me of hiding something in the tree-stump. I didn't, I tell you. I swear I didn't. I haven't even got a tape-recorder, for one thing."

"You borrowed one from the office."

"That's quite true, I did, but only for one day, to polish off some correspondence. All this is nothing but guesswork, and you know it."

"What if I told you my men caught the fellow? And that the tape's in our hands?"

Amelia sat absolutely still, like a hunted deer that freezes when it hears the hunter, hoping to become invisible. "Well?"

"That would be proof, wouldn't it?"

Amelia took a long pull at her cigarette and, with the resolution of a bather plunging into icy water, raised her eyes to Cottrell's face.

"Yes, it would."

"So there's no use in further denials, Mrs. Tripp."

She looked at him quite steadily. "But it isn't, is it?"

"What do you mean?"

"That tape isn't in your hands."

"I'm not bound to disclose our evidence. But I'm warning you that you'd be wise to tell the truth."

"I am telling it."

Alex couldn't withhold his admiration. Amelia had kept her wits and sensed in the Colonel's voice, with remarkably acute antennae, the faintest trace of lack of conviction. Now she'd called his bluff. Of course he hadn't got the tape. And he was trapped by his own weakness—he wouldn't lie directly. No place for gentlemen in this game. For a moment he was silent and Amelia jumped in.

"I know perfectly well that if you had the evidence to convict me, you'd make a charge. You *haven't* got the evidence because it isn't there. Of course one's heard of the police framing people before now. But you can't do that so long as Sir Christopher's here."

She glanced at the Chairman with a look of gratitude, almost affection. His eyes were on the floor.

"I shouldn't be too confident, madam, if I were you," the Colonel said icily. "I'm not prepared at the present stage to reveal all our information. And there's another matter."

Amelia looked straight at the Chairman. "Sir Christopher, does this third degree treatment of one of your Commissioners have your approval?"

Sir Christopher gave her a stricken look and lifted his hands. "It's all terribly distressing. But the situation can't be left as it is. If I may advise you, Mrs. Tripp, much your wisest plan is to tell the truth and shame the devil."

"Some time during this night we're talking of, on Saturday," Colonel Cottrell continued, "the sandwiches were poisoned. We believe the poisoner used the so-called lucky beans—"

"You *believe—*"

"—of which you had a necklace in your possession. The next morning you reported the necklace missing."

"It *had* gone. If I'd really poisoned someone with it, don't you think I'd have kept quiet?"

"Sooner or later, your necklace would have been remembered and we should have asked you to produce it. To have failed to do so would have almost amounted to an admission of guilt. It was much cleverer to throw away the rest of the beans and report the necklace stolen."

"Colonel Cottrell, are you accusing me of murder?"

"I told you, I'm not framing any charge yet."

"But you *are* trying to make me incriminate myself."

"I'm simply stating the facts. You had the means—this string of poisonous beans. You knew they were poisonous. You had the best of motives for wishing Sir Christopher out of the way."

"I had! A motive—? What on earth do you mean?"

"Sir Christopher had already warned you that your past had come to light. Once it all came out, your whole career would lie in ruins and you'd be finished as a public figure—more than that, you'd be in danger of arrest and imprisonment. But if the Chairman came to grief, the whole Commission would probably collapse. Then, in the general confusion, your own personal trouble might get forgotten, as it had been once before. It was a chance worth taking—your only chance. So you took it. And the plan miscarried."

"But the idea never entered my head! In a way, I'm surprised it didn't. I suppose one's ideas run to killing people or they don't, and mine don't. So I poisoned Lord Bagpuse by mistake!"

Colonel Cottrell leant forward in his chair. "Mrs. Tripp, your bedroom door opens on the covered way, that narrow veranda, leading from the dining-room to the kitchen?"

"Yes, of course it does."

"And if you stand outside your door and look to your right you can see into the kitchen, if the door's open, that is?"

"I daresay you could. I don't stand outside my door and look into the kitchen."

"But you did on Saturday night."

"What are you trying to say?"

"In that kitchen there are two refrigerators, one of which contained the sandwiches. There's also a small coffee mill."

"A what?"

"A hand mill for grinding coffee. You knew it was there."

"How did I know?"

"Do you deny it?"

Amelia took out another cigarette and lit it from the first and stubbed out the butt. She was beginning to get rattled.

"I don't deny or confirm anything. Why should I? What right have you to question me like this?"

"Did you know about the coffee mill?"

"No, of course not. Why should I?"

"So you *do* deny it?"

"I don't know what you're talking about."

"In spite of the fact that Sir Jeremy explained how the coffee was made in the presence of everyone staying in the guest-house, after lunch on Friday?"

"Good heavens, do you expect me to remember everything that's said—every triviality about the food and so on? Don't you think I've got more important things to remember?"

"The smallest detail is important to anyone who's planning a murder. You remembered—"

"How dare you say that!" Amelia leapt to her feet looking like a cornered leopard, no longer able to control the shaking of her hands. "You've no right to say those things! If you've evidence then arrest me—but you haven't because I—Sir Christopher, for God's sake help me! He's exceeding his rights. And you sit by—"

"Colonel Cottrell, I really think this has gone far enough," the Chairman said sternly. He was looking acutely uncomfortable. "Mrs. Tripp is within her rights, you know. If there's any question of bringing a charge then of course you should have cautioned her. But I understood from you there was no question of that."

The Colonel glared angrily at Sir Christopher and his face began to darken to a chilblain hue.

"I beg your pardon," he said stiffly, "but you must please allow me to know my own duties and their limits. I've already told Mrs. Tripp I am *not* charging her."

"Then perhaps we can conclude this painful interview—"

"One moment," Amelia intervened, quickly restored. "What's all this leading up to about a coffee mill?" Cottrell said loftily:

"We have reason to believe that this hand-mill was used to grind the so-called lucky beans into powder."

"That's news to me," remarked Sir Christopher.

"The results have only just come through from the labs. Minute traces of powdered bean were found in a small crack in the machine, although it had been washed and used since."

"Remarkable!"

"An exceedingly smart piece of deduction on the part of my Superintendent. We know now how the poison was obtained and prepared, and roughly where and when it was put into the sandwiches."

"But you don't know who put it there," Amelia pronounced, unable to keep a note of triumph from her voice. "Such evidence as you have is all circumstantial."

"If I were you, madam, I shouldn't dismiss circumstantial evidence so lightly. It has convicted many criminals before now."

"If you're calling me a criminal—"

"I really think, Cottrell, that's about as far as we need go. Mrs. Tripp, you've heard exactly how the situation stands. Colonel Cottrell has been extremely frank with you. It's now my turn to be frank also. I'm expressing no opinion one way or the other. But you yourself must be more anxious than any of us to end an intolerable situation. I'm quite sure your only wish now is to resign."

"From the Commission?"

"As you say."

"If I did that, I should be admitting these iniquitous charges."

"There are no charges. You'd be putting an end to a situation that's become intolerable for all of us."

"*You* could put an end to it by apologizing."

"My dear lady, you must see the position you're in. As to the public, everything that's been said will remain within these four walls. We can blame it all on ill-health. There's an element of truth in that, isn't there? I've had a bit of a struggle but I've got London to agree to that. So if that's settled . . ."

Amelia shook her head. "It isn't settled."

"You can hardly mean that you refuse to resign?"

Alex was looking at her with undisguised admiration, Cottrell with mottled incredulity, Jacey impassively. She shook her head.

"I didn't sell the Commission's secrets and I didn't poison Lord Bagpuse so I don't see why I should resign."

"My good woman," the Colonel began, "don't you realize that only a lot of luck and Connor's insistence has—"

"Now, please, Cottrell, let me handle this," Sir Christopher said. "Believe me, Mrs. Tripp, I can understand your feelings. It's not my place to judge you and I'm not doing so. Let's say you're as guiltless as a sucking dove, whatever they are. It's still impossible both for you and for us to stay on after what's been said. And that's bound to be believed by people here, not only the police. In fact, Butterfield . . . But you must see what I mean. And I must repeat my request."

Mrs. Tripp had given up smoking and, with bent head, was rubbing her fingers as if to work on a tight glove. A tear fell onto her hands and to everyone's embarrassment she put them to her face and started to sob, as silently as she was able. Sir Christopher got to his feet.

"Well, this has all been perfectly horrible. I advise you to go straight to your room, Mrs. Tripp, and think it over calmly. Then I'm sure you'll see . . . And let me know your answer, will you, after tea? Say by six o'clock. Look, there's no need to go through the office, you can get through this way, my wife's out. Seeing more schools, poor woman, I'm afraid." He opened the door into the private suite and stood aside. Colonel Cottrell coughed and looked out of the window. Amelia got slowly to her feet, her shoulders still heaving.

"Thank you," she gulped. "I—"

"Never mind that now. Come and see me about six o'clock—or, if you don't feel like it, send a message." Sir Christopher shut the door behind her and heaved a deep sigh.

"That was one of the worst half-hours of my life. You know, Cottrell, you went too far."

The Police Commissioner shrugged his shoulders. "I'm not used to kid-glove methods. That woman's guilty or I'm a Dutchman. Treason and murder—two crimes I'm afraid I'm old-fashioned enough to find extremely distasteful. We'll get the evidence. It's early days yet."

"I still think it's incredible. What's your opinion, Jacey?"

The Superintendent looked slightly taken aback, and glanced at his superior. "As the Commissioner says, sir, it's early days yet. There are other factors we shall have to take into account."

"Such as?"

"Well, politics for one thing. The Triple-P have made a dead set at the Commission from the start. Any of the staff here could have poisoned the sandwiches. Look at the propaganda value to them. And it's in line with their violent tactics and methods."

"We've no proof," Cottrell said.

"No, but we do know that some of the Merry Hippo's staff are Triple-P members. Chisanga's investigating and he tells me he's onto something. I've left him for the moment to follow his own line."

"I doubt if it's the Triple-P supplying our secrets to the enemy across the lake," Sir Christopher said.

"I doubt that too, sir. The two things may not be connected."

"No, I suppose not. A pity your fellows *didn't* catch that man who was prowling about on Saturday night."

"A great pity, sir. They chased him but he got away in the darkness. It's pretty hard in a place like this, with the lake so close. They hide their canoes in reeds and bushes and once you lose sight of them you've had it."

"And you spotted no more prowlers last night?"

"None, sir. But I'm afraid our precautions weren't altogether foolproof."

Colonel Cottrell grunted. "That American fellow getting out. That was a bad show, Jacey."

"I don't know about this, do I?" Sir Christopher inquired.

"I found Dr. Rumble's room empty at about eleven-thirty," Jacey explained. "I was just nosing round. We didn't spot him going or returning."

"That's very odd, isn't it?"

"Well, sir, I'm afraid he's got a secret weakness. Of course if it wasn't for all this trouble, we wouldn't have paid any attention to his private life, so to speak."

"You mean he sneaks off to brothels in the town?"

"I suppose you might call them night clubs or just cafés."

"Niteries," Alex contributed.

"They do the high-life and that sort of thing. He doesn't seem to get into any trouble. Just has a drink or two and looks on. Maybe stands a girl a couple of drinks but that's all, so far as we know."

"And did he find a niterie last night?"

"We're still checking up, sir. So far we haven't traced him but it isn't easy. Europeans aren't encouraged in these Hapanan joints in the town."

"Fancy there being all that night life in Shooting Star," Sir Christopher commented. "I must try it sometime. Meanwhile you don't suggest that Rumble's selling secrets to the enemy?"

"It's the woman, of course," Colonel Cottrell said.

"We seem to have come to something of a dead end." Sir Christopher paused, and smiled wryly. "That wasn't very well put, I'm afraid."

Chapter 19

It was half past five before the Commission wearily adjourned. Dodging his colleagues, Alex followed the path from the bottom of the garden through a couple of hundred yards of scrub and bush to the road. A large Hapanan policeman emerged from the bushes and followed fifteen paces behind.

Alex felt like a convict at exercise. He glanced at the tree-stump Colonel Cottrell had mentioned. The hollows and miniature caverns between its buttress-like roots were just right for the concealment of small packages. The path led downhill fairly steeply, and a two-foot jump landed you on the unpaved road that led, on your right, to the township, on your left to the residential quarter and, beyond, the endless *momombo* bush of Hapana.

Just out of sight, to the left, a drive took off from the road and curled around and uphill to the front of the guest-house. Below the road lay the lake. Alex had already been thwarted in his wish to stroll along its shore, watching water-birds, by a strip of ground scoured by gullies too deep, and bush too thick, for anything but goats—and, perhaps, extra tough-skinned Hapanans—to traverse.

The dam was still imperceptibly rising by a few inches a week. The livid, barren branches of half-drowned trees standing in the water looked sinister and sad. This man-made, unnatural inland sea was killing a wide stretch of country. No doubt in a few years' time, the lake would look as if it belonged there; at the moment, half-created, it was alien and predatory. Insects, animals, vegetation were dying that it might come to birth.

Alex walked a short way along the road but felt a fool with the policeman keeping exactly fifteen paces behind. In any case, the sun had dipped below a low range of hills across the lake in Bonga, leaving an orange glow in the sky. Time for drinks—and for Amelia's answer. Poor Amelia, she was finished: no more politics for her; no more parliamentary gossip, intrigue, drama, boredom, occasional flashes of historical significance.

What, he wondered, had become of Loewenstein? Dead, deserted, still in prison, divorced, disappeared? Or was Amelia still secretly in touch with him? Had she really tried to murder the Chairman? Had the scarlet beans tempted her, and then the coffee mill, the sandwiches so handy—a sudden impulse? One chance in a million had saved Connor and destroyed Bagpuse. Cottrell was right: if the Chairman had died, Amelia's past might never have come out. A thought struck him—how had *Partridge* known about Amelia? Known that she'd been Mrs. Loewenstein?

He scrambled up onto the path and climbed briskly back to the guest-house and its waiting drinks. These were in their place, unlocked personally by Slocombe who would lock them up again before dinner, and himself uncork the wine. Dinner with the Borgias. Alex took a look at the company: Faustus puzzling over a copy of *Horse and Hound,* Sir Jeremy conferring with Slocombe, Zaza hovering like a hawk about to pounce on anyone who'd listen. Hastily, he poured himself a whisky and escaped along the covered passageway to call on Lady Bagpuse.

He found her sitting in an armchair in a blue flannel dressing-gown knitting a pullover, a portable radio by her side. Her face was rather blotchy, her grey hair untidy, but she didn't look exactly ill.

"Where did you get that drink?" she inquired, anxiously.

"From the lounge. Can I fetch you one?"

"No, no, certainly not. My life's of no importance for its own sake but I must guard it until I can warn the Prime Minister. You didn't get that drink from Sir Christopher?"

"No."

"He poisoned Freddy and now he's trying to poison me. But I won't be poisoned until I've warned the Prime Minister. Only, you see, he's keeping me a prisoner. I was to fly home tomorrow but they say I'm not well enough. Of course I'm perfectly well. It's to keep me from warning the Prime Minister."

"About the Polish pigs?"

"They've arrived at the London docks. It was on the wireless. They're all infected. The incubation period can't be more than a fortnight so you see there isn't a moment to lose."

"Surely the vets—?"

"The vets know nothing. If those pigs are not destroyed within the next ten days every British pig will die and the country will be on its knees. And it's worse even than that. Just before my husband died he heard from Percy, that's our head herdsman, that something mysterious had gone wrong with our best New Spot boar."

"Is his name Soviet Ambassador?"

Lady Bagpuse nodded. "Freddy named him after we'd had a tour of young Soviet farmers. I didn't like the name myself, I said it would be unlucky. Freddy was worrying terribly. Suppose he's already *got* the disease? What then?"

"You could send a telegram to find out."

"I'm a *prisoner* here!" Lady Bagpuse had abandoned her pullover and was leaning forward and pounding her knees with her fists. "You must help me, Dr. Burton! They won't let me out, they won't let me go to the Prime Minister. They let me see a young man with a beard who said he'd tell the truth to the newspapers, but I didn't trust him and I'm sure he was a spy sent to watch me. Woodcock, I think his name was."

"Partridge."

"With a beard like that he's sure to be in the pay of the Russians. It was a foreign-looking beard, not the kind sailors have. They keep on trying to make me see that foreign doctor but of course *he'd* poison me at once. I trust Dr. Furneaux, he's a kind man. And Chief Faustus, who reminds me so much of my Freddy, and that nice girl Miss Labouchère, but no one else."

"In a few days, Lady Bagpuse, you'll be able to fly home and put matters right."

"Will it be in time? That's what I'm worried about. Dr. Burton, will you get a message through for me? To save your country?"

"I could try," Alex said cautiously.

"I knew you were a true patriot, Freddy liked you from the start. You must tell the Prime Minister he must immediately slaughter all the Polish pigs and burn the carcasses."

"I'll do my best."

Of course, she was half dotty—but only half. Despite a persecution mania and a pig obsession, she could be shrewd enough—she'd summed up Partridge pretty well, for instance, and was quite right about being more or less a prisoner. Alex doubted if they'd be able to keep her quiet much longer, even with Dr. Furneaux's light sedation.

It was well after six, and he decided to yield to curiosity and find out about Amelia. Hugo Evans was in the office, wrestling with a sluggish telephone.

"You haven't seen Matunda anywhere, have you?" he inquired.

"No. My guess is that he's somewhere within whispering distance of the press."

"They've vanished too, but we think they've gone down to the south-eastern province. Butterfield says the trouble everyone has been expecting there has started."

"The *Sulu Sita* society?"

"Yes. They're getting hold of people now and forcibly baptizing them in their own peculiar way. They've started with that fellow Hook. It's most unfortunate. The sect, or whatever it is, has been declared a prohibited society and of course there's going to be an awful row in Parliament."

"At least it will draw off Sparks and Black and leave us in comparative peace."

"Comparative is right. There's no one with Sir Christopher if you want him."

The Chairman was at his desk, at last showing outward signs of strain and fatigue. A bottle of whisky stood in front of him. He nodded at Alex and looked at his watch.

"Six-fifteen. No sign of Mrs. Tripp. You know, I felt like a mongoose mesmerizing a snake. Or is it the other way round? Ricky-ticky-tavy. Perhaps Thomasina . . ." He pressed his buzzer and, after an interval, Thomasina appeared. She gave a faint, impersonal nod in Alex's direction. Even to feel her presence in the room was excessively painful. He looked the other way.

"I wonder if you'd just run along to Mrs. Tripp's room and ask her if she'd be good enough to see me now?" Could you call his tone ingratiating? Silky, anyway. With a shock Alex recognized, beyond doubt, the desire to please. Lady Connor's acid remarks came back to him. Had something been going on right under his nose? He felt the bitter gall of anger rising again. Thomasina and the boss—thirty years older. No better than a strumpet, not worth losing an hour's sleep over. And he'd lost a whole night.

"We'll hold back the announcement till she's flown home," the Chairman said, "and then of course give out ill-health as the reason."

"Are you satisfied justice is being done?"

"Tell me something that *is* satisfactory about this Commission! And I really thought, you know, I might do a useful public service. I can't help feeling sorry for her. Very few of us have a past so blameless no one could make things awkward for us if they tried."

If Sir Christopher had hidden skeletons, Alex thought, he'd bet they were connected with women. He must have been attractive once—he was attractive now, damn it. And Thomasina—the flattery of an older man . . . He said nothing.

"I do hope Mrs. Tripp isn't going to make difficulties," the Chairman added. "In her own interests she's got no other—"

The door was flung open and Thomasina stood on the threshold, so dead-white her eyes looked pitch-black against a pallid skin.

"There's been—something terrible—we must fetch a doctor but I think it's too late—"

"Oh, my God," the Chairman said. Thomasina made a visible effort to control herself.

"She didn't answer so I went in. She's lying on the bed. I think she's—I don't think she's breathing but I didn't stop—"

Alex took her by the shoulders and pushed her into a chair. When he touched her, all his bitterness and anger and disgust evaporated. Amelia Tripp was dead and his heart was singing: Alex drew back from the abyss of human egotism and poured Thomasina a stiff dose of whisky.

Chapter 20

ALEX PICKED UP a coverlet from the floor and threw it over Amelia's body. One arm hung down limply over the edge of the bed, her head was thrown back on the pillow, her face dead-white. By her side was an empty glass, a small medicine bottle and an ash-tray full of cigarette stubs. He sniffed the glass cautiously and smelled whisky. She had kicked off her shoes; they lay on their sides near the bed.

He waited there while the Chairman telephoned. Outside the day was fading, lights were springing up in the windows, the ritual of evening drinks would have begun. A sudden squawk of birds suggested some disagreement about perching order in a tree. Alex felt his eyes drawn to the still figure on the bed, mutely accusing him, it seemed—of what? Simply of living? "If to her share some female errors fall, Look on her face, and you'll forget 'em all." And perhaps they had not been such very dreadful errors.

In the room's stillness, he thought he caught a sound of low, shallow breathing. He touched her hand: chilly, but not absolutely cold. One should hold a mirror, he knew, up to the mouth to see whether it misted over. While he hesitated, there was a knock on the door and outside stood a steward with a tray.

"This for madam."

"All right, I'll give it to her."

Alex inspected the note and put it in his pocket to hand over to Jacey. He thought he recognized Sir Jeremy's writing, neat and rather cramped—he'd seen it on the margin of a memorandum, and on doodles left at the conference table.

Better not to touch Amelia till the doctor came. He was taking his time. Alex watched the stars coming to life behind the trees, over the lake, throughout the vast arching sky. The farthest galaxy, he'd read, detected through the strongest telescope, was five million light-years away. Beyond that, millions of other galaxies, unrecorded, unknown, continuing forever through infinity. And one human body lying on the bed.

At last there were voices, footsteps, and Dr. Godfrey came in, followed by Jacey and Sergeant Chisanga. The doctor went straight over to the bed to make his examination. Jacey asked:

"When was this discovered?" Alex answered:

"Just after six-fifteen. By Miss Labouchère."

"When did you last see her? Mrs. Tripp, I mean?"

"Not since about three o'clock. She skipped our afternoon session. This came for her a few minutes ago." He handed over the note and Jacey looked round the room, smelled the empty glass and examined the small medicine bottle.

"Were these barbiturates, Doctor?"

Godfrey looked up to say: "There's a chance to save her if we hurry. Ring up the hospital at once for an ambulance and tell them to warn Sister Barclay. Meanwhile—" He extracted a hypodermic from his bag, filled it and pricked the flesh of her inert arm. "There's still movement of the heart. We've a chance, no more."

Jacey vanished to telephone, and returned a few minutes later to take possession of the tablets and glass.

"Barbiturates plus alcohol, Doctor?"

"I can't give an opinion yet."

"How long has she been like this?"

"Impossible to say. These conditions can be quite prolonged, depending of course on the strength of the drug. Anything up to twelve hours."

"Can you put a limit the other way?"

The doctor looked at the inert body. "Not without knowing the dosage. But not less than about three hours."

"Somewhere round about three-thirty, then, at the latest," Jacey concluded. "Odd she didn't lock the door. Suicides generally seem to. And no note or anything."

"I think we should search the room," said Chisanga.

"You carry on, Sergeant," Jacey agreed, "and I'll begin on the inquiries."

"You might start with the Chairman, John," Alex suggested. "She was supposed to give him her reply at six o'clock, you remember."

"Yes, I suppose it all ties up. It might have been better if she . . ." He glanced at the figure on the bed.

Dr. Godfrey was listening to the faint action of Amelia's heart through his stethoscope. "We've not much time," he said. "Superintendent, will you have someone waiting by the entrance to show the orderlies the way?"

Alex went out with Jacey, leaving the Sergeant to his search. They walked along the passage, past Lady Bagpuse's door, to the Chairman's suite. Sir Christopher was sustaining himself with a drink, his wife almost distraught.

"There's a curse on this whole Commission!" she exclaimed. Her eyes looked rather wild. "Poor Freddy Bagpuse, Blanche half off her head, we live in a state of siege, and now this. . . . The only sensible thing is to call it a day and go home."

"Now, Constance, you know we can't do that," the Chairman said sharply. "What's the verdict, Jacey?"

"She's alive, sir. But only just."

"Thank God for that!"

"It's a bit soon for thanks, according to the doctor. It's touch and go."

"I think he ought to see Blanche Bagpuse before he goes," Lady Connor said. "I don't believe Dr. Furneaux knows what he's talking about and I'm getting more and more worried about her."

"But she won't see him," Sir Christopher pointed out. "She says he's a foreigner."

"She never *has* seen him, has she?"

"I don't know."

"She's only *heard* he's a foreigner. If I take him in and tell her it's a Doctor Bull, let's say—a name like that would surely reassure her? —she'd never suspect. He hasn't got an accent, not to notice. It would take a tremendous weight off my mind."

"It's a bit awkward, my dear," Sir Christopher pointed out. "For one thing, she keeps accusing me of murder."

"Dr. Godfrey knows a persecution mania when he sees one. I don't think we've the right to keep her here with no medical attention except that old dodderer."

"Very well, Constance, if that's how you feel."

"He could see her while he waits for the ambulance, it's just next door. I'll go and ask him, anyway." She made for the door as if to allow Sir Christopher no time to raise further objections, walking a shade unsteadily. Her speech was jerky, too. If she'd called in the gin bottle to prop up her morale, Alex felt he'd be the last to blame her.

"Go with her, Jacey, like a good chap, will you?" the Chairman asked. "I don't want Godfrey to feel forced—"

"All right, sir. And then, if you'll give me a few moments—"

"I'll be here. . . . Sit down, Alex, and help yourself to a drink. I hope to God that wretched woman pulls round. I feel responsible. I drove her to it, but what else could I do?"

"I don't see how you were to blame."

"Not intentionally, of course. I was simply an instrument. But I've seen this sort of thing happen before."

"Suicide? In Britain, I believe, one hundred a week."

"Not that I'm to blame for, thank God. And I *was* to blame, on this other occasion, much more than I am now. All conveniently buried in the graveyard of the mind and then this comes along and the ghosts walk."

"If *you* start seeing ghosts we might as well pack up and go home."

"I wish we could," Sir Christopher said sombrely. "We haven't got to the end of it yet, I'm afraid. I suppose this tragic business is more or less an admission of guilt."

"It could be just general despair. And aren't we a bit premature in assuming that it *was* suicide?"

"Good God, Alex, you don't think—" Sir Christopher looked dumfounded.

"Seems plain enough on the surface. But murders can be faked to look like suicide. It's been done. And we've got a murderer around."

"Yes, but . . . You're not much comfort, Alex, are you? I suppose the doctor will be able to help us. Ah, there's Constance. I think probably hers was a good idea . . ."

Lady Connor looked rather less fussed. She helped herself to a drink and said:

"Dr. Godfrey agreed to look in, though only for a moment and non-professionally, whatever that means—afraid of treading on Dr. Furneaux's toes, I suppose. So I introduced him as Dr. George Bull—I thought perhaps *John* would be overdoing it."

"Well, if that relieves your mind . . . She took it calmly?"

"She didn't fly at his throat. Poor Blanche! I wish we could get her away."

"I think in a few days we shall."

Alex's mind was on Thomasina. Her second major shock, and no one comforting to turn to—Hugo Evans, Mrs. Godfrey. Unless that creature Partridge . . . He excused himself and went into the office to find Thomasina still there, tidying up for the night. She looked all in, and the last of his jealous anger went. Too much grand tragedy was in the air for jealousy to seem even decent; but constraint replaced it.

"You're working late," he said. "It's after seven."

"A lot's been happening."

"I'm sorry you had to find her like that."

"I thought she was dead."

"They're taking their time with that ambulance."

"It seems longer than it is."

She hesitated. "I'd like to tell you something, only it sounds so phony you won't believe me."

"About Partridge?"

"I know that if a man's lying on one's bed in the dark at about half past eleven there's only one conclusion to be drawn. But it just doesn't happen to be the right one. I don't expect you to believe me, though."

"I've no right to complain if there are ten men lying on your bed, or in it for that matter."

"There'd hardly be room for me in that case." Thomasina tried a rather unsuccessful smile. "I was doing some urgent work for him, and he'd come to collect it in person."

"Mending his socks?"

"Making transcripts from tape. He came to fetch them, and waited. Of course it was silly of him to go into my room and lie on the bed but I couldn't help that, could I?"

"He's got a nerve."

Her next smile was more successful. "So you do believe me?"

"Does it matter if I do or not?"

She considered. "Yes, I think it does."

"I'm prejudiced against Partridge."

"So I observed. So did he, I imagine. You really shouldn't have done that. He could run you in for assault and battery."

"Is he going to?"

"I don't think so. He's quite harmless really."

"So you think."

"Isn't it rather childish to talk like that?"

"Yes, very," Alex agreed. "I think that's the ambulance."

He drew aside the curtain and watched the ambulance drive into the courtyard. Two uniformed Hapanans got out and extracted a stretcher from the back. A policeman came up, and Dr. Godfrey's driver Jacob, and a couple of stewards, and several others; soon a lively conversation was in full swing.

"I'd better hurry them up," Alex said. "Will you dine with me?"

She shook her head. "I'm too tired, thank you all the same. I'm going straight home."

"A drink before you go?"

"Not even that. Perhaps tomorrow."

"Tomorrow then. And sleep well." He hesitated, looked at her shadowed eyes and weary expression, kissed her gently on the forehead and left the room. Before he reached the courtyard the ambulance men had finished their chat and followed the policeman to Amelia's room.

Alex waited in the courtyard to see them go. The little procession was soon back: Amelia was light and they were stalwart men. They lifted her into the back of the ambulance under Dr. Godfrey's supervision.

"How's she doing?" Alex asked.

Godfrey gestured with his hands. "I should say we have a fifty-fifty chance."

"How soon will you know?"

"An hour, perhaps, after we get her into the theatre. I'll ring up Sir Christopher directly there's any news. Will you be good enough, Dr. Burton, to tell him so for me? I want to follow her straight down in my car so as to lose no time."

"Of course, Doctor. And good luck."

"It's the patient's constitution we must rely on rather than my good luck." Dr. Godfrey climbed into his waiting car and followed the ambulance down the drive and away towards the hospital.

Chapter 21

Alex made for the lounge in a sombre mood. If Amelia lived, what would her future be? We said the purpose of life was the pursuit of happiness and yet we tried to stop people from escaping from an unhappiness they feared more than death. But then, no use to seek logic in human affairs.

It was nearly half past seven and the surviving Commissioners were consoling themselves with their pre-dinner drinks. They were in need of consolation.

"A calamity, a shocking disaster!" Sir Jeremy seemed even more upset than Alex would have expected—personally touched as well as professionally injured. "An accident, of course. These barbiturates are dreadfully treacherous. She hadn't been sleeping—giving herself too generously to the task in hand. One can only hope and pray that Godfrey will save her."

"One's almost tempted to believe in hoodoos and jinxes," Slocombe added. "Never have I known so much go wrong—and *so* wrong. It's—" He made a helpless gesture with his hands.

"There's an old superstition, is there not, that disasters go in threes?" Dr. Rumble, drink in hand, had thrown his jacket over a chair to display a pair of braces with mermaids on them. "But superstition is the enemy of progress, eh, Mr. Zaza? Fortunately the good Hapanans are learning fast to put superstition behind them and face the future with a scientific outlook. Superstition thrived under colonialism. For colonialists emasculated the dynamo of change and shackled the millstone of tradition to the necks of the emergent peoples of this vital continent . . ."

Alex took his drink and retreated to his bedroom where he lay down for a quarter of an hour with the latest volume of the Twickenham edition of Pope. If anything could restore to his mind the comfort of detachment, it would be his favourite Augustan. But tonight even Pope failed. He drew back the curtains to inspect an encircling darkness drenched with myriads of icy stars. A shrill, continuous trilling from the cicadas quivered in his ears, a wave of sound emerging ceaselessly from grass and bush and trees. On a deeper level drummed the throatier, harsher chorus of the frogs, no less countless, from the margins of the lake.

Stars, grasshoppers, frogs—too much of everything, crowding you in, menacing you with their profusion and indifference. A man was no more than a mote of dust, a bead of dew on a morning cobweb. The glory, jest and riddle of the world: between Pope's London and Hapana's bush stretched not only the centuries and miles, but the great gulf between two concepts of life and man's place in it. Here, what was strange or terrible about a murder? Just a brushing aside of something in the way, a twig snapping underfoot. It was a wonder people weren't murdered in dozens every day. Perhaps they were—all these passions and poisons.

Alex brushed his hair more carefully than usual and adjusted his tie. He was not a fanciful man, in fact he prided himself on a disposition exactly to the contrary, but he was full of uneasiness. He'd have called it presentiment if he had believed in such things. He searched his mind for a reason.

There was this ugly business with Amelia—like hunting a stag into the sea; and the constant, nagging fear that something one ate or drank might have been got at. There was the knowledge that someone *had* tried to get at Sir Christopher, and would very likely try again. The awareness of policemen lurking behind bushes, and of someone in their midst selling secrets to an enemy. And, out there in the *momombo,* humans plotting to kill their fellow humans in singularly savage and unpleasant ways.

All that, and something more. Alex frowned, reminding himself of the stupidity of looking for a rational explanation of the irrational. A presentiment was, by its nature, divorced from reason. No doubt Amelia would recover, Lady Bagpuse fly home and respond to treatment, the Chairman look back to say, with the Abbé Sieyès, *"J'ai véçu,"* the *Sulu Sita* fizzle out in a welter of recrimination, and Steyn Consolidated maintain its satisfactory dividends. Relations were restored with Thomasina and tomorrow . . . Perhaps that was it. Fear that, like a foolish quail, he'd let himself get enmeshed in a net from which there was no escaping, a net that destroyed even the will to break free.

Meanwhile it was eight o'clock and nearly dinner-time. It was a reduced party, with the Bagpuses, Mrs. Tripp and Matunda missing. But the Connors had emerged from their suite, no doubt to stiffen morale, and in pursuit of the same end Sir Christopher was telling stories of the first Protectorate he'd steered towards independence. Now the astute young schoolmaster he'd once released from jail was a semi-deified dictator whose bronze statue, twenty-five feet high, holding a torch of freedom that flashed on and off at night, dominated Liberation Square and adorned, in replica, all public buildings —including the jail, which housed the entire opposition.

Alex went up to Sir Jeremy and said: "I'm afraid your note to Mrs. Tripp didn't get delivered. She was unconscious when it arrived."

He had never seen Sir Jeremy caught off-balance before. His colleague actually gave a jump and splashed some of his whisky over his trousers.

"My note? I don't know what you mean."

"I thought I recognized your handwriting. Perhaps I made a mistake."

"Certainly you must have. I never . . . What happened to it?"

"To the note you didn't write?" Sir Jeremy would have to do better than that, Alex thought, if he wanted to lull suspicions of impending take-over bids or record dividends in the City. He said: "I gave it to Jacey."

"Oh . . . It must have looked like my writing, I expect. Mine's almost atrophied, what with the competent secretaries and all these office devices. Ah, dinner's ready. Desmond has opened some Chambertin '53 this evening; we all need a little bucking up."

As they took their places at the table Lady Connor asked: "What about poor Blanche?"

"They're taking her a tray in her room," Slocombe explained. Lady Connor was still concerned.

"I hope she's not moping. I'd better just see she's got all she wants. Don't wait for me."

When they were seated, Sir Christopher asked: "Has anyone heard any news of Mr. Matunda?"

"He's away plotting," the Rev. Zaza said darkly.

"Plotting?"

"Making up plots for London papermen."

"You mean he's gone off with Sparks and Black?"

"He has many debts," the Rev. Zaza said, almost with sympathy. "And the London papermen have a lot of money."

"I was wondering why they've kept so quiet—for the moment. Of course, it can't last. I think Partridge has handled them splendidly. He—"

Lady Connor stood for a moment in the open doorway, clutching both posts to hold herself steady. Her distinguished if rather beaky face was awry, as if someone had pushed it from one side. Sir Christopher's back was to the door and he didn't see her until she gave a sort of croak and he swung round, rising in his chair.

"Constance, my dear! Whatever is it? You must sit down. You—"

The croak developed into hoarse but recognizable speech.

"Something ghastly—Blanche—it's horrible—she's—"

Lady Connor sagged into her husband's outstretched arms. He and Sir Jeremy helped her to a chair. Alex raced along the passageway to Lady Bagpuse's room with Slocombe at his heels. The door was open, the light was on, he went in.

Lady Bagpuse lay on the bed, motionless, her blue dressing-gown rumpled and disarranged. When Alex reached the bedside he saw that her head was twisted back at an unnatural angle. The sight of her face wrenched at his stomach and filled his gullet with bile. Her flesh was a dark mottled red, her bloodshot eyes protruded, her tongue was lolling from contused lips. A pillow lay on the floor by her side. Alex picked it up and put it back on the bed. The pillow-slip was crumpled and stained with moisture and a little blood.

Both men stood for a moment voiceless and stunned. There were steps in the passage. Slocombe picked up the pillow and put it down again.

"What can have . . ."

"Smothered," Alex said.

Chapter 22

"I DON'T believe we'll ever crack this thing except from inside," John Jacey said to Alex. They sat alone in Sir Christopher's office, which had been put at Jacey's disposal.

"Inside what? The Commission?"

"More or less. Now, Lady Bagpuse. She was last seen alive by Dr. Godfrey, and he thinks he left her at about five past seven. Lady Connor found her, dead, at ten past eight. So I've got to get everyone's movements between those two times."

"There's the staff."

"Chisanga's working on that now. Between seven and eight they were to-ing and fro-ing between the dining-room and the kitchen and they might have spotted anyone who went in or out of her room. Or gone in and out themselves."

"I've told you what I did."

"You left the Connors' suite soon after seven, had a word with Miss Labouchère and then saw the ambulance go off with Mrs. Tripp, followed by Dr. Godfrey."

"That's right."

"What happened to Miss Labouchère?"

"So far as I know, she went home. Why?"

"It's all a question of checking."

"You surely don't think—"

"I don't think anything. A woman could have held a pillow over Lady Bagpuse's face just as well as a man. She was lying down and, taken by surprise, she'd be helpless."

"Is Dr. Furneaux sure she *was* lying down?"

"There are no signs of a struggle, and no one person, short of Hercules, could have lifted her onto the bed single-handed."

"It seems a simple way to kill anyone," Alex reflected. "A spur-of-the-moment job, presumably. Not planned."

"It *could* have been planned, but as you say it seems more likely to have been a sudden idea. Another thing—someone Lady Bagpuse knew, and wasn't surprised to see. Otherwise she wouldn't have let him—or her—stand by the bedside."

"A quick end."

"I suppose so. Now, back to your own movements. After the ambulance and the doctor left, you went into the lounge and there you found the following people." Jacey read from his notes. "Sir Jeremy Maxwell-Palmer, Slocombe, Zaza, Rumble, Chief Faustus and Evans. That's all?"

"I think so. I only stayed ten minutes, or less."

"Then you went to your room until just after eight. The same people were in the lounge when you got back?"

"Plus the Connors."

"Who came in about five to eight. Up to then they were in their suite."

"Alibi-ing each other."

Alex helped himself to coffee from a pot standing on the desk. It was getting cold, but he scarcely noticed. "You know, the most obvious suspect, looking at it all objectively, is Sir Christopher. Lady Bagpuse had been going round—or, rather, staying put—and accusing him of murdering her husband."

"She's known to be half-cracked."

"People with bees in their bonnets do have flashes of perception sometimes. It's a queer thing—" Alex stirred his coffee and frowned in thought.

"If I have to arrest your Chairman," Jacey observed, rubbing his lopsided nose, "then I really *shall* have to resign."

"From the start, Lady Bagpuse has had this delusion about the Russians trying to wipe out the British pig industry by introducing a disease. A sort of pig myxomatosis. She swore her Freddy was bumped off because he'd found out about it, and that *she'd* be the next victim. And now she's dead."

"You're not suggesting all that should be taken seriously?"

"Well, this introduction of disease isn't impossible. It's a form of biological warfare. I believe, in the war, there were plans to spread rinderpest all over occupied Europe. We'd even built up a stock of virus in cold storage on an island in the St. Lawrence somewhere, only it was never used."

"But we aren't at war."

"Cold war? It's going a bit far, of course. But not scientifically impossible."

"So some master-mind away in the middle of Africa eliminates both Bagpuses?"

"Not one of the more earth-bound theories, I admit."

Jacey scratched his head and said: "Well, back to our muttons. Some people can be eliminated. Mrs. Tripp can hardly have held a pillow over Lady Bagpuse while in a coma. She couldn't have been faking, could she?"

"You saw her, John. Could she?"

"I shouldn't say so. But then I'm not a doctor."

"Godfrey is, however. He'd have had to be an accomplice."

"There is one point about Dr. Godfrey," Jacey said. "He looked in to see Lady Bagpuse shortly before seven. So far as we know, he's the last person to have seen her alive. We've only his word she *was* alive when he left her."

"I suppose he could have pushed a pillow over her head and then gone back to Mrs. Tripp's bedside. Seems a bit risky, with Lady Connor popping in and out of the old trout's room."

"And a very clumsy method for a doctor to use. But people do take risks and act clumsily. Chisanga's checking up on whether any of the staff went to her room after seven."

Jacey paused, scratched his head again and helped himself to cold coffee.

"Two murders now," Alex reflected, "and the oddest thing of all is that neither seems to have a motive."

"So far we've got a choice of three. The pig plot theory, Sir Christopher trying to stop Lady Bagpuse accusing him of murder, and the enemy agent trying to avoid exposure. All weak as hell. The only one that holds a thimbleful of water is the last."

"And if Amelia really *is* the enemy agent, that's out too because she couldn't have smothered Lady Bagpuse."

"Except, I suppose, with Dr. Godfrey's connivance. Of course he was a foreigner originally."

"Now you're as bad as Lady Bagpuse," Alex said. "Are you really satisfied about Amelia Tripp?"

"No, I'm not, frankly. I think the security people jumped to the obvious conclusion because of her record. But that's them all over—once anyone gets a black mark, it follows him for the rest of his life. Even your Commission's own security man doesn't think she's the one. He's said as much to Sir Christopher."

A light seemed to burst inside Alex's head, revealing in a blinding flash the blatantly obvious.

"Just how blind can you be?" he exclaimed aloud, almost stunned by incredulity.

"What's that?"

"Partridge. He's our security man."

"Of course—didn't you know? Not a lot of use, in my opinion, but we're always supposed to be prejudiced. The sitting duck was Mrs. Tripp and with a great deal of banging they've knocked her over. Well, we shall see. I've set a sort of trap tonight."

"More traps," Alex commented.

"Perhaps not exactly a trap. But I think that last night, after the Chairman had given Mrs. Tripp her warning, the real agent smelt a rat and didn't try to get this information out. Or he may have found our guards too efficient. Though I doubt that—one or two are almost certainly bribed. But he's bound to try tonight."

"Certainly there's plenty of news."

"My men have orders to make no move whatever to scare away the intermediaries."

"Then you won't catch anyone in your trap."

"I've made other arrangements, but I won't go into that now. What I've got to do at the moment is to find out where everyone was between seven and eight this evening. Now, those six people you left in the lounge. Did they stay there all the time or did any of them go off for five minutes—it would hardly take more—and do in the old lady?"

"D'you really think it was one of those six?"

Jacey refilled his cup and made a slight grimace. "This is stone cold. I wouldn't mind a fresh brew. My dear Alex, I don't think anything yet. One of the snags about this wretched guest-house is that anyone can walk into anyone's room at any minute, and there are always two ways in and out. Like this office." He gestured at the two doors. "On the other hand, we have all these guards about and some of them may have seen something."

"Between seven and eight," Alex reflected. "It's a longish time. Can't the doctor narrow it down more than that?"

"Old Furneaux's a bit past it, to tell the truth, and all he'd commit himself to was that she hadn't been dead more than about an hour when he saw her. A pity we couldn't get Godfrey, but he was busy pumping out Mrs. Tripp."

"Furneaux got here about half past eight, didn't he?"

"A bit after."

"That would mean she was done in after seven-thirty. That lets Godfrey out, because I saw him leave myself just before then."

"Well, thank you very much, Alex; probably you'd better not stay while I question these people. Who shall I start with? It doesn't matter. Perhaps Sir Jeremy."

"That reminds me," Alex said. "That note I gave you for Amelia. I thought I recognized the handwriting. Was it Sir Jeremy's?"

Jacey extracted a paper from his pocket and handed it to Alex.

Dear Mrs. Tripp,

You asked me for some figures about the Company's wage bill over the last decade, broken down into the various categories and differentiating between Hapanans and Europeans. I've put our statisticians on to this and told them to present the data in the form of graphs wherever possible. In the past I have been struck by the fact that very few women can read graphs, but you are clearly an exception—as in so many ways.

Please don't hesitate to call on me for any further assistance you may need. It is a pleasure to be of some service. I shall not easily forget your quick and thorough understanding of the essential principles of the electrolytic treatment of blister in reverberatory furnaces on the Haley-Pratt system, and of the Ziervogel wet method of extraction of silver nitrates.

I wonder if you would dine with me tonight at the Pig and Whistle? There are some points about our homecraft courses for the wives of our metallurgic laboratory workers on which I'd very much value your advice.

Sincerely yours,
Jeremy Maxwell-Palmer.

Alex handed the letter back gravely. "Say it with sulphuretted cuprous oxides, do you suppose?"

Jacey grinned. "Sex rears its head among the reverberatory furnaces. I've often wondered how top people lead up to the point my young Inspectors reach in a bound with 'How about it, Lil?'"

"He hotly denied having written it," Alex recalled.

"Everything's so mixed up I daresay it's in code and all about pig diseases, or Russian rifles for the *Sulu Sita*."

"That's a new one on me."

"It's my Commissioner's idea. Now, do you think you could ask Sir Jeremy to come this way? You look remarkably cheerful, Alex, considering."

Alex felt ashamed, with Lady Bagpuse cold and stiff in the next room, and his own monumental idiocy to deflate him. But somehow it didn't. Partridge was in the security racket and it was really a business partnership. Thomasina hadn't been free to explain. He owed her, and would deliver, a handsome apology.

Chapter 23

A ROOM had been set aside for Chisanga in the staff quarters just behind the kitchen. It contained a good solid table with six chairs and it belonged to Mazozo, one of the senior stewards, a man with Negroid features and a black skin who'd worked for ten years at the Merry Hippo without getting the promotion he believed to be his due. He looked sullen until he smiled, when his grin almost spanned his face and made him suddenly gay and even youthful; but he did not smile much.

Chisanga noticed that Mazozo's wife was comely and extravagantly dressed. He put her down as a flirt, and perhaps the cause of Mazozo's sullenness. Her earrings were expensive and she was the kind of woman who'd wear a different dress every day. But she kept the room clean and brought him tea in a big earthenware pot, with plenty of sugar, so he gave her the reward of a smile.

"This is a nice room you have," he said to Mazozo. "I can see you have a good wife."

Mazozo looked surlier than ever. "All women are alike. If you beat them they behave for a day or two. If you give them a new dress, they use it to attract a lover and ask you for another one next day."

Chisanga laughed. "I think your wife has a good spirit. She keeps things clean. Now, I am asking you about the death of the fat white woman. You know that someone killed her tonight."

"I don't know anything about that."

Mazozo was not only sullen, he was clearly stubborn as well. Chisanga decided that he was like a rock at the mine, you would have to force the truth out of him with a pick or a drill. So he would ask questions as sharp and powerful as the miners' drill, though not so noisy.

"What were you doing," he began, "between the hours of seven and eight?"

Mazozo looked at him with some contempt. "Do you suppose that I was drinking tea or lying on my bed or visiting a beer-shop? That is the hour before the Europeans eat. I was getting everything ready."

"You were walking about between the kitchen and the dining-room?"

"Am I a bird? Was I flying?"

"It is better not to speak like that to an important policeman," Chisanga said ominously. Mazozo said nothing.

"When you were walking about between the kitchen and the dining-room, you passed the door of the room of the fat white woman. Now, you must think carefully. Did you see anyone either coming out or going in?"

"I'm very busy. I don't have time to stand as idly as a crane and look at doors." As Mazozo's voice was now a little more respectful, Chisanga decided to adopt a different attitude.

"I'm not saying that you are idle, Mazozo. On the contrary, I think you are a man with keen eyes and a clever brain. Therefore you may have noticed something that people who are less alert would not have seen."

"That is true," Mazozo agreed. "Yes, now you speak of it, I did see someone come out of the fat white woman's room—it was about half an hour before the Europeans started to eat."

"Ah! This is important evidence." Chisanga sounded impressed, and began to write in his notebook. "A European or an African?"

"It was a European. A woman."

"Another woman! Which one?"

"I don't know her name. She has no husband, and works as a clerk for the chief white man."

"Did you see her go in and come out?"

"No, only come out. She went across the grass outside, she didn't go into the lounge to join the other Europeans."

"Do you think she was going to meet someone?"

Mazozo picked his nose reflectively. "She may have had a lover out there. I don't know. Why don't you ask the night-watchman?"

"The night-watchman? Did he see her?"

"How do I know, policeman? It's no business of mine."

Chisanga paused to sip some tepid tea. Now he must move very carefully, like a man stalking an antelope. The least false move would scare away Mazozo's willingness to talk. He had the feeling that he was getting close to something important, like a hunter who comes on the fresh track of an elephant.

"There are two night-watchmen here," he ventured. "One is called Mlombo and the other Simon. I don't suppose she saw them both."

Mazozo shrugged his shoulders. "Perhaps she didn't see either. Mlombo is getting old, he might stumble in the darkness going up and down the path. The other watchman, Simon, is younger."

"Ah! Going up and down the path."

"That is all I can tell you," Mazozo said, as if regretting that he had spoken at all. "I know nothing about this affair. There is more tea if you want it."

"Your wife makes good tea," Chisanga replied, "and you have been wise to answer questions. The bird that leads the hunter to the tree, eats the grubs from the honeycomb which the hunter finds there. Now you must go and fetch this night-watchman called Simon."

When Mazozo had gone his wife took away the tea and left Chisanga to smoke cigarettes and meditate. He hoped Mazozo wasn't leading him off to chase a spirit or a bird. He didn't trust Mazozo; but then, indeed, was anyone to be trusted? Anywhere?

Just when he was deciding that Mazozo had cheated him; the steward appeared, followed by a thin, middle-aged man in an army great-coat and sandals, who had about him a smell of the bush. But his face, with a narrow, pointed chin, was intelligent, his manner self-assured.

"Mazozo says you want to see me," he began, quite boldly. "I am on duty, so I can't stay. I am a night-watchman."

"Yes, I know," Chisanga said coldly. The impudent man should have waited for his superior to speak first.

"Night-watchmen have very important duties, to guard everything against thieves and see that there are no fires or sorcerers. Now the bushes are full of policemen, but they wouldn't see a fire unless it burnt their feet."

"I didn't call for you to listen to impudence," Chisanga snapped. "Mazozo, go away, I wish to speak to this man alone." Mazozo went out without a word.

"I am making a very important inquiry about the murder of a white woman and you must answer my questions truthfully if you don't want to get into bad trouble."

"I know nothing about the murder of a white woman," Simon looked the least bit uncomfortable.

"You know something about another white woman, one who is young and thin, who came out of the guest-house tonight at half past seven and went to meet someone in the bushes."

Simon shook his head. "I know nothing about that."

"It will be no use to lie to me, Simon. I have information here—" he tapped his notebook "—which tells me things which you believe are hidden. They are not hidden."

"I am telling the truth, policeman. I did not see any white woman coming out of a door. But about that time you mention, I did see a white man."

"Where did you see him?"

"He was walking through the bushes towards the house. I didn't see him go into the house as I was on the look-out for thieves and criminals. I saw he wasn't a thief so I didn't follow him."

"How did you know he wasn't a thief?"

"I have seen him before. But I don't know his name."

"What does he look like?"

Simon shrugged his shoulders. "Fairly thin and fairly old. What do Europeans look like? They are all much the same. It was dark and I didn't look carefully. This European may have just been going into the bushes to relieve himself. I don't know."

"Are you sure you can't remember anything more about him?"

Simon considered. "Well, he's a man who has an instrument that he puts into his ear."

"Puts into his ear?"

"Yes, one end goes into his ear."

"Is he deaf, then?"

"I suppose so, but it's only what I've been told. I am a night-watchman, and I only see lighted windows and locked doors. Once there was a fire that started—"

"Never mind that, I don't want to hear about fires. I want to hear about messages that are carried up and down the path to the lake."

"Messages?"

"Messages that are sometimes hidden in the stump of a tree."

"I don't know anything about that at all."

"Then you are a very poor night-watchman if you don't know what is going on under your eyes."

"It's not my job to follow people with messages, if such people exist, as you say they do. It's my job to stop thieves breaking in and fires breaking out and snakes climbing up drain-pipes—"

"Yes, I know your duties. It is also part of them to know who prowls about at night through the bushes. If there are messages, someone must carry them."

"You are as wise as a schoolmaster," Simon said sardonically.

"You have been seen going up and down the path to the lake."

Simon shook his head. "You are quite wrong, policeman. Others may go up and down that path but I don't. I am paid to stay and watch the guest-house and that is what I do."

Something in Simon's tone, its confidence, told Chisanga that the wall of rock was not going to give way to the drill. Or perhaps Simon was like a fish, he slipped through the hand. The right way to go about the business was to find a hook and pull him out of the water, and then he would struggle and gasp and tell everything he knew.

"Very well, Simon," he said impressively. "That is enough for the moment; I am very busy, and have an important conference with the Commissioner of Police. I shall have more questions to ask you later. And it's no use trying to run away, because the police will find you."

Simon laughed and said: "Why should I run away? It is others who will run, the Shiwa and the Mongu and the Europeans. Soon we Chuma people who own the country will have it all. Even policemen will have to do what they are told by Moto Mguu."

"So you are also a politician, night-watchman."

"No, I'm not a politician, but I don't like this talk of running away. Good night, policeman, and be careful of paths with rocks in them that bruise the feet in the dark." He pulled his great-coat round him and walked out of the room.

Chisanga put away his notebook thoughtfully, and looked at his wrist-watch. Nearly eleven o'clock. In the police force there was no resting, no off-duty, only work. He had eaten no proper meal, only tea and buns. But he was so conscientious that he didn't mind, so devoted to duty that he wouldn't go to bed, even now. He would find the Superintendent and tell him some of the important facts he had discovered.

Some, but not all: not until he could reveal the whole story to the Superintendent complete, like a new bicycle. It was no good giving someone a bicycle that had been taken to bits and not reassembled. He would not say much about Simon the night-watchman, for instance, who knew more than he would reveal about messages going down to the lake in the dark. But he would mention the young white woman seen by Mazozo, and perhaps the European with an instrument in his ear. None of these important facts had been discovered by a European, and yet Chisanga was only a Sergeant, and Jacey a Superintendent with three or four times more pay. It was unfair, but it wouldn't last much longer. Soon, he, Chisanga, would have crowns on his shoulders, a motor-car, and a lot of money in the bank.

Chapter 24

THOMASINA's shadowed eyes suggested a poor night. She was nervous, and kept glancing at Sergeant Chisanga, who sat at a small table smoking cigarettes and studying his notebook with an air of impassive importance. They were using Amelia's bedroom as a temporary office. Jacey kept rubbing his twisted nose with one finger and looking out of the window. She wondered whether he'd seen an interesting butterfly.

Outside, in the morning sunlight, everything looked normal and serene. And yet there were spiders tearing live flies to bits, ants devouring grubs, buzzards pouncing on voles; the cycle of pain, destruction and rebuilding went on endlessly. She thought of the frog-pond with its ferocious little crocodile, and every night the frog chorus growing weaker. Yet the pond looked calm and beautiful, the frogs croaked happily until a single snap silenced them forever.

"Now, Miss Labouchère, a few routine inquiries. When did you last see Lady Bagpuse?"

Thomasina hesitated. She looked at Jacey—the crocodile, his jaws momentarily at rest?—and decided to take the plunge.

"Last night, round about half past seven."

Chisanga looked up and gave the Superintendent a significant glance.

"Can you fix the time more precisely?"

"Not really. After the ambulance arrived—"

"One moment, please. Let's get this down. The ambulance arrived at seven-fifteen approximately."

"Yes, I was with Dr. Burton in the office. We saw it come and he went out to hurry up the men."

"And you remained in the office for how long?"

"I should think about five minutes. Then I decided to look in and say good night to Lady Bagpuse before I went back to my billet. Just for a few minutes."

"Did anyone see you?"

"No, because I went round by the garden. I didn't want to go through the lounge and get involved in having a drink."

"And you found her quite normal?"

Thomasina gave a faint smile. "I'd hardly say that. She's been very odd lately, hasn't she? I mean—"

"Did she show any special signs of peculiarity last night?"

Thomasina hesitated. "Well, I thought she was a bit hysterical. You know she has—had—these wild suspicions and delusions. They were in full spate."

"Directed against any particular person?"

"I don't think one could take any of that seriously. She had a persecution mania."

"The fact remains that she was murdered."

"Yes, it's so extraordinary, apart from being horrible. Why *her,* of all people? Why?"

"That's what I'm trying to find out. You may have been the last person to see her alive."

"Apart from her murderer, of course." Thomasina looked at him steadily and then away. She was kneading a handkerchief, and as taut as a coiled spring.

"Apart from the murderer, yes. Did she say anything to suggest she might have been afraid of any individual? Or had some knowledge that might have made her dangerous to anyone?"

Thomasina moistened her lips. "She spent most of her time accusing people of plotting against her and killing her husband."

"Accusing Sir Christopher, you mean. I can understand your reluctance to repeat these sort of accusations and I think we all know how much value to set on them. It was the mixture as before, in fact?"

"More or less. Except that she'd rather changed the direction of her fire, so to speak."

"What do you mean by that? She was accusing someone else and not Sir Christopher?"

"She got confused. She said there was a plot to poison her and she'd thrown all her medicine bottles into the bath and smashed them. She really didn't make much sense."

"How long did you stay with her?"

"Not more than ten minutes."

"Was she lying on the bed when you left her?"

"Yes." Thomasina shivered and shut her eyes.

"Do you know if she locked the door?"

"I don't suppose so. It wasn't locked when I went in."

"When you left, it would have been about twenty-five or twenty to eight?"

"I suppose so. I didn't look at my watch."

"And you went back the same way?"

"Yes, I avoided the lounge for the same reason. I wanted to go straight home—to my billet."

"There was a car waiting for you?"

"Yes, there's always one of the Company's cars available to ferry any of us about. I found one in front and the driver took me back to the Godfreys'. I suppose I got there about ten to eight."

"Did you see anyone when you got in?"

"Mrs. Godfrey was there. He was at the hospital, of course, with Mrs. Tripp. We had an early dinner and I went straight to bed."

"I see." Jacey doodled with his pen on his note-pad. "This hasn't got us very far."

"I'm afraid it hasn't."

"Have you any ideas yourself, Miss Labouchère? I mean, as to why Lady Bagpuse was murdered within, say, twenty minutes of your seeing her?"

There was a steeliness in his tone she hadn't heard before. She looked at him with foreboding.

"I'm afraid I haven't. She was so *harmless*. Even if she was a bit unhinged by her husband's death, I don't see what harm she could do to anyone."

"Even the people she was accusing of murder?"

Thomasina looked startled. "You mean Sir Christopher? It was a sort of joke, almost. No one could possibly take it seriously."

"You said there was someone else."

"Well, she was lashing about in all directions."

"Supposing one of those directions had been the right one?"

"Oh, I don't think it was."

"Suppose you tell me who she mentioned and we can have a think, too?"

Thomasina shook her head. "I told you, she didn't mention actual names. It was all about a plot, and poisoned medicines, and pigs and Russians."

"It mightn't be wise to keep anything back, you know."

"Wise? Well . . ."

"Two people have been murdered."

"Is there a connection, Superintendent? There must be, surely? Why *both* Bagpuses? Do you think there can possible be anything in this business about pigs . . . ?"

Chisanga cleared his throat and intervened. "May I ask some questions, Superintendent?"

"Certainly, Chisanga. Go ahead."

Chisanga had been listening with impatience to his superior getting nowhere with this suspect, letting the quarry escape—shooting with a blocked arrow.

"Madam, when you left the victim's room, who did you go to meet?"

"To meet?"

"Yes, in the bushes?"

"I met no one in the bushes!" Thomasina said indignantly.

"You were seen walking in the garden in the dark—"

"I told you I went round to avoid the lounge!"

"And there was someone you met."

"That's completely untrue!"

"Do you know a night-watchman called Simon?"

"A night-watchman? Of course not."

"This night-watchman knows you."

"I don't know what you're talking about."

"Where's all this leading, Chisanga?" Jacey asked.

"The object of my questioning will be seen, sir," Chisanga replied with dignity. "Did you see in the bushes a European with an instrument in his ear?"

"In his *ear?* No, I didn't, but what sort of instrument?"

"Do you mean Sir Jeremy Maxwell-Palmer?" Jacey inquired, intrigued despite the lamentable course the inquiry was now taking.

Chisanga nodded. "That is the man. He is deaf."

"Was *he* in the bushes, too?"

"He was seen there."

"This is getting like a game of consequences," Jacey said. "Did you meet Sir Jeremy in the bushes, Miss Labouchère?"

"Certainly not!"

"Why do you think Miss Labouchère met Sir Jeremy, Chisanga?" Jacey inquired.

Chisanga frowned. It was not the Superintendent's place to interrogate him, Sergeant Chisanga; it was the Sergeant who was questioning a witness. "I have my sources of information," he replied loftily. "I do not say that he met this witness definitely. He may only have been going to relieve himself."

"I really think we've asked Miss Labouchère all we want to for the moment," Jacey said, swallowing hard and with his mouth twitching. "You seem to have discovered a great deal of activity in the bushes, Chisanga. I congratulate you, but I think we'll release this lady and talk to some of the others."

Chapter 25

When Thomasina had gone, Jacey looked at his Sergeant with mingled amusement and reproof.

"We mustn't press these people too hard, you know, at any rate at this stage. We've got nothing against any of them yet."

"That lady was holding things back."

"I think you're right there. Who's this night-watchman? He seems a mine of information."

Chisanga now regretted mentioning Simon; he had intended to keep the night-watchman to himself. He had, as yet, lacked an opportunity to give the Superintendent more than a brief summary of his previous night's inquiries. At eleven o'clock Jacey had still been questioning everyone in the Merry Hippo about their movements, and then he'd disappeared to sort out and summarize his information. The upshot of it was that the six men who'd been together in the lounge alibied each other, except for one vital omission: somewhere between twenty to eight and eight o'clock each one of them had gone separately to his room to tidy up for dinner.

Only Zaza, who'd been away for twenty minutes, and Alex Burton, had taken longer than was necessary for a wash. But each of the others had taken five or ten minutes. And, at a pinch, five or ten minutes would have been time enough to nip into Lady Bagpuse's unlocked room, smother her, and return to the lounge. It was discouraging, and Jacey had cursed a good deal when he'd worked it all out. And now Thomasina had destroyed another possible lead.

The only unusual objects he'd found during his search of Lady Bagpuse's room had been the smashed medicine bottles in the bath. He and an assistant had spent the best part of an hour sorting out the muddle and setting aside samples for analysis.

All sorts of theories had passed through his mind. There'd been a struggle in which all the bottles had been swept into the bath; Lady Bagpuse had caught someone in the act of tampering with them and had been silenced. The simplest explanation, of course, was the one he hadn't thought of—that she'd smashed them all herself. The medicines had gone off to the labs in Umpah, but Jacey had little hope that they would yield anything.

Lady Bagpuse had been alive at twenty-five or twenty to eight—that is, if Thomasina hadn't killed her—and no one, apparently, had been seen to enter or leave her room after that. Thomasina, of course, could easily have held a pillow over her face and suffocated her. But why?

"I can't help feeling that *someone* must have seen this murderous visitor either slipping in or out of Lady Bagpuse's room last night," Jacey remarked. "After all, stewards were going to and fro all the time."

"I have questioned the senior steward, Mazozo," Chisanga said. "He saw no one, except this lady we have just questioned. Why don't you arrest her?"

"Miss Labouchère? Because we've no evidence."

"She was seen coming out. Soon after that, the corpse was discovered."

"I know, but in that twenty minutes or so after she left . . ."

"In a cell, she would have a clean breast."

"But if she's innocent?"

Chisanga shrugged his shoulders. "Women kill like snakes when they're angry or jealous. It's the lioness who hunts, more than the lion."

"Miss Labouchère can hardly have been jealous of Lady Bagpuse."

"Who knows? Perhaps she loves Sir Christopher. This fat woman calls Sir Christopher a murderer. So she kills to please him."

"That's a theory, anyway," Jacey said. "I'd better see Dr. Rumble next. While I talk to him, will you check up on the rest of the staff? Make sure no one saw *anything* between seven-thirty and eight?"

"Very well," Chisanga said. He was glad of the opportunity to question people by himself. His own methods were much more successful than the Superintendent's, which were feeble and out of date.

Dr. Rumble displayed no reluctance to talk. "This is indeed a melancholy occasion," he began. "Little did I think, when I joined this group of dedicated men and women—"

"We'll get straight down to cases, Dr. Rumble, if you don't mind. I want more details of your movements. Where were you at half past eleven the night *before* last? Monday night, that is?"

"I've told you my movements last night, Superintendent, in detail. I don't follow you when you ask about my movements on the previous evening. Surely no murder was committed then?"

"But at half past eleven, Dr. Rumble, you were not in your room."

"And may I inquire the source of that information?"

"You may. I looked."

"Sir, this is an admission of a gross breach of personal liberty. Without a search warrant—"

"No search warrant is needed to knock at a door, receive no reply and look in. I would remind you that one murder had already been committed."

"You're not suggesting, Superintendent, that I have some connection with that?"

"I'm just asking a plain question."

Dr. Rumble was silent for a moment. Then he pulled out and lit a small cheroot.

"I guess you're doing what you believe to be your duty," he said handsomely. "Just for the record, I would remind you that your duties don't extend to questioning good citizens about their private affairs, especially when they aren't citizens of Hapana or any part of the British Commonwealth. However, I don't think the question of diplomatic immunity need be raised between us, Superintendent."

"I don't think it need."

Dr. Rumble drew on his cheroot. "All too many visitors, I fear, to underdeveloped countries, content themselves with a superficial view of the problems perplexing these less fortunate members of the human family. What can be seen from costly hotels, from country clubs, from the back seats of expensive automobiles? What do such observers know of the true lives of the peasants in the field, the toilers in the swamps, the delvers in the mines? Nothing!"

"So you like to find out."

"I like to find out. That is it exactly. I have a profound curiosity, Superintendent, about the different ways in which the countless members of our human family go about their business. How they conduct their government, their industries, their private lives. About—"

"The beer-shops of Shooting Star, for instance."

Dr. Rumble nodded. "You have hit it off exactly, Superintendent. Such studies deepen and extend an understanding of the forces motivating human action. They do, it's true, expose the observer to some of the uglier aspects of colonialism. I am often appalled—"

"So at half past eleven on Monday night you were in a beer-shop in the town. Right? Which one?"

"To tell the truth, Superintendent, one beer-shop is very much like another. I go to talk to the people. And although these excursions, Superintendent, are undertaken purely in the interests of sociological research, I would rather you kept this conversation to yourself. Some of my colleagues might misinterpret my intentions. Perhaps they aren't accustomed to our informal American ways. In my country the democratic way of life—"

"How often have you been to these joints?"

"On two occasions only, Superintendent. I found the experience tiring and arduous, sordid perhaps at times, but well worth while. From a sociological angle, that is."

"What interests me is how you managed to elude the guards."

Rumble smiled blandly. "That is my secret, Superintendent. Sometimes even the keen eye of Cerberus winks."

"Well, you'd oblige me by not trying it again. For one thing it's dangerous. My men are armed and sometimes they get jumpy—trigger-happy, even."

"Thanks for the warning. I reckon my researches are pretty well complete."

"We don't want any more tragedies," Jacey added. "I'm supposed to protect you Commissioners and I'm having half my men taken away, just when I need them most."

"Why, that's tough, Superintendent."

"It's this outbreak of violence and religious mania in the south-eastern province. Reinforcements have to come from somewhere. So I'll just have to do the best I can with my men far too thin on the ground. I'm telling you this, Dr. Rumble, in the hopes of getting your co-operation. If you sneak off—I'm sorry, go down-town on sociological investigations—you not only may get shot at, but you add a lot to our difficulties."

"Well, that's frankly put. Very frankly put. I like frankness, Superintendent. I'll certainly co-operate."

"Thank you, sir. I appreciate that. Incidentally, please regard what I've just said as confidential. For obvious reasons, I don't want it to get about."

"Naturally I shall respect your confidence." Rumble rose to go and Jacey walked over to the door to open it for him. "Just one small point, Dr. Rumble, I see you're a cheroot addict. Do you ever smoke cigarettes?"

Rumble took a long pull at his cheroot, withdrew and inspected it, and glanced thoughtfully at Jacey through his rimless lenses.

"For myself, I prefer the pure leaf of the *nicotiana* plant uncontaminated by burnt paper. May I ask the reason for this inquiry?"

"Idle curiosity."

Dr. Rumble smiled. "I wouldn't put you down as an idle man, Superintendent. While I myself prefer cheroots, I respect the taste of others. For example, on these little sociological expeditions of mine down-town, I armed myself with packs of cigarettes to break the ice, as it were, when making the acquaintance of the good Hapanans. I found cigarettes very effective ice-breakers, Superintendent. The good Hapanans don't appear to smoke cheroots. Does that answer your question?"

"I think it does," said Jacey.

Chapter 26

"THE FUNERAL's fixed for two o'clock but God knows if it can be rushed through in time."

Hugo Evans' forehead was puckered and his expression hunted. He sat by the telephone with a lot of cigarette stubs in an ash-tray and a pile of files in front of him. Alex watched him with an unworthy trace of *Schadenfreude*. Hugo added:

"They keep the ordinary sizes, but this! Naturally there's nothing in stock. First I tried a Goan who does most of the hospital work but he's attending his daughter's first Communion. Then they put me on to a Hapanan outfit, the Kutprice Koffin Kompany, but they've just rung up to say the carpenter's gone off with the keys of the timber store—gone to a funeral, of all things. What a country!"

"It might be worse," Alex said consolingly. "We nearly had two more funerals. But Mrs. Tripp's going to recover."

"I never imagined, when I got my transfer to African Affairs, I'd be chasing coffins in a mining town for a twenty-stone cadaver. I wish now I'd gone to the Home Office." The telephone rang and Hugo took up the receiver. "Oh, they've found him, have they? Good . . . Yes, of course I know it'll cost more. For God's sake hurry, you've got less than two hours . . . A deposit? Oh, for goodness' sake stop quibbling and get on with the job!"

Hugo wiped the sweat from his face. "In all my born days . . . The Chairman's alone now if you want him. Lady Connor's suffering from shock and wants to go home."

The Chairman, Alex thought, was looking pretty rough. Not

that his smile was less welcoming, but his complexion had grown more sallow and his eyes more sunken; he blew his nose constantly and had taken to fiddling with things on his desk. He was fiddling now with a pen, an inkstand, an ash-tray, a bottle of paludrine. Jacey had wanted to provide him with a personal bodyguard, but Sir Christopher had rebelled. And now even his wife had packed up.

"If you don't mind my speaking frankly," Alex said, "you oughtn't to see anyone alone, as you're seeing me."

"I can only say that if you're a murderer, Alex—well, if my judgement's as bad as that, I've forfeited the right to live."

"Nor ought you to leave medicines lying about on your desk." He indicated the paludrine.

"That lives under lock and key, I've only just taken it out. With Constance *hors de combat* I keep forgetting it. Normally she's marvellous at reminding me." He extracted a tablet and poured some water from a jug on his desk into a tumbler, but instead of swallowing the tablet he rolled it between finger and thumb while his thoughts moved on.

"You know, Alex, the situation's really grim. The P.M.'s given me discretion to call the whole thing off if I think it's best. He's left it to me. It's such a tremendous responsibility. . . . Suppose I decide to carry on and there's *another* disaster—well, it doesn't bear thinking of."

"And if we pack up and go home . . ."

"That's unthinkable, too. I'm making no decision for twenty-four hours. In a long experience I've found that snap judgements are wrong at least fifty per cent of the time. Meanwhile, look at these."

He passed over a sheaf of papers. Fleetway Black and Mervyn Sparks had gone to town and the *Clarion* and the *Popular* had splashed their stories all over the front pages. Two murders—all pretence about Lord Bagpuse had been abandoned; an attempted suicide; a fear-riddled, heavily-guarded Commission; rising political tension; above all, the sinister secrets of the *Sulu Sita:* all these, indeed, amounted to a rich Fleet Street feast. Fleetway Black's dispatch concluded:

Through sources I cannot reveal I am about to make contact with the leaders of this midnight cult. In my next dispatch I shall make known for the first time the secrets of its dark practices, hitherto considered unprintable. . . .

Alex put it down. "Of course the unrevealed source is our friend Mansfield."

"Quite right. He went off with the press to the south-eastern province yesterday. And now the press is after me, too. My hideous past, anyway."

He handed Alex a cutting from the *Popular*. It announced a new series: *"The Famous Cases of Sir Christopher Connor, K.C.M.G., Q.C."*

Sir Christopher Connor, former Governor of two British liberated colonies, started his meteoric career as a barrister. Many of his cases caused sensations at the time and made legal history. In a series of articles specially written for the *Clarion* we shall recall the most controversial of these cases, starting tomorrow with his defence of the slayer of an unborn baby and a mother-to-be of fifteen. Make sure to order your *Clarion* from your newsagent EVERY DAY.

"I shall read these with interest," Alex said.

"That's more than I shall—throw it away, will you? That sort of thing upsets Constance and God knows she's upset enough already. If only she'd fly home . . . What do you really think about all this, Alex? *Why* Blanche Bagpuse? That's what I can't understand."

"The obvious reason is because she found out who murdered her old man."

"How *could* she have, sitting in her bedroom and anyway half off her head? She was accusing me of the crime and no one paid any attention. Suppose she accused the real murderer, no one would have paid attention either. He only had to laugh it off."

"There is another possibility," Alex suggested.

"There must be. What is it?"

"Our trouble is that two separate wires have got crossed. There's the leakage of information, and there's the attempt on your life that misfired."

"You think they *are* two separate things?"

"They must be if Amelia Tripp's the spy. She couldn't have murdered Lady Bagpuse. Among our party here, she and Mansfield are the only ones who can be definitely ruled out for that."

"But supposing the spy *isn't* Mrs. Tripp . . . Alex, I wish you'd go and see her in the hospital as soon as you're allowed to. It really was suicide, apparently—she's admitted it. Find out if she tried to kill herself because she was guilty and feared the consequences, or because she was innocent and couldn't face a ruined career."

"I'll try. Let's suppose, for a moment, X is the spy—not Amelia. Now, we've jumped to the conclusion that Lady Bagpuse was smothered because she suspected who did in her Freddy. But suppose it was X she was on to, the spy, and not the murderer?"

"Can you really see her as a smeller-out of spies?"

"She'd got them on the brain. And her brain sometimes worked quite logically. And of course she might have seen something suspicious and put two and two together."

"To make about twenty-five, I should think. And if it's not Amelia Tripp, who's X the spy?"

"We're pretty certain X must regularly attend the Commission's meetings. Leaving out Amelia and Matunda, that makes nine."

Sir Christopher ticked the names off on his fingers. "You and me, Jeremy, Rumble, Zaza and the Chief, and then Evans and Miss Labouchère. I make that eight."

"And Partridge. Nine."

"Oh, yes, Partridge. But as he's our anti-spy attachment, wouldn't it be a little labyrinthine to cast him as the actual spy?"

"Double agent?"

"I suppose it's possible."

"We'll eliminate the Chairman, and for the time being me, though I'm not quite clear why. That leaves six."

"Surely we can tick off Jeremy?"

"On what grounds?"

"A director of one of the largest mining groups in the world—a bastion, as our press friends would say, of the capitalist system—surely he isn't likely to be working for the Communists?"

"None of this is likely, if it comes to that. Take Chief Faustus."

"No, I can't honestly see him in the role either. That leaves Rumble and Zaza among our colleagues, plus Hugo, Thomasina and, I suppose, Partridge. Hugo's a highly respectable civil servant who's had many confidential jobs."

"So was Donald Maclean."

"That's true. Hugo was specially picked after the most stringent checks, and the same applies to Thomasina. But the security people do slip up. They did with Mrs. Tripp."

"I rather fancy Dr. Rumble. He's always taking side-swipes at colonialism."

"Surely the Americans wouldn't send us a *spy?* He's got a long, blameless record in half a dozen official bodies. They're always knocking us about our security."

"There was Alger Hiss."

"It's rather tempting. I suppose, though, if you come down to it, Zaza's the strongest candidate."

"A turbulent priest."

"For goodness' sake don't say that, Alex! I don't want anyone to rid me of him, even if he is a spy. I've always thought it would be easier for one of the Hapanans to pass out information than for one of us colonialists. Probably half the guards are party members and delighted to pass on messages."

"And Faustus," Alex said. "He's by no means a fool, even if his English is limited. *He* could have found out something and passed it on to Lady Bagpuse. She seems to have had some mysterious way of communicating with him."

"Just suppose," Sir Christopher said, with a return of some of his normal alertness, "that Zaza's our X. Faustus gets on to him, and warns Blanche Bagpuse. Then Zaza gets to hear of this and holds a cushion over her face—in that case why doesn't he do in Faustus, too?"

"Perhaps he's waiting for an opportunity. Or he may have somehow blackmailed Faustus into keeping quiet."

"At any rate it's worth talking to Jacey about this. Zaza's always been something of an enigma. Although, somehow, I can't quite see him deliberately smothering poor Blanche to death."

"I can't see anyone I know doing it," Alex said, "but someone I know must have."

The telephone rang and Sir Christopher's expression became apprehensive. "Ah, Butterfield, yes, no more bad news I hope? . . . There is? Oh, dear . . . In the south-eastern province? As bad as that? . . . To us? . . . At the funeral this afternoon? I'm sure Colonel Cottrell . . . They did *what?* . . . What an extraordinary thing . . . Well, really that's most unusual . . . Of course I realize it's serious . . . Yes, I'll do what you say . . . All right, we'll talk about it then."

He hung up. "That was Butterfield."

"So I gathered."

"Really, people in this country do the most extraordinary things!"

"I can't wait to hear."

"To begin with, the trouble the Government expected has broken out. Butterfield thinks Matunda hatched it with his press friends to discredit Zaza by sending the rising off at half-cock. And the press get their story—two birds with one stone."

"Who'd think he'd be so Machiavellian?"

"If you ask me, Machiavelli would be outclassed here in a week. Everyone knows that Zaza's mixed up in the *Sulu Sita* and if the rising fizzles out so will he."

"I'm almost sorry for Zaza. *Has* it fizzled out?"

"It was a flop in Umpah, the police arrested the ringleaders while they were still asleep. But out in the country districts no one seems to know what's going on. Except that Butterfield says there's a plot to seize all of us at the funeral this afternoon and forcibly baptize us all, according to the rites of the society."

"Surely they can't . . ."

"Butterfield says we're to take it seriously. Forcible baptisms have been going on all over the country. And apparently—"

Sir Christopher's face displayed signs of inner conflict. Concern, fear, incredulity. . . . Then he gave up the struggle and laughed.

"I know it's serious, but do you know what they've done, Alex?"

"No?"

"Raided the dispensaries and stolen all the enemas."

Chapter 27

THE FUNERAL followed its normal course until the coffin, carried with difficulty by eight strong men, was lowered into the grave. Then Chief Faustus stepped forward, raised one arm and, with great dignity, delivered a funeral oration. The Bishop of Hapana looked startled and indeed displeased, but bowed his head and waited, if not with resignation, at least with self-control. A row of armed police almost encircled the mourners, and behind them a concourse of Hapanans stood in a silence ominous rather than respectful.

"Have they been searched for enemas?" Mr. Butterfield whispered to Colonel Cottrell.

"Not exactly searched, sir, but they're fairly bulky things and without buckets—"

"Quite so, quite so."

All the same, there had been an atmosphere of tenseness, even hostility, until Chief Faustus stepped forth. In his red gown of a Master of Arts of the University College of Llandudno he was easily the most impressive figure there, not excluding the Bishop. As his words rolled on Alex felt a change of atmosphere, as if the mists of hostility were being sucked away by a rising sun. A murmur from the crowd caused the police to grip their rifles tighter, but the sound expressed sympathy; the Chief was carrying his audience along as smoothly as his native waterways bore the Shiwan barges on the crest of the annual floods.

When he reached the peroration he raised one arm and called for a response. Three times this came: a deep, throaty, lion-like roar.

Then he bowed his head, spoke a few soft words and stepped back. The crowd stood in silence for a few moments and quietly dispersed, leaving the Bishop to resume his functions with the best grace he could muster. So Lady Bagpuse had been laid to rest next to her husband in the bleak and shadeless cemetery of Shooting Star.

"I really must congratulate you, Chief, on your magnificent oration," Sir Christopher said. Tea in the guest-house lounge was dispelling some of the party's gloom.

"Very happy." The Chief, who had disrobed, gave his delightful smile.

"Almost Roman in style. She was deeply attached to you, Chief."

"Very happy."

"I'd like to know what you actually said."

"Very happy."

"Well, perhaps in the circumstances that would hardly have been . . . Never mind. Once again, I congratulate you."

The Chief shook hands, bowed formally and withdrew. He was not in the least arrogant but carried with him an air of authority and wisdom, whether or not derived from a long line of kings.

Jacey took his teacup across to Alex and said: "I want your help this evening, if you don't mind. I'm going to make one more attempt to catch your spy, on the assumption that Mrs. Tripp's a false alarm."

"Well, good luck to you, John. I'm busy."

"Two funerals are enough for one week, don't you think? I want you to sit up all night, if necessary, and watch two of your colleagues."

"Which two?"

"I'll tell you later. I'll be along about ten. And don't have a fit if I black my face."

"The broken-nosed policeman, his face black as soot . . ."

"In the morning it'll probably be red."

Alex took Thomasina out to dinner, but the evening didn't go at all well. The aftermath of the funeral subdued them both. Even Alex had begun to wonder when the next disaster would strike, whether Sir Christopher was safe, whether the next person he spoke to was a killer. It was like having a poisonous snake moving about your room and being unable to locate it.

"I shall be thankful when we're all safely home," she remarked.

"To a waiting mother? A suburban residence? A London flat?"

"A flat off the Fulham Road. Not much, but my own."

"By yourself?"

She smiled. "Sometimes. There's a spare room. A Greek restaurant down the street. A delicatessen next door and a bus stop opposite. It's very cosy."

"Then be careful."

"Of what?"

"Of contentment, leading to complacency."

Thomasina showed signs of impatience. "I'd rather be complacent and content than mixed up in all these murders and suicides and revolutions. While we're sitting here, someone may be poisoning Sir Christopher."

"The devoted P.A."

"Well, he's a good boss. Never flaps, always considerate, a sense of humour. And knows it all."

"He puts on a wonderful act."

Thomasina looked at him half in amusement, half in exasperation. "First you were jealous of poor little Stephen, now it's Sir Christopher."

"Has he ever made a pass at you?"

She flushed a little. "You've no right to ask that."

"He'd be inhuman if he hadn't."

"He's human all right."

"Then you've answered my question. Dirty old man."

"If you talk like that I shall go straight home." Thomasina was really angry.

"Well, isn't he?"

"No, he's not. He's under sixty, and very young for his age—anyway it's nothing to do with you. You smear everything."

"It's to make you angry, Thomasina. Because you look like a vitriolic rose."

She couldn't help laughing a little but not with real enjoyment, and the evening never recovered from its bad start. Anyway he had to be back by ten to start his wild-goose chase with Jacey. He dropped her almost with relief at the Godfreys'.

His wing of the guest-house had three windows: his own, Rumble's next to him, then Zaza's. Through uncurtained panes Alex caught a glimpse of Rumble in his shirt-sleeves, with a green eye-shade and a profound expression, studying a blue-book. He knew the one: *An Economic Survey of Hapanan Resources,* 1961, by Professor Untermayer. Zaza's curtains were drawn but a light shone through the chinks. These were the two he had to watch. Jacey had muttered their names conspiratorially into his ear just as he was leaving for dinner. ✓

But Jacey hadn't issued instructions about man-watching techniques. He was out there somewhere in the darkness presumably, with his commando-blackened face. No moon, a black night, a sky encrusted by stars. A storm was gathering somewhere and, from the distance, came an occasional thunder-rumble and a fulgurous orange glow. The frogs on the lake were nearly silent. Waiting for a moon, perhaps. Did frogs croak to the moon? That busy, pampered little crocodile in the Merry Hippo's pond came to mind again, gorging and growing. Alex couldn't suppress a slight shiver as he put on rubber-soled shoes, old trousers and a dark jacket and made his way as silently as he was able to the silent garden.

To watch the two windows seemed the obvious thing. Zaza and Rumble. Could either really be the spy? It seemed so far-fetched. Probably he'd draw a blank. He stood against a clump of bushes, invisible—or so he hoped, anyway. What about his face? Perhaps that, too, should have been blackened, like John's.

Midges pinged in his ears and savaged his neck and irritated his ankles and the backs of his hands. He swore at them silently; this neither relieved his feelings nor discouraged the gnats. His feet ached. He kept shifting his weight. Like all people of sedentary habits and active minds, he lacked the art of physical repose and was unused to standing upright. Assuming he could keep as keen a watch sitting down as standing, he lowered himself carefully and hugged his knees. Rumble was still studying the economic survey. Zaza was walking about: at any rate, through a chink in the curtains, movement could be discerned.

Where were John, Chisanga, the guards? The garden was strangely still. Alex felt very much alone and full of fears. Something nipped him in the bottom, quite hard. A scorpion? With an effort he checked a convulsive movement. Only an ant, probably, but who would have thought so small a body could have so much formic acid in it?

At last he saw Rumble get up, stretch, close his blue-book and draw the curtains. Alex scrambled to his feet and approached the windows with caution. A flower bed checked him, but he was close enough to hear sounds in both bedrooms. Rumble was cleaning his teeth, Zaza seemed to be moving furniture about. Why, at this hour? Getting out spools of tape from secret hiding-places? It was frustrating not to see through the curtain.

Alex waited for a little and then returned to his bush, spread a handkerchief in the hopes of fending off ants, and sat down again. Midges, ants, mosquitoes. Had he remembered his daraprim? These were the bad kind of mosquito, the *anopheles*. Yes, he'd taken it on Sunday—the day Lord Bagpuse had died. Incredible, only four days ago but it seemed an age.

Alex's mind, lacking anything to grip on, coasted into a pleasant, relaxing glide. He thought about Thomasina. He recalled her eyes and lips and movements and body, and his thoughts became voluptuous. Like a damned adolescent, he told himself: daydreaming about women, imagining conquests and responses as if he were suffering from sex-starvation. Perhaps he was? If so, this was no place and time to apply palliatives. He tried to switch his mind back to a paper he was writing on the influence of Italian humanism on English political thought in the seventeenth century; but he failed dismally.

At last Zaza's light went out. In bed? Or waiting for nefarious visitors? A little later, Rumble's light vanished, too. Now an insect had got into his shoe. Cautiously, with slow movements, he took off the shoe and shook it, put it back and tied the lace. Then he looked up and froze. Something dark was slipping through the darkness near the guest-house. He heard a very faint sound, perhaps the movement of clothing, or a footfall on grass.

He tried to watch the figure but a shrub intervened. The shape had moved away from the house and vanished. Alex cursed viciously, if silently; through fiddling with his shoe, he'd missed the one vital moment. In those few minutes—two, at most three—someone had either approached the guest-house from the garden, or had slipped out of it and gone away. Which? Rumble or Zaza leaving, or a go-between who'd taken something from one of them? Perhaps through a window? Or might it have been one of the guards?

He couldn't see more than ten or fifteen paces. Was that a rustle by the clump down there? Treading very cautiously, he set a course in that direction, moving so far as possible from bush to bush. His heart was pounding in a way you read about, but normally experienced only after a fast sprint, and blood was throbbing in his ears. He wasn't cat-eyed, he didn't know the layout of the garden, anyone could cosh him with a blunt instrument.

He blundered into a bed of cannas whose thick leaves rasped as loudly in his ears as a train going through a tunnel. The quivering of the cannas subsided, he stood still and listened for a length of time impossible to specify. If he'd been asked how long he'd stood there he wouldn't have known whether to say two minutes, or twenty. Anyone could thus experience the relativity of time.

I've muffed it, he thought—I told John I was no good at this sort of thing. All the same it was infuriating. That bloody shoe. To his surprise, he felt the spirit of the hunt mounting in him. He wanted to track someone through the bushes, to spring remorselessly in the dark, to bear the quarry down.

He advanced more boldly, though without a precise objective. A sound from behind, and to his right, raised the hairs on his scalp and he swung round, instinctively crouching. Then a colossal weight landed on his back and flung him to the ground with such force that every bit of air was punched out of his lungs. He felt the life being ground out of him on the hard turf; he couldn't even writhe and twist to throw off his killer. His sinews torn apart, his body wrenched by agony and his soul by protest, a last despairing thought went through him like an electric shock—this is it, this is finality. Blood roared in his ears; a rumble of thunder from across the lake didn't even reach his stunned mind.

Chapter 28

So AFTER ALL he wasn't dead, but every bone felt pulverized and a light blinded his eyes. Someone was bending over him—to finish the job? The light shifted and caught in its beam a glint of bronze flesh, and a hand gripped his shoulder. He gulped in shuddering lungfuls of air and tried to be sick. Dimly, through the pain, he recognized the symptoms of being winded. Panic subsided as he found he could move his limbs.

"How can I know you when you walk about in the bushes?" a voice said in aggrieved tones. "Can you rise?"

Alex was still gasping for breath but his lungs were working. Were his ribs cracked or his back dislocated? A hand grasped his and he heaved and stood on his feet, still sick and dizzy. A distant flare of sheet lightning rose and fell and in its half-light two other figures close by, apparently embracing, sprang into view and then vanished again.

"I think I'm going to be sick," he said shakily. "You're like a hippopotamus, Sergeant Chisanga."

There was a soft chuckle. "I learnt that at the police college. Why didn't you say you intended to walk about in the bushes? I nearly snapped off your neck." He sounded self-satisfied.

"Very nearly."

"You come with me out of the bushes where you make a lot of noise. We want all quiet tonight."

Sore, aching, sick and above all crestfallen, Alex followed the Sergeant towards the staff quarters. The other two men, he now saw, had not been embracing; one had his wrists tied behind him and he was in the grip of a policeman. The evening's catch—apart from Alex, the fish they had to throw back.

Sergeant Chisanga rapped briskly on a door and a woman opened it. She wore a printed cotton cloth, and the light glinted on her ear-rings and copper bangles as she stood aside to let them pass into a small room lit by a low-powered bulb dangling from the centre of the ceiling. A charcoal brazier gave out heat and acrid fumes. The table was covered by a lace cloth and on it stood teacups and buns.

"This is where I shall conduct my inquiry," Chisanga said. The man with tied hands shook his head, like a dog emerging from a river, and glared angrily at Chisanga.

"What right have you to seize me? Am I not night-watchman here? Wasn't I doing my duties, night-watching? And then you seize me like a chicken. You will suffer for this, you policeman!"

"Silence, rat!" Chisanga commanded. "Now you will tell me who gave you the parcel you hid under the tree-stump. And if you don't speak at once, and speak truly, you'll be beaten till you're broken like a pot smashed on stones." He sat down, took out his cigarettes and nodded at another chair. "Be seated, mister. This is the night-watchman I caught hiding something in a tree-stump. Yesterday he lied to me. That was foolish." He glared at Simon, who was rubbing his wrists with a look of resentful anger.

"I told no lies," Simon said.

"Don't speak until I command you," Chisanga snapped. "The woman here makes good tea," he added to Alex. "We will drink first." He took out his notebook and pencil, lit a cigarette and settled in his chair. Presently Mazozo's wife brought a large pot in which used tea-leaves, sour milk and about a pound of sugar had been boiled up together. Alex didn't really share Chisanga's enjoyment, but the shock had exhausted him and it was certainly reviving. What with the tea and the glowing brazier he soon felt overheated, unlike his companions, who became more animated as the temperature rose.

"Now, night-watchman," Chisanga began in a tone full of menace, "I am ready for you. Who told you to put that parcel in the tree-stump?"

Simon had evidently decided, on reflection, that blank denials were useless. "I am a good night-watchman," he said, "and I protect the house against thieves. If a man asks me to put something under a tree-stump, is that wrong? Is it against the duties of night-watchmen? I do not know what was in the parcel. Perhaps it was a charm to keep away evil. That is all I have to say."

"Fool, imbecile and hyena! Are your ears full of mud? Did you not hear my question? Who gave you that parcel?"

"Truly, I don't know," Simon replied with every appearance of honest candour. "It was very dark. How could I see the face of the man who gave it to me? I didn't ask questions, either."

Chisanga gazed at him as if he'd been an insect crawling over a boot.

"You are so great a fool, Simon, that I am wasting my time talking to you. The time has come for the whip to talk, to help your memory. Don't you understand that we, the police, know you have been putting parcels in that tree-stump every night? And that the parcels are collected by fishermen? All right, if you insult me by your foolishness it doesn't matter; we shall catch the fishermen, and you will be beaten so that even vultures won't be able to pick your bones."

Simon had been considering. "I am a man of peace, and I know it's right to help the police, even sergeants who shout and bully people. I'm willing to help you if you are polite. Is it polite to attack me when I am night-watching? To seize me as if I was a wild animal? I have done nothing—"

He was interrupted by the arrival of Jacey, his blackened face streaked by dirty grey patches due to sweat and exertion—queer enough to frighten the birds. His tunic was torn and his hair standing on end.

"Good work, Chisanga," he said. "You got your man. I'm afraid mine got away."

"How was that?" Chisanga inquired sternly.

"He came up the path all right, and took the packet. Just as I made a dive for him something warned him, and he took off a split-second too soon."

"What can have given him this warning?"

"I think it was my stomach rumbling. I've had hardly anything to eat all day. I gave chase and we went hell-for-leather down the path, but I couldn't catch him. A bare-footed man can always out-pace a booted one."

"There was a constable stationed on the road," Chisanga pointed out.

"This fellow got into the reeds and vanished like a water-rat. We picked him out later with our torches, paddling like hell in a canoe. If we'd only had a motor-boat—but we hadn't. Anyway, he'd jettisoned the cargo by then."

"He had . . . ?"

"Thrown away the package. We caught a glimpse of it with our flashlights spinning into the reeds."

Chisanga looked disapproving, but at the same time rather pleased. He had succeeded where the Superintendent had failed.

Jacey sat down and poured himself a cup of tea. "This ought to stop my tummy rumbling, anyway. Shutting the stable door . . . What's the night-watchman said?"

"He is very obstinate," Chisanga answered.

"Who gave you the packet of cigarettes to hide in the tree-stump?" Jacey inquired. Simon looked at him and shrugged his shoulders.

"Is it wrong to put a packet of cigarettes in a tree-stump?"

"Not wrong at all, but foolish. A waste of good cigarettes. Now tell Sergeant Chisanga everything and you won't come to any harm. You've committed no crime so far. Or at any rate not one I know about."

Simon gave a brief grin and directed a look of triumph at Chisanga.

"Of course there is no crime in hiding cigarettes in tree-stumps," the Sergeant said crossly. "Only in obstructing the police in the execution of their duties."

"Did you get the package from that European who talks all the time?" Jacey asked. "The American?"

Simon hesitated briefly while thoughts of great importance evidently passed through his mind.

"It wasn't him. It wasn't a European."

"Ah!" Jacey said.

"It was the man who preaches, the man who won't agree with Moto Mguu."

"You mean the Reverend Zaza?"

"Yes. Zaza."

Chapter 29

ALEX LAY AWAKE and thought about the murderer. Shouldn't one be able to ignore all these confusing cross-currents caused by spies, secret societies, political intrigues and the like and reach right down to a solution by a grasp of *character?* Nearly everyone had motives, even opportunities, to kill others, but very few people actually did so. The reason lay in their characters, not in their circumstances. They weren't cut out to be killers.

What was the character of this particular killer, as revealed by his actions? Ruthless—you had to be that. Secretive, deep, a good actor. Above all, Alex thought, a man—or woman?—with the quality of recklessness. Both crimes must have been committed on the spur of the moment, not as a result of calculation and planning.

The killer had seen the chance and taken it, acting with tremendous speed, precision and nerve. Accepted great risks and got away with it. A gambler by nature, the sort of man—or, again, woman—who might have made a brilliant if erratic games player. Who filled that bill? How could he tell? Everyone wore disguises. What did he really know about his colleagues—about Sir Jeremy, for instance, or about Rumble and Zaza, about Hugo, Slocombe, Sir Christopher for that matter—or, least of all, Thomasina?

What, after all, did the pin know about the magnet? She had a curious quality of aloofness. Whenever he put out a feeler towards anything intimate she evaded him like a sea-anemone folding up for self-protection.

Alex got out of bed to draw a glass of water from the tap and a breath of fresh air at the window. Gentle sounds hummed from the next room. Dr. Rumble was snoring. A clear conscience? Guilt, Alex thought, didn't keep you awake—only fear and uncertainty.

At last he slept. Dr. Rumble snored peacefully on, dreaming perhaps of the incidence of hookworm among the aborigines of Ecuador. The Rev. Goliath Zaza awoke with the dawn and read aloud a chapter of his favourite Book of Revelation. His great, shining spirit floated magnificently among the seven flashing stars and the seven golden candlesticks before the emerald throne with a rainbow round about it.

> And I beheld when he had opened the SIXTH SEAL, and lo, there was a great earthquake; and the sun became black as a sackcloth of hair, and the moon became as blood: and the stars of heaven fell unto the earth, even as a fig tree casteth her untimely figs, when she is shaken of a mighty wind; and the heaven departed as a scroll when it is rolled together; and every mountain and island were moved out of their place.
>
> And the kings of the earth, and the great men, and the rich men, and the chief captains, and every bondman, and every free man, hid themselves in the dens and in the rocks of the mountains. . . .

The Rev. Zaza read on with mounting exultation until the time came to put aside his Bible and resume, until breakfast, his revision of the eighth manifesto of the Forever Forward Group, setting forth demands for independence back-dated to March, 1960.

With his early tea, Alex studied a schedule, circulated the day before, of the Commission's tour of the mine workings, due to start at nine o'clock that morning. Sir Jeremy and Slocombe had fixed it up a week ago. Better to stick to the programme, Sir Christopher had decided—either carry on regardless or pack up altogether; besides, a day off from the conference table, to see what really kept Hapana ticking over, would be good for everyone. So there it all was on the schedule: the pneumoconiosis research centre to start with, next the crushing mills and giant smelters, the electrolysis plant and research laboratories; then the underground workings; in the afternoon a tour of housing estates, welfare centres, hospitals and schools. A very full day.

Desmond Slocombe, at breakfast, was like an eager sheepdog keeping his flock assembled for an orderly move into the pen.

"We have seventeen churches of eight denominations—built out of beer-hall profits, incidentally, a valuable source of income. Our boys' choir won the Anglican championship at Abidjan last year. Over thirty bursaries to Scandinavian folk high schools . . ."

His audience was depleted and rather glum. Besides Alex, only Rumble, Zaza and the Chief were there. Alex couldn't help looking at Zaza with a certain curiosity. Was his mind a-bubble with thoughts of fishermen and tape-recorders, of Marxist ideals and funds for his party? Did he act for gain or from muddled idealism, with innocence or vanity, or just to keep one jump ahead of Matunda and Mguu? Zaza was restless and on edge, Alex thought—preoccupied. His eyes glittered and he displayed a meagre appetite.

Did he know, or guess, that his game was nearly up? At this moment, while he gulped his coffee, Jacey was probably waist-deep in mud and reeds, searching the lake's margins for the jettisoned packet. "It's an outside chance," he had told Alex, "probably one in a thousand. But I'm going to spend all day there if I have to—set on by leeches, I expect, ravaged by mosquitoes. It's my own damned silly fault." Without some solid evidence, he could make no charge—not on the unsupported word of a night-watchman.

After breakfast, Alex strolled across to Hugo Evans' office. The desk was littered with dispatches and telegrams. The rising in the south-eastern province seemed to be fizzling out; the Prophet had vanished, and many of his chief disciples been arrested. The future of the Connor Commission had been considered by the Cabinet. *"HMG appreciate and endorse your decision to continue inquiries,"* the Cabinet office had cabled. *"Urge that you will observe most stringent security precautions bearing in mind . . ."*

"Did anything come through on Moscow radio yesterday?" Alex inquired.

"Quite a lot, and all about the rising—ruthless imperialist storm-troopers armed with nuclear warheads and flame-throwers, all that sort of thing. No inside dope about the Commission. It looks as if the leak hasn't leaked anything since Mrs. Tripp was put out of action."

"Or as if the leaker saw the trap."

"One odd thing," Hugo added. "A cutting from the home papers that's just come in. It's on the back of one of those articles muckraking about the Chairman's legal past."

He slid over a cutting and went on studying dispatches with a preoccupied frown. *"New Pig Disease Spreads,"* Alex read.

Britain's pig producers are seriously alarmed by a new disease believed to have been introduced from the Continent. Many pigs have died and the epidemic is spreading.

"This is a direct result of the Government's agreement with Poland under which Iron Curtain pigs are entering this country," said Mr. Higginbottom (46) of the British Pig Federation yesterday. "The British pig industry is threatened with total disaster." A deputation is due today in London to see the Prime Minister.

IS THIS OUTBREAK OF A HITHERTO UNKNOWN DISEASE PART OF A COMMUNIST PLOT TO WEAKEN BRITAIN'S ECONOMY? This startling suggestion was made yesterday by an official (39) of a livestock society who has asked to remain anonymous. "Frankly, I'm scared for my life and that of my family if I reveal what I know," he told our representative. "The late Lord Bagpuse warned the Government. What happened to him? Dead in mysterious circumstances in Africa. If their arm can reach out to Africa how safe am I in Norfolk? I have my three daughters to think of—Jane (13), Mary (10) and Cordelia (3)."

A standstill order on all further importations has been imposed by the Ministry. All foreign pigs still in quarantine are to be slaughtered forthwith.

Underneath, in black type, was the note: *"Lady Bagpuse dies mysteriously—is she another victim? See page 7."*

"This is going to be quite a story," Alex commented.

"It is already."

"How's the Chairman this morning?"

Hugo gave a quick and slightly wolfish grin. "Still alive, if that's what you mean. Worried, though. Lady Connor's none too good and he's trying to make her fly home."

Alex turned over the pig cutting and glanced at the article on the back. There was a photograph of Sir Christopher in a wig, thinner in the face and perhaps more predatory; the wig altered his appearance and, anyway, most press photographs were all but unrecognizable. The story was a sordid one, involving the seduction of a Lolita-type teen-age girl, a back-street abortionist, a respectable but errant married man, a shifty landlady and a glamorous young blonde wife standing by her guilty husband, the abortionist. Sir Christopher—Mr. Connor then—had been defending. Pretty thin stuff, thought Alex; most barristers who'd practised at the criminal bar had handled dozens of such cases. Sir Christopher had wisely transferred to the Chancery bar and made his name, and his money, in a less sensational manner.

A smudged photograph caught his eye. It seemed vaguely familiar. He studied it more closely and with a deepening frown. Then he read through the article and studied it again.

A sort of flash-bulb seemed to go off in his mind. In a moment he saw everything, or thought he did; the sense of conviction was overwhelming. The motive had been missing; now he held it in his hand. Then he thought again, and saw that his solution was impossible. And yet it *must* be right. There was only one chance of finding out.

"You look as if you'd seen a ghost," Hugo commented. "Are you all right?"

Alex slipped off the table, feeling numb. "Yes, but if Lady Bagpuse . . . There's no time to lose."

"There's another ten minutes. Slocombe's fussing so much we shall be early anyway. The Chairman wants to know if you can find time to go up to the hospital this morning to see Mrs. Tripp. He thought possibly it wouldn't break your heart to skip the pneumoconiosis centre and join the party at the rolling mills."

"I'm going there now. Will you do me a favour?"

"What kind?"

"Keep a close eye on Thomasina till I get back."

Hugo laughed. "Our Thomasina's pretty good at looking after herself."

"I hope so," Alex said, and loped from the office towards the waiting cars.

Chapter 30

Everyone but Alex gathered at the pneumoconiosis centre, including Sir Christopher, who looked worried and drawn. Sir Jeremy was on one side of him, Slocombe on the other. This was their day, and despite the low spirits of the Commission they were going to make the most of it.

The only Commissioner to display high spirits was Mansfield Matunda, who had rejoined his colleagues with the air of a fat spaniel after demolishing a particularly succulent bone. The Rev. Zaza pointedly looked the other way and asked a lot of questions of Dr. Godfrey, their guide and conductor.

"We X-ray every one of our employees on recruitment, and again at least once a year. If we have the slightest ground for suspicion we test their rates of breathing, intake of oxygen, level of metabolism . . . Here's our new electron microscope, with powers of magnification up to two hundred thousand. If you will look at this screen you will see the magnification of single dust particles."

Lights flashed on, knobs were revolved, switches depressed and several large, quivering, yellowish objects sprang to life on the screen.

"Those are oranges," observed the Rev. Zaza.

"Specks of dust, magnified by one hundred thousand."

"How can we believe such lies? They are oranges."

"Tck, tck, tck," observed Chief Faustus.

"The two cultures appear to be just as widely separated in Hapana as in Britain," Sir Christopher remarked. "I never can understand anything scientific. It's all beyond credulity."

Thomasina's first impression of the crushing mills was of remorseless, soulless, terrifying power. Power that terrified because it lacked mind or heart, and was on such a huge scale: great, revolving, vibrating steel cylinders, each fifteen or twenty feet in diameter, each filled with tons of steel cannonballs; rows and rows of these cylinders revolving evenly, steadily, ceaselessly, all pounding to fine powder lumps of rock dragged up from the depths of the earth.

What most alarmed her about the mills was their cold, rhythmic existence apparently outside human control. Very few human beings were to be seen, and those few were not doing anything; they were just standing on a platform looking at the machinery. Beneath their feet, with deafening noises, revolved the cylinders. One slip, one attack of vertigo, and over you might go into mills grinding not even slowly, but exceeding small.

Thomasina felt giddy and stood well back from the rails. Hers, she supposed, was a purely feminine reaction. Men, presumably, liked, or at least admired, all this machinery; it gave them a vicarious sense of triumph. One of their kind had created these miracles from symbols in the mind. It was like a woman looking at a baby. She mightn't have created that particular one, but it was the kind of thing she did create, and to do so was miraculous. Instead, men created all these ghastly crushers and crankshafts and flywheels and dynamos. She didn't even know what they were called.

For the first time, Thomasina felt consciously glad of being female. The very wish to invent this sort of thing seemed to her perverted. No wonder men made wars and always would, however much some of them might recoil from the results of their sex's impulses. Someone shouted something in her ear. It was Dr. Rumble. Something about Bethlehem, Pennsylvania. Or was it Bethlehem, Jordan? No, almost certainly Pennsylvania. She nodded and smiled.

Sir Jeremy was bellowing too, into the ear of Sir Christopher. He had detached his deaf-aid, and no wonder. Stephen Partridge had joined them with Fleetway Black and Mervyn Sparks in tow. The newspapermen were looking bored. No doubt they had seen lots of machinery. They had their eye on Zaza, probably. Was he the brains behind the *Sulu Sita?* No one seemed sure. Perhaps it hadn't any brains behind it anyway, only muddled hopes and frustrations.

Everyone clambered up a long, perpendicular steel ladder. If you were to lose your foothold, you'd go hurtling down into those rotating cylinders below. The visitors moved cautiously past enormous pipes, pale with dust, from which a sort of throbbing came. These, murmuring like arteries, led to a double row of tanks that ran the whole length of the shed, divided by a steel slatted platform. Down through the slats you could see the revolving cylinders and flywheels and shafts and roaring, hungry machinery.

It was lucky, Thomasina thought, that Mrs. Godfrey had warned her to wear flat rubber soles. To look down made her feel sick, to look up made her feel dizzy. To look anywhere at all made her feel miserable. She closed her eyes.

"In these tanks," Desmond Slocombe was saying, "the process of flotation separates the sulphide grains containing copper from the tailing by means of air forced up through the cells . . ." She opened her eyes with caution, to gaze at the rows of tanks. They were filled with a swirling, mercury-coloured slime full of great air-bubbles, like livid pustules forming and bursting, forming and bursting, swelling and popping—like something in a horror film. She remembered a lot of Things from Outer Space hatching in a laboratory tank, to the shocked dismay of Professor Quatermass. It was just like that.

"The resulting concentrate averages about thirty per cent of copper and the next stage is to thicken it in readiness for smelting. A vertical spindle revolving in the centre of a tank to which are attached radial rakes . . ."

To Thomasina's dismay yet another perpendicular steel ladder led up to a platform above the flotation tanks. Couldn't she stay on the lower level? Clearly not. Up went Sir Jeremy, up went Sir Christopher with Slocombe behind him. Suppose someone were to give him even quite a gentle push, tread on a hand, dislodge a foot? Of course there were people all round him, safety in numbers, but even so . . . She felt someone brush against her leg, and looked down in a sudden panic. Zaza was clambering up behind her with a strained look on his face and his glasses misting over. Behind were half a dozen men she didn't know—managers, engineers.

They reached the topmost platform and looked down at rows of slime-filled cells and cylinders, and at the huge round tanks full of glistening, moving sludge. The tanks were as large as—she couldn't think how large they were. Cathedral domes? A push, and in you'd go, to drown in that sinister grey slime which, it seemed, hid and disguised the copper as someone, perhaps someone with her on this platform, hid and disguised a secret guilt and hate. Stupid fancies, she thought, but they made her mouth dry, her heart thump like the machinery which shook her eardrums, pulverized her nerves.

"Mixed with the copper sulphides in the concentrate we find smaller quantities of iron, silica, lime, alumina and magnesia as well as minor constituents . . . Careful going down, ladies and gentlemen. The rails get a bit slippery . . . Accidents? Very seldom, since we introduced our system of accident-prone tests. One can never eliminate the human element, you know. But our safety record is one in which we take considerable pride . . ." Down they went, getting hot and dusty. Sir Christopher was ladder-clambering with a young man's agility, still flanked by Slocombe and Sir Jeremy. He was at any rate pretending to enjoy it.

All this for copper, and Thomasina didn't even know what it was used for. Sheathing ships' bottoms, someone had said. Surely there couldn't be enough ships' bottoms in the world to need so much sheathing? She thought about those heavy, shiny casserole pans—excellent inventions, but worth all this? Electricity, she supposed, motor-cars, airplanes—the world was full of factories taking in each others' products. All, really, to keep men busy, doing something, out of mischief. No, not out of mischief: whatever else they didn't do, they always found time for that.

At last the party reached ground level and Thomasina brightened up. Perhaps it was only the height and the noise, but up there she'd felt a sense of menace, of impending disaster. If, among them, was the hunter of Sir Christopher—the individual who, in the last three days, had blotted out two people without hesitation or scruple, a man perhaps by now growing reckless—wouldn't this give him his quick chance? A bump, a slip—perhaps even a prepared loose board or sawed-through rail?

At the back of her mind she couldn't quell the feeling that somehow she herself was involved. Did something Lady Bagpuse had told her hold the key to the puzzle? Why had that harmless, half-crazy old thing been killed? For the tenth time Thomasina went over everything that had been said, most of it nonsense. The pigs, the spy obsession, the hysteria, the smashed medicines, the . . . A thought sprang into her mind and things clicked together like a combination lock releasing its spring. All supposition, but then this morning . . . it *could* be the case? But why, why? There seemed no sense in it. She must be wrong, and yet . . .

"Does all this excite you as much as it does me?" asked Stephen Partridge, coming up behind her. "That's to say, as much as an end-of-term concert in the school hall on a wet December afternoon? Or is copper your secret vice?"

"It's too noisy." Thomasina frowned, not wanting to be interrupted. But Stephen paid no attention.

"No wonder Slocombe and Sir Jeremy have boxed the Chairman in between them. One little push, and . . ."

"Don't!"

Stephen laughed. "Nervous? What a din! Where's the boy friend?"

"Do you mean Dr. Burton? He went to the hospital. I don't think he's back yet." She looked round suddenly, wishing, to her own surprise, that he was near her, and wishing it badly. He was taking a long time. Had something gone wrong? What could go wrong in a hospital? Probably Amelia Tripp was pouring out her life history. A little sourly, she hoped he was enjoying the experience.

"Things were pretty hectic down there with Black and Sparks," Stephen Partridge was telling her. "I must say the fun and games Matunda's been up to . . ." He gave her a lot of details she didn't hear.

They'd come now to the smelting plant, the largest—or was it the second largest?—in the world. In furnaces of unimaginable ferocity, the concentrate was heated to some fantastic temperature and separated into its many components. After that it was further refined by a process called electrolysis.

Now they had to climb another ladder, this time to reach a wooden inspection platform even more dangerous, it seemed to Thomasina, than the steel-slatted ones above the flotation tanks. In places there was not even a rail. This platform ran the whole length of an enormous, high, fume-filled shed—over a thousand feet long, she heard someone say. Here the concentrate was roasted in furnaces and finally run off into moulds to solidify into copper bricks.

This shed was even noisier than the last but much more active and, as it were, demoniac. You thought at once of Thor and his thunderous hammer, the one-eyed Odin, of Vulcan in his forge. Above them, huge tubs or ladles swayed about on overhead cables. They seemed to be conducting a monstrous, demented gavotte—dipping and bowing, halting, reversing, sliding and shivering, all to the discordant, pounding music of machinery and half-hidden by swirls of acid fumes and gouts of gas. Somewhere, men must be working levers and pressing switches, somewhere there must be control, but the controllers were invisible and could be deduced only from the behaviour of the cranes and tubs and ladles.

It was not much good trying to understand it all. Sir Jeremy and Slocombe had conducted Sir Christopher to the far end of the narrow platform. There they stood, poised high above some vast furnaces and in the lee of a mass of pipes, shafts and flywheels. People were moving about in small groups with a stunned look, trying to take in the eager explanations of engineers. "Reverberatory furnaces . . . reagents . . . rotated on trunions . . . molten matte . . ."

Across on the other side of the shed, and fifty feet or more below them, stood a rank of enormous steel cylinders. These exposed to view, as they slowly rotated like huge sea-monsters turning on their ocean bed, a red, fiery, gaping mouth from which long flames shot out alarmingly from time to time. Over them, suspended by steel cables, hovered a line of black cauldrons or tubs. These were ladling substances into the gaping red mouths of the great cylinders—feeding the sea-monsters. They tipped out molten metals run off from the furnaces and, now and then, ladlefuls of scrap metal taken from heaps of jagged slag somewhere below them, under the platform.

Thomasina watched with uncomprehending awe. Propelled by an invisible force, seemingly of its own volition, a tub would come swaying down the cable out of a murky mist of fumes, hover above the open red mouth of a slowly-revolving steel drum, and suddenly up-end itself. Out would tip a great gobbet of molten metal, straight into the red hole—like a hideous, elemental vomiting of some primordial beast. Or rather not primordial—the first of things, primitive—but the reverse, something belonging to the end of a long story nearing its finale in a mechanized, armoured, inhuman decadence.

When the rotating drum received this tribute, the red glow in its mouth faded for a moment and then roared up with a flaming spurt of triumph. Long flames shot forth like the tongues of devils. The industrial Moloch had accepted his ritual sacrifice.

While Thomasina watched, something even more alarming occurred. A scoop appeared above the rotating cylinder below her, just across the aisle. Slowly it tipped, and opened its jaws to disgorge a load of scrap metal into the glowing aperture.

There was a pause, a low hiss from the cylinder, then a tremendous, booming belch. A fountain of sparks and a cloud of sulphurous fumes billowed upwards. The empty scoop swayed on its purposeful way along the cable, and from farther down the shed came another echoing, deep-throated boom. Thomasina peered down to see a human figure, dwarfed by the machinery, moving about. When the man looked up he offered, through the swirling fumes, a blank, grey, eyeless, flattened visage. He wore a mask.

"Is that all right?" Thomasina shouted at Partridge, who was standing just behind her on the platform's edge. "I mean, intended? Those explosions?"

He smiled, his teeth white in the gloom—almost like a vampire's. People looked strange and sinister in this lurid atmosphere, derived partly from the red glare of molten fires, partly from a harsh kind of neon lighting, all clouded over with smoke and fumes.

"Gases igniting in the converters," he shouted back. "Goes on all the time. Blowing out sulphur dioxide." Another explosion drowned most of his words but she caught ". . . heated up to well over two thousand degrees centigrade . . . like to fall into one, would you?"

Thomasina peered gingerly over the edge. In fact, if you fell you wouldn't go into a converter, as apparently the hungry cylinders were called, but onto heaps of slag just below. This slag, Partridge tried to explain, was mixed in the converters with molten matte and with something called fluxes, to be run off, eventually, in wonderful orange-red, glowing streams, like liquid fire from the veins of pagan gods of unimaginable ferocity. And then it set into red-gold blocks of solid "blister" copper.

"It isn't very safe up here," Thomasina shouted. She was feeling sick again and the platform seemed to tremble with every explosion. Between her and the drop was nothing but a single wooden rail.

She drew back a little and looked round for the rest of the party. Sir Christopher was still at the far end of the platform flanked, as ever, by his two faithful guides. Had it really been wise to bring him up here? Had he—apart from other dangers—a good head for heights? Mightn't his enemy be able to contrive some feint to distract everyone's attention: to betray, even for an instant, the vigilance of Slocombe and Sir Jeremy, and in that instant to push or trip his victim? Suppose that either Slocombe or Sir Jeremy himself . . . but that was absurd.

No sign of Alex yet. Why so long in the hospital? Hugo Evans stood with Godfrey and Rumble, who was no doubt telling them about some even finer smelting plant in some other part of the world. Zaza and Matunda were looking rather glum, perhaps concluding that great industries planted in their country like vast, exotic trees should be owned and operated by Hapanans, not by colonialist exploiters and capitalist thieves.

A head appeared above the top of the ladder by which they'd all climbed up to the platform. Alex at last! Thomasina was amazed at her own sense of relief. As usual, his tie was twisted and his hair rumpled; he seemed out of breath. He came up to her and she shouted in his ear:

"How's Amelia?"

"Getting on well. What a din! Where's . . . ?" He looked round and evidently saw someone he wanted. Another hollow roar from a converter drowned what he was saying; she only caught: ". . . near the edge. Back in . . ." Alex walked towards Sir Christopher, one hand on the wooden rail. Thomasina wondered why his hair always got untidy and why he wore those loose, brightly-coloured ties. Still, in a way they suited him, as curly pipes suited certain types of men.

Then everything vanished except the cancer-clasp of terror as a grip fastened on Thomasina's wrist and she felt herself jerked backwards so violently that her arm seemed to have left its socket. Her legs lashed out, one foot hit something, her head jerked back and a pale distorted face appeared, upside down—a mask of savagery, a nightmare flash. Terror, protest, fumes, an explosion that seemed the last cry of an expiring world: and she was falling, falling backwards into space. Her scream choked in her throat, the hollow boom of an explosion flowed over her like the great, the final, the exterminating wave.

She lay on the hardness: nerveless, disintegrated, numb. Was this death, an agonized reawakening in a purgatory of din and darkness? Dimly, but with gathering consciousness, she understood that she was still on the platform and still alive.

What made Alex turn his head as he walked away from Thomasina he couldn't say—perhaps a general wariness. Turn it he did, in time to see an arm shoot out to seize her wrist and jerk her backwards, robbing her of balance, so that only one quick twist was needed to hurl her over the edge. The single wooden rail splintered and gave way. Alex must literally have leapt the few paces between them and pulled back with such force it was astonishing he didn't rip away all the tendons of her shoulders.

The man, jerked off balance, staggered and let go of Thomasina to save himself. His arm stretched out to grip the rail but the rail wasn't there. He tilted backwards, let out a screech that was drowned by a boom from a converter and toppled headlong into space.

Alex dragged Thomasina clear and looked down. Below, limp

among the jagged death-grey lumps of metal, lay a heap of rags. Overhead a scoop swung slowly round, performing its part of the inhuman, mechanized gavotte, and hovered on the end of its cable. Its jaws opened, slowly the scoop descended, the jaws dug deep into the scrap and closed with a deliberate, an unhurried bite.

Up went the scoop, and looking down again Alex saw no heap of rags, only a pit-marked crater where a load of scrap had been torn away. Up went the scoop, swung across the aisle, again descended to spew its contents into the converter's glowing mouth. Then came the hollow, responsive roar of the fed monster accepting its morsel: a hiss, a cloud of acid fumes, and the final bellowing explosion. A man had gone to his Valhallan end.

Chapter 31

"You knew all the time, didn't you?" Alex asked.

Sir Christopher stared at the carpet as if he lacked strength to raise his eyes.

"I think I knew he was after me, but I couldn't be sure. It all seemed so unlikely—so long ago. And why, in God's name, did he go for *Thomasina?*"

"Because she knew something dangerous, something Lady Bagpuse told her just before she died. I don't know what it was yet but we'll find out. So he had to silence her, as he silenced Lady Bagpuse."

Sir Christopher looked all in—drained of vitality, deflated, like a cushion deprived of its stuffing, an oil-disabled bird. Eaten, apparently, by remorse. It would be ironical if his morale were to snap just when the danger was lifted. They were in the Chairman's office, breaking a rule by drinking whisky in the morning.

"Alex, how did *you* know?"

"I didn't, until I saw that newspaper cutting this morning. There was a photograph, a bad one and twenty-three—is it?—years old, but I thought I recognized him. His name was Gottfried then."

Alex extracted the crumpled cutting from his pocket and looked at it again. There was the smudged photograph—a face less monkey-like and lined, but a younger Godfrey's. He'd been a refugee doctor then, making a new start in London. And he'd been fool enough to get mixed up in an abortion case. The girl had died three days after he'd operated.

According to the defence, conducted by Sir Christopher—plain Mr. Connor then—a quack had attended to the girl after the operation, and she had died from this quack's remedies, not from Gottfried's surgery. But both the girl's landlady and the man involved denied the story, and all Connor's skill and persistence had failed to shake them in the witness-box. *"Connor Loses a Case but Wins a Name,"* said the headline. Gottfried was found not guilty of murder but guilty of manslaughter and got five years—a light sentence for those days.

"Is that all it says?" asked Sir Christopher.

"It adds a rather sad postscript. Gottfried had a young, attractive wife. She stuck by him, and later on she threw herself out of a window in Bayswater. Quite a bit later, though, a couple of years."

The Chairman was plainly crushed beneath a weight of recollection, it seemed, of guilt. But why? He'd tried his best, and done his client well. "No fault of yours, surely," Alex added.

"It was, though." Sir Christopher took a gulp of whisky. "That was it."

"You don't have to tell me this, you know. It's over and done with a long time ago."

"About an hour ago, Alex. No one knows it—no one did but Gottfried, that is Godfrey, and he only guessed. Of course, she came to see me about his defence—his wife, I mean. She was very lovely and in great distress. The combination, you know, is pretty formidable. I was young, I'd been working too hard, I'd made a mistake in my first marriage. She knocked me off my feet. Well, I'm just making excuses. It was unforgivable, appalling. I can only say—I suppose you've been in love. The way it hits you for the first time."

"A gruelling experience," Alex agreed.

"It's unbelievable, looking back. A sort of madness. It wasn't only, you see, that I fell in love with her. Just as the case was ending, a new witness came forward. He would have sworn to the quack. If I'd put him in the box the prosecution's case would have collapsed."

"And you'd have won."

"Yes, but I was past caring. I was insane. I had only one thought

—with Gottfried out of the way, I could do what I liked with the wife. Nothing else mattered. I tell you, I was insane."

"So you suppressed the witness?"

"I said it was too late to introduce new evidence. There was only one thing, Alex—I swore that if a murder verdict was brought in, I'd get the case retried. So I was risking my own career as well as Gottfried's life. I don't think I've ever made a better closing address before or since. Gottfried's life was safe but . . ."

Sir Christopher shrugged his shoulders, sagging in his chair. "If I was a religious man I could draw all sorts of morals. Dead sea fruit and all that. I got what I wanted but it didn't work. She was in love with him. After a bit we started quarrelling and in the end . . ."

Alex didn't know what to say, so he said nothing. Sir Christopher finished his drink and added:

"Queer, if you come to think of it. They both died the same way. I mean, by falling. And even after more than twenty years . . ."

Alex got up and prowled round the room with his hands in his pockets. To pry into Sir Christopher's past hadn't been his intention and the role of confessor embarrassed him acutely. Also his ribs were sore and a corn hurting.

"Did you recognize him?" he inquired.

"Godfrey? The face seemed vaguely familiar but I see a lot of faces, you know. Naturally he'd changed, and in a different country, far away, at first the penny didn't drop. But of course he knew me. And the ironical thing was that he was afraid of *me*."

"I suppose he'd been struck off the register."

"Of course. After he came out he got a new start in Cairo, and then he came down here with references and a first-rate medical reputation. No one, I suppose, thought of checking up. He married, had a family. A word from me could have blown it all sky-high—for good, at over fifty. I suppose you could scarcely blame him for panicking."

"So it wasn't revenge he was after—self-preservation, really."

"Perhaps a combination. He must have hated me and feared me. Perhaps it all fused together and sent him a bit out of his mind. Poor devil."

"And poor Bagpuses."

"Yes, I know. There were so many red herrings. Our famous leak, for instance. And then—he could have got hold of all the native poisons with no trouble, why steal poor Amelia's necklace? I suppose that's what he *did* do?"

"That's what makes it all fit. He was a man who acted on impulse."

"Yes, I think he was."

"His wife told me he threw up his practice and everything in Cairo literally at a moment's notice," Alex said. "I don't believe he'd thought out in advance a scheme to poison the sandwiches. I think he came here that night, the night before the fishing trip, for some quite legitimate purpose—a patient, possibly—and saw Amelia leave her room. He knew she had the necklace. Do you remember, he gave us a little lecture about lucky beans at the Pig and Whistle?"

Sir Christopher frowned slightly and shook his head. "I expect you're right. I'm getting confused. I've had too much whisky."

"He knew she had the lucky beans, and he knew the layout of this place thoroughly. He treated the staff for one thing. So he'd know where the fridges were, and the sandwiches. It wouldn't take him more than ten minutes at the most to nip into Amelia's room, take her necklace, run some of the beans through the coffee mill and poison your particular sandwiches."

"It was a gamble."

"That exactly fits his nature. He got away with it, but the thousand and one chance came up and the wrong man died. And then there's Lady Bagpuse. Unfortunately she looked out of her room in the middle of the night and she *did* see him. But she thought it was you."

Sir Christopher looked up. "That was why she accused me of poisoning Freddy?"

"D'you remember, she wouldn't let Godfrey see her because he was a foreigner? She'd only see Furneaux. She never *had* seen Godfrey, not until Lady Connor insisted, just after Amelia Tripp tried to commit suicide. Then she recognized him. You're both about the same build and it would be easy to make a mistake in the dark."

"But Godfrey *couldn't* have killed Blanche," Sir Christopher objected. "Thomasina saw her alive after he'd left for the hospital with Amelia and the ambulance. In fact, several people saw him go off in his car. That must have been about half past seven. And Blanche was alive at twenty to eight."

Alex was relieved to see an ingrained interest in a factual point beginning to overcome the Chairman's remorse. He shook his head.

"Godfrey set off for the hospital, as you say, about twenty-five to eight. No one checked the time he arrived."

"You mean he came *back?*"

"I saw the sister, this morning, who admitted Amelia to the hospital, and the surgeon on call. They both said Godfrey wasn't with her when the ambulance arrived. He turned up soon after, they're not sure *how* soon—the sister thought about a quarter of an hour. Time enough to have stopped his car on the road, nipped back up that path, and rammed a pillow down on Lady Bagpuse. A big risk—true to form again. Luck was with him, and he was at the hospital about a quarter of an hour after the ambulance."

"To save Amelia when he'd just murdered Blanche. We're queer creatures. . . . You'd have thought, being a doctor, he'd have chosen a less obvious way. An injection, or something."

"That was his cunning. There was nothing to suggest medical skill."

"Yes, I see. . . . Well, Alex, the police will have to start recruiting their detectives in the Redbrick senior common-rooms. I like your point about his temperament."

"It struck me from the first that of this bunch of people—and it really had to be one of us—only three had the right temperament for this kind of murder: impulsive, risky, unplanned and entirely successful."

"Godfrey and . . . Who? Matunda?"

Alex shook his head. "Mansfield's a political chess player who thinks out his moves in advance. Rumble's too ponderous, Sir Jeremy far too cautious and careful, Slocombe hasn't the initiative, the Chief's much too decent, Hugo Evans—well, he's a borderline case, but there again I think he's too much of a planner. Our friend Zaza's the type and I thought for a while it might be him. But the murders weren't carried out in his style. They didn't match his half-mystical, half-cracked religious fervour. If he murdered anyone he'd do it chanting incantations and calling on prophets."

"That still leaves your third candidate."

Alex smiled. "I'll mention no names."

Sir Christopher raised his swan-like brows and gave Alex a quizzical look. "I shouldn't have been a good colonial Governor—and I honestly believe I was—if I didn't think things out a bit more thoroughly than that. However . . ."

There was a knock, and Hugo looked in.

"Jacey's here," he said. "He'd like to see you, if you're free. And I've got a draft statement for the press you might like to look at. A third 'accident.' The press are beginning to think we're unlucky."

"They're damn right," Sir Christopher said. "Tell Jacey to come in, will you?"

"There's only one good thing about it," Hugo added. "At least there'll be no third funeral."

Chapter 32

Jacey hadn't been able to wash off all the camouflage. Traces of black remained in his neck wrinkles and round the ears. Elsewhere mudstains, partially dried, suggested a morning by the lakeside and no time to change his trousers. Behind him marched Sergeant Chisanga, a much tidier figure, with a small tape-recorder in his hand.

Alex looked at the tape-recorder and asked: "Any luck in the swamps?"

Jacey nodded. "We hunted about from dawn onwards and I was just about ready to give up when we found an old water-logged canoe, half submerged. And what we wanted right inside it. If it hadn't been for that, it would have sunk like a stone. Sheer luck. Well, we were about due for some."

"You mean you've really solved our little mystery?" Sir Christopher inquired.

"I'll leave you to be the judge of that, sir, in a moment. May we clear up this other matter first?"

"Of course. But I'm afraid I can't help at all. I saw nothing."

At the critical moment in the smelting shed, Sir Christopher said, his back had been turned to the platform's edge and his eyes fixed on a piece of machinery whose virtues Slocombe was extolling. He'd not even heard anything above the clatter. "In fact if I hadn't been told, I wouldn't know to this moment that anything dreadful had happened. I imagine that everyone else is in the same boat. So I think we can stick to our accident theory, can't we, Jacey? It's so much better for all concerned."

"That's in the hands of Dr. Burton, sir. And Miss Labouchère."

"It was an accident all right," Alex confirmed.

"Then I suppose that closes the case," said Sir Christopher. "Thank God."

"A few loose ends need tying up," Jacey suggested. "Sergeant Chisanga's been making some inquiries."

The Sergeant cleared his throat. "Yesterday I questioned a steward called Mazozo, also another man, a night-watchman called Simon. Both these men saw a lady coming from the room of the corpse. They saw the lady who belongs to Sir Christopher."

"Miss Labouchère," Jacey elucidated.

"They saw her go into the bushes in the dark, and they saw a European in the bushes also, with something in his ear to make him hear louder."

"Sir Jeremy!" the Chairman exclaimed.

"That was exactly the mistake we made," said Jacey. "Jumping to conclusions."

"A mistake . . . ?"

"There's something else besides a deaf-aid you can put into your ear to make you hear louder. Or that certain people can."

"You speak in riddles, Superintendent."

"A stethoscope."

"Of course!"

"The locals are always intrigued by stethoscopes, and they've often seen Godfrey use his. If someone describes a stethoscope they know at once he's referring to a doctor. We were just slow. I was, rather." Chisanga said nothing, but looked severe.

"That confirms your guess, then," Sir Christopher observed to Alex. "Godfrey must have stopped the car and walked up the path and reached Lady Bagpuse's room just as Thomasina was emerging. He may have waited in the darkness till the coast was clear. So he *was* seen, after all."

"That could be checked with Godfrey's driver," Alex suggested.

"I have done so," Chisanga said briskly. "His name is Jacob. He was driving behind the ambulance when the doctor told him to stop. He was at the bottom of the path. Jacob knows this path well—"

Chisanga was reflecting that Jacob was the lover of Mazozo's plump wife, who made good tea. He had found that out, and now he wasn't worrying. A man so soon to become a Superintendent needn't bother about a cook's son who drove for a European who was dead. "Jacob knows that path, and the doctor also. The doctor used it when he came to the guest-house by night to see the cook's son who was ill."

"What cook's son?" Jacey inquired.

"Joshua, the son of Annunciation. He was ill one night a little time ago and the doctor used that path to visit him."

"Was that on Saturday?" Sir Christopher inquired. "The night before the fishing trip?"

"That is right," Chisanga confirmed.

"So Godfrey *was* here. And took Amelia's beans . . . That all ties up. Jacey, don't keep me in suspense any longer. That package you found: was it a spool of tape?"

"It was, sir."

"Decipherable?"

"Luckily the metal case was watertight."

"Then for goodness' sake—"

Jacey took the tape-recorder from Chisanga and fiddled with it for a few moments. The spools started to revolve. The silence was broken only by Chisanga lighting a cigarette. Sir Christopher's worried expression gave way to one of fascinated interest. A voice began:

"All meetings of the Connor Commission have been cancelled following the liquidation of the Vice-Chairman's widow by British secret agents as she was about to flee from imperialist oppression to the people's Republic of Bonga. Revolt in the south-eastern province spreads rapidly as long-oppressed Hapanans rise against the iron heel of British colonialism. Against the sticks and stones of desperate patriots, ruthless imperialist forces . . ." The voice droned on and there was no mistaking its Horatian rumble.

Alex looked at Sergeant Chisanga, and said: "Your friend the night-watchman swore it was Zaza who gave him the packages to hide in the tree-stump. Was he lying?"

"Certainly he was lying. That night-watchman Simon is a liar and a savage and a hyena. He is also a fool to give that talk to a police officer. I knew he was lying."

"Has he got a grudge against Zaza?"

"He is a supporter to Moto Mguu. Zaza is the enemy of Mguu, so Simon the night-watchman is against Zaza. So he told me it was Zaza who gave him the packages. He was a fool, because I was too clever to believe his story. He is sorry now," Chisanga added ominously.

"I can see one has to know one's way about Hapanan politics to succeed as a detective," Sir Christopher remarked. "But now we *are* in a fix about Rumble. I must get on to Butterfield, he'll have to talk to the people in London and work it out with them. Alex, be a saint and see if Thomasina's recovered, will you? And if so, ask her to get the private line to Butterfield's office . . ."

Thomasina had been resting in Amelia Tripp's empty room, recovering from the morning's experience. She'd resisted firmly all suggestions that she ought to go to hospital to be treated for shock, and now she was back in the office. "Things are piling up," she insisted, "and anyway it's better to occupy one's mind." Alex tried to look at her dispassionately, but couldn't. It had been so near a thing.

"Thomasina, will you—" He found it difficult to speak.

She glanced across the room at Hugo Evans, who managed to look disapproving without any overt expression. From her desk she took a note and handed it to Alex.

"A steward brought this in about ten minutes ago. Will you give it to Sir Christopher? It's marked urgent."

"Have you had any lunch?"

"I don't feel like it today. Anyway, it's too late now."

"I'll give this to the Chairman and then I'll be back. I want to talk to you," Alex insisted.

"I'm so hopelessly at sea. I can't . . ."

"Then navigate, Miss Labouchère, navigate," Hugo Evans put in. "Storms are brewing, gales blowing up. To start with, please get

Butterfield on the private line. There's going to be a major international crisis if we don't look out."

The note was from Dr. Rumble. Sir Christopher read it in silence and handed it to Alex.

Dear Sir Christopher,

On my return here this A.M. after our distressing experience I found an urgent telegram awaiting me from my Government, requesting me to proceed forthwith to Hapana's good neighbour the Republic of Bonga in connection with negotiations for a development loan which have run into trouble there. You can understand with what reluctance I have decided that this must take precedence, for the time being, over the labours of our important Commission. But a good soldier must obey his commanders and I have no choice but to leave immediately for the airport, where I have ascertained that a plane for Bonga leaves in under the hour.

I should have preferred, of course, to come first to you to obtain your blessing on this mission, but the circumstances are such that I felt I could best serve your interests by taking my departure with as little fuss as may be. Please give my salutations to the other members of our harmonious team and to your good lady. I shall, of course, speed my return to Hapana just as soon as these delicate negotiations have been finalized.

With my warmest greetings and thanks, sincerely,

Horatio A. Rumble.

Jacey looked at his watch. "He'll be away by now, sir. There's a scheduled flight to Bonga and on to Addis Ababa at noon. I'm afraid my Commissioner will be disappointed."

"No one to prosecute," Alex commented. "Nothing but a cinder and a fugitive. He'll have to concentrate on the *Sulu Sita,* with their unorthodox methods of worship."

"I must say, Rumble's escape is a relief," Sir Christopher remarked. "It's saved us all a great deal of embarrassment. I simply don't know what we'd have done if he'd stayed. The Prime Minister . . . I think all we need say publicly is that Rumble's gone on a special mission and will rejoin us later."

"If we can get away with it."

Sir Christopher looked judicial. "You know, I've been thinking . . . I've some hopes that after this we may settle down to a more normal existence as a Commission, if we can only shake off our press-hounds."

"They're baying for blood," Alex remarked.

"Well, hungry hounds must be fed. Do you ever see those fellows Black and Sparks, Alex?"

"Not if I can help it. But they're around."

"Suppose you were to drop a hint, just a hint mind you, about this mission of Rumble's—something behind it all—I imagine they'd find even the scent of a story there more promising than our own rather mundane activities."

Alex looked with admiration at his Chairman. "Draw them off? Rumble will certainly give them a better run than we shall. I'll see what I can do."

"It would be a relief to get rid of them."

Jacey put his spool safely in his pocket. "I'm afraid we failed dismally to protect you, sir. It was luck, not our efforts, that kept you alive. Though if we'd had a little more time, I think we'd have done our stuff. Chisanga got onto the trail all right and if Dr. Godfrey hadn't lost patience we'd have been asking him some awkward questions later on today."

Sir Christopher shook hands with Chisanga and thanked him, too. Thomasina put her head in at the door to say: "Mr. Butterfield's on the line." Sir Christopher vanished into his office.

"I shall take this tape down to Umpah personally," Jacey said to Alex. "In a way I'm sorry there'll be no case. Just to finish up with. I'm off in a month or two."

"For good?"

"Yes, Chisanga's taking over my job. We've just heard that Hapanization's to be speeded up. Roll on the golden bowler—I can't wait."

"What are you going to do with it? Collect butterflies?"

"I can't afford that. Not with three boys to educate."

"I should think there's plenty of police jobs going in our own peaceful little island," Alex suggested.

"I've had enough of police work. I've always had rather an absurd ambition and now I hope to gratify it."

"Go into Parliament? Sail round the world?"

"The artificial jewellery trade. I like things that really *glitter*. Besides, look at its future—so long as there's sex there'll be jewellery. Can't go wrong. My compensation will just about fix me up with a partnership in a small business in Birmingham. You must come and see us when we're settled in."

"I'll do that," Alex promised.

"I shall miss Hapana sometimes, I daresay. But Chisanga will carry on splendidly." He smiled at his successor, who smiled back with a magnanimity he felt he could afford. He looked with disapproval at the mud on Jacey's uniform, and with approval at the neatness of his own clean trousers. It was for lesser fry to hunt about in swamps, not Superintendents. And it was Chisanga who'd struck the criminal's trail, Jacey who'd confused a deaf-aid with a stethoscope. Next time there'd be no such mistakes.

Chapter 33

"I'M AFRAID we're a sadly depleted party," the Chairman said, gazing round at his colleagues assembled in the board-room at the Merry Hippo. "The events of the past few days have been exceedingly distressing but now, I'm sure, our troubles really are over, and we can get down to business again."

"Hear, hear," said Sir Jeremy. He was sitting next to Amelia Tripp, who looked thinner and somehow more distinguished, less highly-strung, more at ease. She took out a cigarette, fitted it into her holder and Sir Jeremy quickly held up his lighter. Alex noticed that their glances met and that they smiled simultaneously.

He caught Thomasina's eye across the room and winked. She was back in her corner with her pad, but last night, at the Pig and Whistle and then afterwards, she hadn't looked nearly so demure. Sir Jeremy and Amelia had been dining at the next table, Sir Jeremy attentive, Amelia setting out to entertain.

"Odd that it needed a stomach-pump to bring them together," Alex had remarked.

"Must you be so coarse?"

"The kitchen-sink school."

"Well, I'm against it. It's a poor job if you can't forget the sink and see the stars even when you're in love."

"Do you think I'm in love?"

"Why are you trying not to be?"

Alex shrugged his shoulders. "Why should Afro-Asian countries be the only ones to want freedom?"

Thomasina shook her head slighty, sampled the dish that had just been put in front of her and remarked: "Not bad, but this cook isn't as good as Annunciation. *Are* you free, incidentally?"

"Matrimonially? I think so."

"Hadn't you better find out?"

Alex had intended to look at her severely, but the look changed its nature as it went on. A warm, slow fire, nourishing and not destroying, was creeping like a lit fuse through his arteries; he felt helpless, sinking in delectable waters, or rising on a golden fountain. The rabbit, he thought despairingly, surrendering to the stoat's call.

"Hadn't you better find out?" Thomasina repeated.

"Yes, I suppose so. Yes, I will."

Amelia and Sir Jeremy, who'd dined earlier, had paused by the table on their way out.

"I want your support," Amelia had said. "Jeremy's got a marvellous idea."

"He's a marvellous man," Alex agreed. Sir Jeremy smiled doubtfully.

"We're scheduled this week-end to inspect experimental tapioca cultivation. Interesting, of course; some of the genetic work on cross-fertilization, I believe, has given startling results. We must see it some time, but just this week-end— Jeremy thinks we might all fly down to the game park for a couple of nights instead."

"He has my vote," Alex said.

"Mine, too," agreed Thomasina.

"Then we'll tackle Sir Christopher tomorrow. We all need a break, I think, don't you?" She had smiled at her companion in a way that already seemed a little possessive. And here they were at a plenary session very nearly holding hands.

"I'm glad to be able to tell you," the Chairman continued, "that a new Vice-Chairman is joining us. I'm only sorry such a ghastly tragedy brought it about. But I know our work will be immensely strengthened by the addition to our numbers of Dr. Ford Bayford, the well-known Oxford pundit on constitutional law."

"Mr. Chairman, we should have been consulted," the Rev. Zaza protested. "It is not at all democratic to appoint a new Vice-Chairman without consulting first."

"Mr. Chairman, we should have an Hapanan Vice-Chairman," Mansfield Matunda pronounced. "This is a Commission that is dealing with Hapanan affairs. Are there no Hapanans to fill this office? I wish to propose—"

"Mr. Matunda, I think we're faced with a *fait accompli*. The Prime Minister was acting quite constitutionally and I'm quite sure that we'll all find Dr. Bayford a tremendous help. Now shall we—"

"If we are to have a new member, Mr. Chairman, he should be someone who will give us spiritual guidance to keep our feet in the paths of God. I think we—"

"The Reverend Zaza doesn't know the Prophet has been arrested," Mansfield interrupted in a tone of triumph. "It's no good his thinking he can get the Prophet onto this Commission. The man we want is Mr. Moto Mguu. Mr. Chairman, I propose that we—"

"Mr. Matunda, we really cannot discuss this." The Chairman tapped sharply on the table with an ash-tray. "Dr. Bayford will join us on Monday. Now—yes, Chief Faustus?"

The Chief spoke so seldom that any incipient signs of wanting to do so received encouragement. He had consulted Thomasina and, with her help, prepared a little speech.

"Mr. Chairman, we are all very sorry to lose through deceasing our Vice-Chairman and his dear wife. We loved them very much and we wish to keep them alive in our hearts. I think there should be a memorial. A statue. A very big statue to show he was a very big man, and she too, his wife. Two statues. May we hear from you, please?"

"That's a very nice suggestion, Chief. Of course I do agree entirely that something should be done in the way of a memorial. But whether a statue—"

"Two statues."

"Whether two statues is the right way to go about it I'm not so sure. In any case we hardly have powers as a Commission—what do you think, Sir Jeremy?"

"An excellent idea. But, as you say, not quite within our terms of reference. But I think I can see a way round. I can't, of course, commit my co-directors but I'm pretty sure the Board of Steyn Consolidated would be very glad to commemorate these two public-spirited people who came to such untimely ends. There'd be nothing against Steyn Consolidated putting up a statue. Two statues if necessary. Perhaps it would be appropriate to have them made of copper."

"They'd go green," Alex pointed out.

"We have a process now whereby the oxidation of copper can be avoided. To carry things a stage further, we might hold a competition for the best design, thus offering to Hapanan sculptors an opportunity to contribute to their country's culture."

"That is an idea with some merit," Mansfield said graciously. "There would be a prize, of course."

"Mr. Chairman, I cannot agree," the Rev. Zaza protested. "These big statues will be idols. They will be graven images. Chief Faustus speaks like Aaron who made the golden calf. And after the people worshipped the golden calf, Moses came and gathered together the sons of Levi—"

"Lord Bagpuse is not a calf," Mansfield interrupted firmly, "and we are talking of copper, not gold. Nevertheless, I think Mr. Zaza has a little bit of sense in what he says. If there is to be a copper statue why must we think about Lord Bagpuse? The right man to be a statue is Mr. Moto Mguu. In Accra, President Nkrumah—"

"Mr. Chairman, may I make a suggestion?" Mrs. Tripp intervened. "Evidently there's a good deal of doubt about the wisdom of a pair of statues. I'm sure Lord Bagpuse himself would have much preferred some more practical memorial of use to his fellow men, preferably connected with agriculture. Couldn't we set up a scholarship, or foundation, connected with the breeding and improvement of Hapanan pigs? That would have been very close to his heart, I know. At the—"

"Mr. Chairman, there are no Hapanan pigs," Mansfield pointed out.

"In that case there's all the greater need for some foundation to see that there are. No better memorial—"

"Who is this lady addressing as Hapanan pigs?" thundered the

Rev. Zaza with a wrath worthy of Jehovah. "Does she come here to insult us by—"

"Order, order!" cried the Chairman, rapping energetically. "Really, you know, we mustn't go off at a tangent like this. May I remind you that the main item on today's agenda is a paper on the double transferable vote? Dr. Burton, could we—"

"Just a moment, Mr. Chairman!" Mansfield Matunda held up a majestic hand. "We must settle first about the Chief's proposal. I do not support copper statues. I do not support a scholarship for pigs. Is this the latest trick of colonialism—to give scholarships to pigs when there are thousands of Hapanan children who do not go to school? This suggestion is cruel and undemocratic. I propose—"

"Mr. Chairman, I really must point out that Mr. Matunda has completely misunderstood me," Amelia protested frantically. "I never suggested giving scholarships to *pigs*. The scholarship would be for young Hapanan graduates to make a study of the breeding of Hapanan pigs, and the best ways—"

"There it is!" the Rev. Zaza cried excitedly. "Once more, this lady calls Hapanans pigs! Madam, do you not know that Hapanans are made in the image of God and that God is not a pig? Are Europeans—"

"Order, order, order!" the Chairman cried.

"Two statues," said the Chief gently.

"These traitors who are spreading tapioca which—"

"And the Lord said unto Moses, go get thee down—"

"—to the double transferable vote—"

"Mr. Chairman, I propose—" Sir Jeremy's voice rang out above the hubbub "—Mr. Chairman, I propose that we adjourn for coffee."

"I second that," Alex said.

"An excellent suggestion! Mrs. Tripp and gentlemen, shall we adjourn?"

In the lounge Sir Christopher, looking crestfallen, remarked:

"I'm afraid we don't seem any calmer. I'd hoped that now the cloud hanging over us had been dispelled, tempers might have been less frayed. Perhaps after our week-end in the game park we shall all settle down."

Alex looked round for Thomasina. The coffee had arrived on a trolley, and she was handing out steaming cups.

"I'm told the game park's full of malaria," Amelia said. "But I don't suppose that matters if we're all taking our pills."

Sir Christopher looked guilty. "I'm afraid the events of the last few days have driven them entirely out of my mind. Constance was seeing I behaved, but since she's been seedy . . ." He felt in his pocket with a contrite look, and then with an air of triumph extracted a bottle from the inside pocket of his jacket. "I can remedy the defect right away." He shook one of the tablets onto his palm, put it in his mouth and washed it down with a gulp of coffee.

"When we—" he began, but the sentence was never finished. Thomasina stood transfixed, her mouth half open, and dropped a cup to drench a valuable rug with scalding coffee. Stepping forward, she brought her clenched fist down as hard as she could on the back of Sir Chistopher. He choked, staggered, and coughed the remnants of his coffee over his trousers.

"Well, really—" Sir Jeremy protested.

"Quick, quick!" Thomasina cried, continuing to pummel the Chairman's back. "*Do* something, for God's sake! An emetic—life and death—"

"You'll choke him!" Sir Jeremy was outraged.

"Poison!" Thomasina cried.

There was a moment's shocked pause, then a confused period of action and ejaculation. Sir Christopher was still choking, but the tablet had gone down.

"A stomach pump—"

"Mustard and water—"

"They say salt—"

"Feathers—"

Amelia Tripp seized the Chairman firmly by the arm. "Let *me* deal with this. I've brought up a child." She marched him off to her bedroom and the door closed behind them. Everyone looked at Thomasina, who sat down shakily, out of breath.

"It's in the paludrine," Alex said. "Lady Bagpuse warned you, didn't she?"

"Yes, but I didn't take it in. I was an appalling idiot. I thought she'd gone queer in the head and paid no attention."

"How did *she* know?"

"I think she just guessed. You know she saw Dr. Godfrey that night when he put the poison in the sandwiches? Only she thought he was Sir Christopher. And then when Dr. Godfrey came to see her, she realized it was him."

"Yes, I'd got as far as that," Alex said.

"I told you she'd smashed all her medicine bottles in the bath? She kept saying, 'He'll get me, I know he will. He's going to put that poison in all the medicines. I've destroyed every one of them.' I tried to soothe her. I said something like: 'He can't do that, we've all been given new, sealed bottles of things like paludrine.' And then *she* said: 'What's the use of that? Where do they come from? *He* issues them. He's put the poison in the bottles. I'm going to warn Sir Christopher.'"

"But the paludrine and stuff came from the Government stores," Alex pointed out. "Dr. Furneaux issued them, not Godfrey."

"I told her that, but she paid no attention. And of course she *was* going to warn Sir Christopher. That's why Dr. Godfrey killed her—a few minutes after I left her, before she'd time to tell anyone else."

"And then he tried to kill you," Alex said. "But how did he know that Lady Bagpuse had warned you?"

"I was blind, an idiot, I deserve to be drowned! It was yesterday morning, at breakfast—just before we went to the smelting works. Dr. Godfrey handed me one of his paludrine tablets and that reminded me of all those medicines she smashed in the bath. I can't remember exactly what I said, but it was something like: 'The poor thing had a delusion about her medicines. She thought that the paludrine was poisoned and she was going to warn Sir Christopher.' I remember now—thinking back—that he looked at me in a funny sort of way but I paid no attention at the time. It went right out of my head. But why didn't I think of it before?"

"Traumatic shock. Being all but pushed over a fifty-foot drop *does* drive things out of people's heads. Luckily the sight of Sir Christopher taking his pill brought it back—let's hope in time."

"I've rung the hospital," Sir Jeremy said, coming back into the room. Thomasina added:

"There's one thing I still don't understand. Surely the new paludrine *was* issued by Dr. Furneaux from the Government's stores? Then how could Dr. Godfrey have poisoned it?"

"I can explain that," volunteered Sir Jeremy. "This Government keeps its hospitals very short of drugs. They simply haven't the money, and the hospitals quite often run out. On such occasions, they borrow from our stores. In fact, to tell the truth, Dr. Furneaux's got into the habit of leaning pretty heavily on us and of course we're glad to help out in that way."

"So you think these new, sealed paludrine bottles," Alex inquired, "actually came from Dr. Godfrey's stores?"

"I should think almost certainly."

"It makes one's blood run cold," said Thomasina. "A delayed-action murder, like one of these awful wasps that lays its eggs in the body of a caterpillar, and then when the grubs hatch out they eat the wretched caterpillar alive."

"No wonder Godfrey wanted to get rid of you," Alex reflected—somewhat too impersonally, she thought. "The poison was in Sir Christopher's paludrine and the next tablet he took was bound to finish him. Lady Bagpuse rumbled Godfrey's plan and so he silenced her for keeps before she could warn Sir Christopher. And then he discovered that she'd passed on her warning to you just before he held a cushion over her face. So to save his own skin he had to eliminate you. . . . There's a moral there in reverse. If Sir Christopher hadn't been so forgetful, he'd have been dead."

"We're by no means out of the wood," pointed out Sir Jeremy. "The ambulance will be here any minute but these poisons act with terrifying speed. We must hope and pray that Amelia's remedies . . ."

"Tck, tck, tck," came from the Chief.

They waited in a silence heavy with anxiety. At last footsteps approached and Amelia and Sir Christopher appeared in the doorway. He looked pale and shaken, but indubitably alive.

"Victory," he reported, smiling wanly, "thanks to Amelia's effective, if unattractive, form of first aid."

"You should be all right now," Amelia confirmed.

The Chairman went up to Thomasina and patted her shoulder. "I'm doing this a lot more gently than you did it to me, but thank you all the same. You saved my life. I'm not sure whether that was wise or not, but I'm quite sure I don't fancy that particular kind of sticky end. Thank you, my dear. And I hope you'll be very happy."

"Happy?"

Sir Christopher looked across at Alex. "He's a bit heavy-footed at times, and can be prickly, but he's not a bad fellow. You could do worse. And as for Alex—if I was twenty years younger I'd do everything I could to cut him out. But I'm not, and that's that." A shadow passed over his face.

"He hasn't asked me," Thomasina said.

"Silly idiot. But he will. Now, after this interlude, are we all ready for the double transferable vote?"

"The ambulance is just arriving," Sir Jeremy said.

"Well, send it back, will you? I don't think we shall need it now."

While the Commissioners were drifting back into the board-room Alex took Thomasina's hand and pulled her up.

"The Chairman doesn't content himself with organizing his Commission, he arranges our private lives. I suppose, as usual, he's right."

"Your enthusiasm is remarkably restrained."

"Only during office hours. I'll call for you at six and move your things up here."

"Oh! Where to?"

"Rumble's room. It's next to mine."

"I never said—"

"We'll make it respectable."

Thomasina laughed. *"We* will?" Hugo Evans put his head through the door. "We're starting, Burton. Please come along, Miss Labouchère."

In the board-room, the Chairman was saying: "Now, before we see a deputation from the Seventh Day Adventist Industrial Missions, we really must dispose of this paper on the double transferable vote. Dr. Burton—"

"Mr. Chairman, I don't think we should consider anything so undemocratic. Any departure from the principle of one man one vote—"

"Mr. Chairman, I think it is a very good suggestion that everyone should have a double vote. It is better to have two, in case anything should happen to one of the votes. Also—"

"Mr. Chairman—"

"Order, order, please . . ."

Alex started to speak. But Thomasina gave up taking notes after a few sentences. It was lucky, she thought, he had a pleasant voice because she would be hearing a lot of it. Were her shoes strong enough for the game park? Perhaps you didn't need thick shoes nowadays, only air cushions for the seats of Land-Rovers. Still, she must try to get down to the town first thing in the morning. Her pencil was again busy, as she drew up a shopping list.